I0629739

# Hidden Secrets

## The Chronicles of the King
### Book One

KIM KOUSKI

Hidden Secrets | The Chronicles of the King
Book One
Copyright 2016, 2022 Kim Kouski
All rights reserved.

SECOND EDITION
V03302022

This book or parts thereof may not be reproduced in any form, stored in a retrieval system, or transmitted in any form by any means without prior written permission of the publisher, except as provided by United States of America copyright law.

The following is a work of fiction. Names, characters, places, and incidents are fictitious or used fictitiously. Any resemblance to real persons, living or dead, to factual events or to businesses is coincidental and unintentional.

ISBN: 978-0692673041
ISBN-10: 0692673040
Little Roni Publishers | Clanton, AL
littleronipublishers.com
@LittleRoniPublishers
facebook.com/LittleRoniPublishers/

Cover, model image © DepositPhotos/Konradbak
Cover, additional graphic elements © DepositPhotos/Smmartynenko

PUBLISHED IN THE UNITED STATES OF AMERICA

"I dedicate this book to the members of the King's Pen Writer's Group, my second family whom I love dearly. Thanks, gang!" ~ Kim

# Hidden Secrets

The Chronicles of
the King
Book One

# Cast Characters

**Attiyq** – *Att-eek* – God of the land, also, *"The Attiyq"*

The Prince's Party

> **Moji Conell** De Caprise - Prince *Coo-nell*, next in the line of the throne
> **Lord Émer** Muiris Amgets- *Ee-mer* - Conell's best friend and Maúl guard
> **Frigg** – *Fr-ig* – Conell's friend and advisor
> **Imogene** (*Chuoha*)- Imogene, a woman from Peoria, Illinois. (*Chew-o-ha* meaning princess.)

The Great Beasts of the Attiyq, also known as angels

> **Áepoo** – *Awe-poo* – the man/horse
> **Asechi** – *As-e-chi* – the eagle/horse
> **Etta** – *E-ta* – The lion/horse
> **Oota** - *Oo-ta* – the bull/horse

Additional Characters/Names

> **Jezebel** – regent-queen of Ezasu
> **Argus** – *Ar-gus* – a demon, consort to Jezebel
> **Brón** – *Brr-on* – Demon daughter of Argus
> **Amhras** – *Am-ras* – Demon son of Argus
> **Ruárc** – *Ru-ark* - a guard
> **Toál** – *Too-al* - Ruárc's younger brother
> **Anu** – *An-ou* – The (deceased) leader of Émer's people
> **Broden** – *Broo-den* – First king of Ezasu
> **Aho Cian** – *Awe-ho* – Priest, *Ky-an* – priest of a small village
> **Voobo - Maúl** – *Voo-bo - Mah-uel* - Émer's people, from the Southern lands.

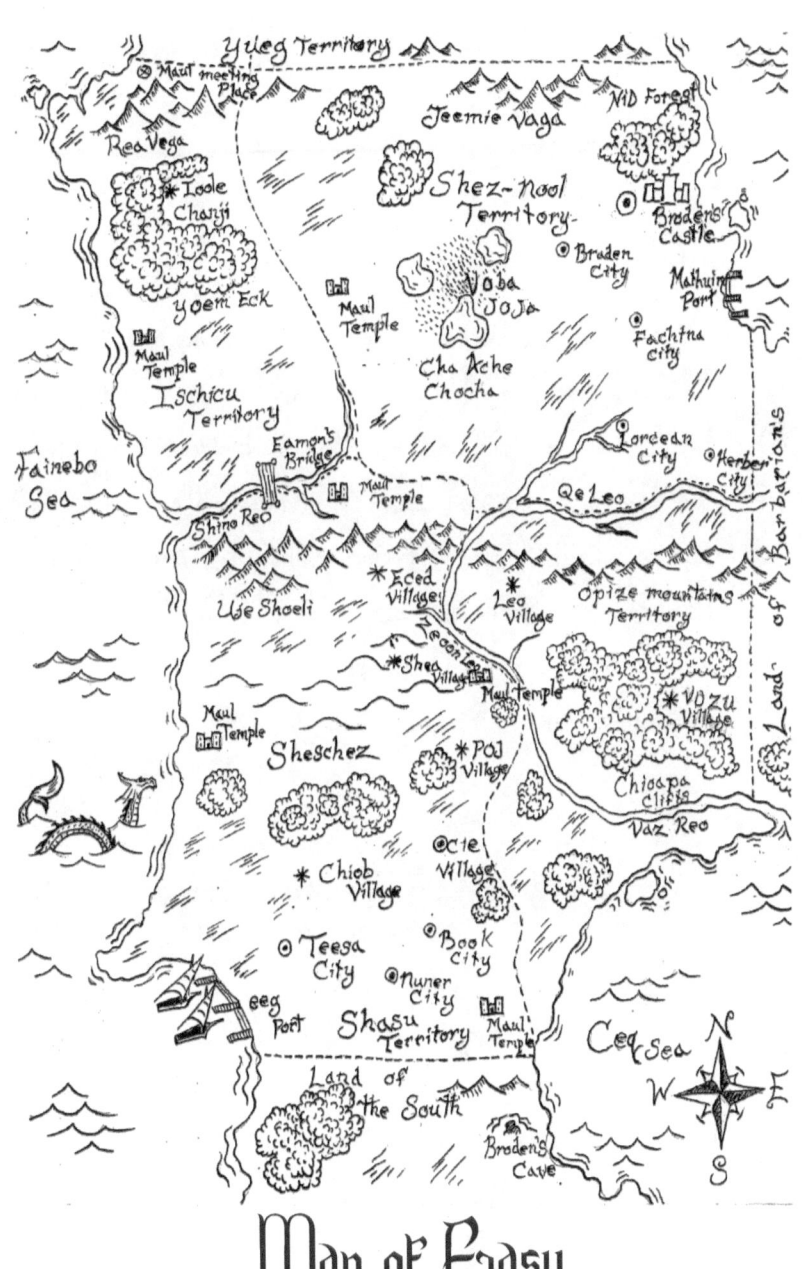

# Map of Ezasu

"You broke your vows, oh son of the morning star. Your eyes desired what you could not have and your hands stole what did not belong to you. Poisonous words seeped from your lips. You would make yourself like the Most High and your throne would rise above the heavens. You longed to be Our God and us, your servant. We cast you from our sight and threw you into the pits of hell."

The Book of Ueje,
the Words of the Attiya,
the Ancient of Days

"Hidden secrets betray us and become our masters."

~ King Broden,
first King of Ezasu in the year
256 from the The Chronicles
of the King, Volume I,
Passage 16.

1

Prince Conell DeCapris pressed his back against the cold stone wall and stared at the cell's spider-webbed ceiling. He flicked off the cockroach that dropped onto his shoulder, his castle now a cell where the reek of mold and rotting corpses hung in the cramped chamber no bigger than a child's bedroom. Five long years imprisoned by the regent-queen who betrayed him and now ruled Ezasu from what should have been Prince Conell's throne; and the blame lay at Conell's feet.

Another prisoner's scream ripped through the prison corridor.

Conell pressed his hands against his ears and grimaced. Eleven years had passed and still, each shriek sounded like his mother begging the barbarians, *"Please do not harm my baby!"*

"Father, forgive me," Conell whispered.

Conell's tired eyes looked to his young captain of the guards who had risen up the ranks of the king's army to become Lord Émer Muiris Amgets of the Third Council of Opize, Maúl Commander of the King's Army, and son of Lord Cadoc Ailill Amgets of the Second Council and Maúl Commander of Father's army. Now, his captain was simply known as Émer. Ranks and forgiveness no longer mattered. Getting Frigg and Émer to safety became his main goal. What was to happen to him afterward depended upon the kindness of cheap wine.

He rubbed his forehead, brought up his leg and dangled his wrist over his kneecap. This nightmare would only end when they escaped. He hoped that safety hid beyond the prison walls.

"Did you say something?" Émer slid the last brick into the stonewall and brushed the dirt from the surrounding bricks. He smoothed down the filling and gently blew away the residue "There. Hopefully, they will not see the lines."

Conell gave his captain a slight grin at his minor obsessions. "It was nothing. You have made cracks invisible."

Émer gauged the dim light in the small cell and stepped back. "I can still see the lines from the pulled bricks, but I don't think the guards will notice."

The young prince raised his eyebrows but nodded. "Still, the Maúl would be pleased."

"My clan is dead, so it makes no difference if they are pleased." Émer stuffed more dirt into the cracks.

"As I said, it will be good to leave this place tonight." Conell averted his gaze.

Seeing his friend day and night fueled his shame. The words, *if only,* haunted him like his mother's frantic tears. Faces of those who died in the midnight raid peered into his cell and accused him constantly. If only he'd spoken the words that would've saved his mother and father and all those in the castle. If only he hadn't remained silent. If only he'd told someone. That same silence now wrapped her arms around him and became his cursed companion.

But the songs of the past no longer counted. His father always said, "Focus on the present, not the past."

"What of Frigg?" His captain stepped back and surveyed his work.

Hours ticked by since the guards hauled Frigg, his young advisor, from his prison cell. "I fear they torture him for sport. He's strong, but I hope his strength holds. I refuse to leave him behind."

"I know, My Moji." Émer smiled at him. "We did not leave him behind after the attack. We will not leave him behind now. He'll survive as we have."

The cell lock jingled. Émer whirled towards the door, brushed the dirt from his hands, and crossed his arms over his chest. The door swung open.

Ruárc, the prison sentry, had a stout body that filled the doorframe. A sneer crossed the guard's thick lips. His younger brother, Toál, stood behind him, his husky hand latched around the squirming arm of a small frame.

"Let me go!" yelped the prisoner's panicked voice.

Émer straightened. Conell raised his hand and kept his captain in his place.

Ruárc tossed the prisoner into the cell. "Here's company for you, Your Highness. *Her* name is Chuoha."

Conell eyed Émer who mouthed, *her?* A woman in Queen Jezebel's prison? The queen refused to have women in the penal for they did not last long. Why was she here?

Émer shrugged.

The girl stumbled then whirled to face Ruárc. She stiffened, but trembled in the weak light. Conell raised his eyebrows. A sign of defiance or fear?

Ruárc blew her a kiss and slammed the door as he exited the cell; the sound vibrated through the stone walls.

Émer leaned over Conell. "Who is *Chuoha?* Why put her here?"

"My name is Imogene Katherine Reazley!" The young girl rushed to the door, pounding with her small fists as the hollow sound reflected her worthless effort.

Émer chuckled and nodded toward the girl. "Look at her short sleeves; they do not cover her arms or hands." He nudged Conell with his elbow and winked. "She is a *Zuuho.*"

Conell rubbed his chin as his eyes roamed over her petite frame dressed in blue trousers and yellow short-sleeved top. The girl's curly, long blonde hair framed her smooth face. She could have been a maiden in his father's castle, except for her indecency. "She dresses as a man, not as a proper woman. She is not a *TTishos.*"

"Her sinning mother forgot to teach her noble ways. No respecting *TTishos* dresses in such a disrespectful manner. Is it a wonder that she's here?" Émer grunted and shook his head. "She is a disgrace to the noble line of King Broden."

"My mother would expel her from Father's courts and hide her *Zuuho* foulness from the children." Conell flashed a grin to Émer. "'Do not expose the children to such nudity,' she would say."

"My mother would beat her and drag her out into the streets where she belongs."

Conell rose from the bench. "Let's see why Ruárc's little *Zuuho* has come to visit us."

The girl grew quiet and leaned her forehead against the wooden door. Soft whimpers crossed the room.

"Tell us, *Chuoha,* what brings you to our humble dwelling?" Conell asked.

The *Zuuho* slowly faced them. The cell's torch spread its dim glow over her curling tresses that spilled down her shoulders. Her blue eyes were swollen from weeping and tear tracks stained the youthfulness of her cheeks. The girl's gaze followed the walls to the ceiling where the spider webs dangled like skeleton

4

fingers. She cringed and covered her head.

"Please help me." She shielded her eyes from the torch's harsh light. "That horrible man brought me here. I'm not supposed to be here."

Conell raised an eyebrow. *Not be here? Ruárc's spurred lover angry over her new accommodations? Perhaps Ruárc's soft warm bed would better suit this tainted creature. Not supposed to be here?* Conell paced around the female with certainty, devouring the precious distance between them. "My, my, my, a *Zuuho* who thinks she is better than me? Perhaps you prefer Ruárc's bed instead?" He dragged his dirty fingertips over her bare arms. "Or has he thrown you from his embrace?"

She recoiled and slapped away his hands. "Don't touch me! I want to know where I am. Why am I here?"

He blinked. How could she not know she sat in Jezebel's prison? Everyone within the land feared this place of hell. Some even embraced the sword over the death stench clinging to this nightmare.

Her watery stare lingered on his eyes until she lowered her head and swallowed. To enjoy the fresh perfume of a young woman's cleaned locks again made him smile and his fingers intertwined in the golden ringlets. The girl tried to move away, but he shoved her back against the door.

"Where are you?" He whispered in her ear. "*Ioole Chaj, leep to aeepa vozo.*"

Her brows knitted together and her lips moved, but said nothing.

"Be careful, Moji," Émer called. "Do not let the stones hear you using the forbidden tongue. You know the witch forbids us to speak it, even here. Speak the queen's tongue so the *Zuuho* will understand."

The prince flipped his fingers. "I will not let Jezebel rule me. I will speak as I please."

"Again, mind your tongue." Émer leaned against the wall and grinned. "You might find it missing one day."

Conell grunted.

"I don't understand what you said," the girl whispered.

He stepped back. Jezebel prohibited her slaves from speaking the ancient language of the Attiyq, but even they understood the forbidden tongue. *How could she not understand? What did her eyes seek?* The guards planned to execute him and Émer tomorrow. *Why send a watcher now?*

Conell said to Émer in his language, "The girl could be a watcher, be careful what you say."

"Witch prison, home of the forgotten," he said to her.

"Why am I here?" A tear inched down her young face and her dry lips trembled.

Conell sneered. Many women had used tears to break his heart; Ruárc's *Zuuho* would fail in her quest. He placed his forearm against the door and locked her in place. "I am sorry, *Chuoha*. I did not hear your words. You must speak up."

"I want to go home. I want my mother." Her trembling arms knocked against the wood.

"Your mother?" Conell laughed. "The sinning *Zuuho* begs for her mother." He lifted her quivering chin; his thumb stroked her cold cheek. "What you ask, *Chuoha Zuuho*, is quite impossible. Jezebel does not allow mothers to enter here. You are alone."

She cringed and tried to move her face away from him. "Stop! I don't know a Jezebel!"

His fingers slid under her chin and held the girl's face close to his. "Jezebel is now the queen of this land. She has sat on my father's throne for ten long years. Or have you forgotten? Perhaps, I could refresh your memory?"

She swiped his hand away. Her whimpering voice grew into a panic pitch. "I don't know what you're talking about. There is no queen. Let me go!"

Conell flicked his fingers and strolled away. "Ruárc must have picked an insane lover."

The girl's face twisted. "I'm not his lover! You're disgusting! And you don't touch me like that ever again!"

He spun and laughed. "Touch you? You are a *Zuuho*, now you care of touching?"

The girl shrank against the door. "I don't know what that means, but don't you touch me again!"

Émer grabbed Conell's arm. "My Moji, there are other ways of finding information."

Conell raised his hands in defeat and leaned against the wall next to the bench. "The *Zuuho* is all yours, Captain."

Émer led her to the stoned bench. "Maybe you should sit down."

A large black rat scurried from under a blanket tossed over a pile of dirty hay and disappeared into a hole in the wall. She squealed and jumped onto the seat; her shrieking voice bounced around the cell.

"I'm not doing this. I can't stay here."

Conell shook his head.

Émer chuckled and helped her to sit. "My name is Émer Muiris Amgrets, son of Cadoc Ailill Amgets, Captain of the Prince's army. And he is Moji, *Prince* in your tongue, Conell DeCapris, son of Efuko DeCapris, last reigning King of Ezasu. King Efuko is dead now."

"Is this hell?" She brought up her legs and wrapped her arms around her shins.

"Some have called it hell." Émer took a seat beside her. "You are in *Iool Chaj* a prison for those who fight against the Witch-Queen Jezebel, whom—as the Moji said—now rules this land. You must have wandered into *Yoem Eoko*, Demon Forest. Those who escape from the prison or rebels seeking to attack the guards wander into the forest."

She rubbed her forehead. "I don't know a Jezebel and I didn't wander into any forest and I'm not Nasty Guy's lover. I was in Glen Oak Park. Then I was in those weird woods. There is no Demon Forest around here."

"What is this Glen Oak Park you speak of?" Émer asked.

"It's a park where people go to have fun. You know picnics, Frisbees, playing with dogs—fun stuff!" Her voice rose with each word.

Conell nudged him in the shoulder. "What is *frisbees?*"

His captain shrugged. "What were you doing in this *park?*"

A look of shame crossed the *Zuuho*'s face. Her babbling words tumbled from her shaking lips and her wringing hands trembled. "I broke the law. I did what the judge wanted me to do and followed all of his orders. This isn't supposed to happen. There was an hour left of my probation and I was going home for my sweet sixteen birthday or what was left of it. *That's* where I'm supposed to be now. Home, not *here!*"

"Calm down." Émer patted her bare arm. He grimaced and wiped off her polluted touch.

Conell straightened. "What orders?"

"I know it was wrong." She brought her knees closer to her chest as a cockroach scurried across the straw-covered stoned floor. "But I wanted the others to like me, so I went along with them. They wanted to spray graffiti on the school building. It was wrong, but I wanted to be cool. When the cops showed up, they found a bag of weed on my friend and they arrested us. The judge said since this was my first offense, he'd let me off with a hundred hours of community service. I did what they wanted. I was cleaning the park, when *this* found me."

She took a medallion from around her neck and passed it to Émer. Conell's gaze flickered to his captain. The gold trinket encompassed Émer's palm and faint light caught the edge of the shining surface. A large wine-colored stone in the middle of the ornament reflected the torch light. A circle with strange letterings ringed the jewel.

Émer peered at the markings. "I am not sure, My Moji, but I do believe this writing could be of the Old Priests."

"I was picking up the trash," she said. "And I saw something in a bush. I reached for it and the chain…well…grabbed me. Wrapped around my wrist. I fell into a pit or something, and I landed *here.*"

Émer looked at Conell, then back to the *Zuuho.* "What do you mean? I do not understand the words with which you speak. *It grabbed me?*"

"Grabbed. Me." She squeezed Émer's wrist. "Grabbed."

Émer pulled free from the *Zuuho's* stained hand and scoured off her depravity.

She looked at his wrist. "Why do you act like I'm dirty?"

8

Émer blinked. "You are a *Zuuho*."

"What's a *Zuuho*?" she asked.

"*Zuuho* are stained women who are improper with men."

"You mean a woman who does... *things* with men? I'm not... I mean, I'm not one of those."

Conell chuckled and spoke in his native tongue. "Insane, she is."

Émer pursed his lips and raised his fingers. "You dress as one."

She looked down at her clothes. "I don't understand."

"You bare your arms with no shame and you wear a man's clothes. You must be as you said, a woman who does *things*."

"What?" Her quaking voice was above a whisper. "No, it was hot at the park and this is what I wear when it's hot out. Why would you think a summer top means...that? I really want to leave now."

Émer's strong purple eyes held her as a snake holds a bird. "As my Moji has said, you cannot leave."

More tears danced on the rim of her blue eyes. "I can't help it that you find it offensive, but please, I'm not...I just want to go home."

"Tell me," Émer said. "Where are you?"

"I don't know," she whispered. "I think I'm dead."

"Who is Queen Jezebel?"

"I told you, I don't know."

"What crime did you do to put you in this place?'

Émer's strong gaze made her inch away. "I was at the park, picking up trash."

"If I were to offer you freedom from this hell and from the guards for pleasure with you, would you take it?"

The *Zuuho*'s pale face fell and she focused on her trembling hands. "Please don't make me do this, please; I just want to go home."

Émer sat back and gave her a small nod. "A normal *Zuuho* would take my offer with gladness. Yet, you are one who shies away. Forgive me, My Lady. I am Maúl and should not treat you this way. You are not as I had thought. I ask for your forgiveness if I have offended you. Please, go on."

The prince moaned. "Captain?"

The captain held up his hand. "My Moji, please! Please, My Lady, continue."

The girl rubbed her palm against her forehead. "I know this isn't happening, I know it isn't. None of this is real."

Émer strong eyes softened. "My Lady, please forgive me for frightening you. I must know who you are. I must protect my prince."

"Protect your prince?" Her amazed face lifted and she held up her palms. "Look, whatever you two do on your own time is your business, but I don't want to belong to it. Just let me leave, please, I won't tell anyone."

Émer inched towards her and she jumped from the seat.

"You guys are insane," she said. "I want to go now. I don't know who put you up to this, but this ends now."

Conell grinned. This frightened maiden had great spunk. Whoever owned her must have paid much. If she belonged to Ruárc, Conell could understand why the guard put his prize in this cell. Her pretense made her as a mouse that sits under the table and waits for scraps. This small golden mouse sat in the captain's hand and could gather anything she pleased.

"Sit." Conell's eyes motioned to the seat.

She plopped onto the bench and forced her shaking hands into her lap.

"What happened?" Conell asked.

Her frightened gaze jumped from him to Émer. The words tumbled. "I don't know what happened. That thing grabbed me; I fell into secret, weird Never-Never land! The chain was around my neck when I hit the ground. That guard, whoever he is, found me. He put a knife to my throat." A haunting covered her face as if feeling the blade. "Oh God, I don't want to die here."

Émer look up at Conell and spoke in his own language. "Moji, I do not believe this girl is *Zuuho*, but I do believe she is ill."

Conell moaned and snatched the medallion from the

captain. "Because she is a woman you believe her words? She lies to you, Captain. She has you in a snare." The warm pendant tingled in his palm. His fingers traced the old engraved writings. *But why would Ruárc try to kill a prized possession if he wanted the girl to spy on us?* He shrugged. She lies. *But does she look like she's lying?* "It looks ancient, but I am unsure of the age. The writings look like those in my father's ancient scrolls."

A memory raised its ugly head and jabbed at his heart. He shivered and tried to shove it away, but it stormed into his mind as they all did.

*Father sat in his study listening to the Maúl elders reciting these archaic words. The wind blew the thin white curtains into the room.*

*An angry Maúl elder jumped from his seat and pointed to the draperies. "The angels of the Attiyq stretch out their hands to the disobedient!"*

*Father cringed as Mother called Conell from the room. The seven-year-old boy stepped out into the hall, but peeked back to catch a glimpse of the angel's hands. They sought him and a chill slipped down his back—an omen for his childish defiance. Those same revenging cherubs lunged for him today. He should have said something, anything.*

He shook the memory away and gave the medallion to the girl. "But I cannot read it. The language is of the old tongue."

"I don't want it." She pushed it way. "I wanted to sell it, get some cash for it. But I've changed my mind."

"I think it should hang around your pretty neck, not mine." Conell slipped the chain over her head.

The medallion dropped with a thump against her small chest. Father had often said that one could see a man's soul through his eyes. Her fearful child-like face reflected the carnage of Father's citadel, the blood flowing across the clean castle floors and dead eyes staring at the freshly painted ceiling. The haunting past of young maids' dying screams and the weeping children were silenced by the prison door swinging open. Conell stepped back.

Ruárc strutted into the room like the king who ruled the palace. His fat belly jiggled under his sweat-stained black shirt and his sword swung from his hip. Toál stood in the doorway. A limp Frigg slouched in his strong grip. The captain rose from the bench and planted his feet before the guard. Conell drew the wide-eyed girl from the bench.

Ruárc spread his arms. "Tell me, Prince Conell, will you miss your royal accommodations?"

Toál tossed Frigg into the room and he landed with a sickening plop. A deep moan escaped the young man as he tried to rise. His elbows buckled. The girl moved toward Frigg, but Conell held her arm.

Conell's stomach ached as a boulder had fallen on him. The fault lay on him. It was his hand that lashed Frigg's back—his fault Frigg was left as an orphan and now the young man paid for his foolish mistake. His closed his eyes. His goal feathered before him, to take Émer and Frigg to the safety of the Southern Borders. He studied the girl. *What to do with her?*

Ruárc smirked and bowed before Émer. "Lord Émer Muiris Amgets of the Third Council, how good it is to see you again." Ruárc placed his dirty hand over his mouth; a feign shock covered his face. "Forgive my poor manners, I have forgotten, the queen stripped you of your title years ago. Now, it is only the poor, dirty, peasant Émer."

The young captain let out a bored sigh.

Toál leaned his fat body against the door and cleaned his nails with the tip of his knife. "Take care, big brother." He grinned at Ruárc. "You stand before a *brave* Maúl."

Ruárc grunted. "I do not fear this tiny Maúl fly."

"Well, well, well." Émer crossed his arms over his chest. "Jezebel's dogs have come to visit us. Did the witch run out of scraps for her pets?"

Ruárc narrowed his eyes. "Perhaps, I can give a message to your father and brother warriors? I am sure they would love to hear from one who is forgotten."

He shook his head and frowned. "Forgive me again, Captain. I am the one who has forgotten. They met such a tragic end, slaughtered by the barbarians. How tragic that you are the last of your kind." Ruárc clicked his tongue.

Toál laughed. "Brother, what did the legends say? The great and mighty Maúl warriors could rise like ghosts from the ground and defeat their enemies. No man could stand before them. Where are they now? Where are these ghosts?"

Ruárc shrugged. "Perhaps, haunting the castle? Maybe if we found a witch, she could summon them. Summon your father, Amgets? Your clan?" The guard sneered. "How will you ever learn the ways of your people now that they are dead? Whatever will you do?"

"Yes, Captain, give us your plan for your future," Toál said. "Oh, of course, you die tomorrow. But be of good cheer. Now, you have no need for training."

Émer narrowed his eyes, but said nothing.

Conell's hands tightened into fists and he gritted his teeth. "Do not allow their words to hurt you, Émer."

Ruárc took a step towards the captain and chuckled. "Poor little Émer. You will die tomorrow knowing you die as a Maúl child, not a Maúl warrior. What does it feel like to see your dream die?"

Émer's purple eyes pierced Ruárc.

Ruárc's chuckling ceased. He broke Émer's challenge and winked at the girl. "Hello, *Chuoha*, I apologize for the poor dwellings. Perhaps we can take a walk along the path again?"

Toál licked his lips. "I know you would enjoy it."

An ash-white spread across her soft features and she grabbed Conell's arm as her legs buckled.

He furrowed his brow. Did she play the part of the woman in distress or did Toál and Ruárc really hurt her?

Émer took a small side step and blocked Ruárc's view. The guard's smile disappeared.

"I heard you enjoy placing your steel against young maidens' throats. Are you man enough to place the knife against mine since I am forgotten, a peasant and the last of my kind?" Émer bowed and spread his arms.

"The brothers who dance with swords," Conell snickered. "Well said, Émer."

Toál reached for his weapon. "Do not speak to my brother with such ill words!"

Ruárc dragged his younger sibling from the cell. "Save your anger, Toál." He stood in the safety of the doorway and grinned. "Tomorrow our swords will taste their blood." Before leaving, he wiggled his dirty fingers at the girl. "Do not fret, Tiny *Chuoha*. Tomorrow you will share my bed as well as my brother's."

The girl dropped to the ground and pressed her palms into the floor, struggling to breathe. The guards slammed the door; the loud click from the lock bounced off the walls as their muffled laughter drifted away

Conell and Émer rushed to Frigg. Gingerly, Conell rolled him over and brushed back his red hair. Frigg's young, freckled face wrinkled in pain.

"Frigg, what happened?" Conell asked.

A soft groan rose from his chapped lips. "My Liege, I do not... know what they seek. They... beat me... with staffs... yet... asked no questions."

The girl crawled to the men and squeezed in between them. "Here, let me help him. I know first-aid."

Conell shoved her back with his elbow. "First what?"

Despite her fear, a determination sat in her eyes. "Please, I can help him. I took a class last year. I made an A..."

"What?"

"You need to move," she said.

Conell rose and frowned at the small intruder.

She gently rolled Frigg to his side and lifted his shirt. Blood dripped from the thick purple slashes crossing his shoulders down to his lower back.

"I will get you some water," Émer said.

"No. The water here must be dirty. If we place it on the wounds, they may become infected. He could die. I need something to stop the bleeding, a clean cloth, if you have one." The girl grimaced. "I've never known of a prison that beats a juvenile inmate like this."

Émer and the young prince exchanged confused glances, but said nothing.

The captain slipped off his gray shirt and handed it to her. "I have nothing else. It is not clean as you asked."

A blush covered her cheeks as she quickly averted her eyes and placed Frigg over onto his stomach.

Conell tried to examine the young man's wounds, only to have his hand slapped. She gently pressed the fabric against Frigg's back. His wounded body jerked and painful groans escaped him.

"I'm sorry," she said.

After a time, she lifted the cloth. The bleeding stopped and she lowered his shirt. Émer and Conell led him to the stoned bench and laid him on his stomach across the cold surface.

The girl sat beside him and felt his pulse. "Be careful. He may start to bleed again. He really needs to see a doctor."

"A doctor? What is a doctor?" Conell growled. This game grew tiring.

"A doctor. You know, someone who heals others using medicine." Her eyebrows rose as she emphasized the words. "Have you heard of med-i-cine?"

A snicker escaped him. "You are a stranger to hell, *Chuoha*. 'Doctors' do not live in *Ioole Chaj*." He snatched the cloth from her hand, lifted Frigg's shirt and gently dabbed his friend's back. The barbs of guilt throbbed in his chest.

"Stop." She pulled the bloody shirt from his fingers. "You'll make it bleed again. He needs to rest so he can regain his strength."

Émer frowned. "Moji," he said in the forbidden tongue. "The girl's mind has fled and you know I cannot leave her behind to suffer from the hands of Toál and Ruárc. You know what they will do to her. Listen to her words, My Moji. They are strange—insane. No one with a well mind would speak such things. We *must* take her with us."

Conell glowered at him. "Has your memory left you? Remember how Jezebel befriended us? And her betrayal? How she confined us in Father's prison? Do her betrayal and the betrayal of those who followed us flee *your* mind? I will not give my hand to another so easily."

"I made an oath before the elders of my tribe when I sat at my father's knee." Émer crossed his arms over his chest. His purple eyes darkened and his soft face hardened. "And I will not break my oath even though they are dead. The girl is ill and the Attiyq demands I show mercy to the ill. I will follow His words. Do not make me choose for you know my answer."

Conell understood the captain's determination. It would lead the young Mául to the executioner's slab, his young neck pressed upon the bloodied block and a sharp axe removing his head from his body. Prayers to the Attiyq would fall from his dying lips until he no longer spoke. Conell looked away from the thought. *Yes, he did know the answer, but to trust another?* His last mistake cost the lives of those in the castle.

"Okay, enough of this." The girl jumped to her feet and shoved her small hands on her hips. "It's obvious you're talking about me. Please have enough courtesy to say it to my face."

Conell rubbed his chin. For a spy, this little one had a great spirit. Ruárc would enjoy taming her. "Well, Little *Chuoha*, we speak of escaping tonight and what to do with you. Émer thinks your mind has fled and the ways of the Voobo-Maúl demand he cares for you, meaning we must take you with us, yet." He cocked his head. "I wonder if you truly are insane."

"I don't understand." Her small body dropped onto the bench. The spy now became the child, her small frame trembling.

He towered over her. "Jezebel sent you. Or perhaps your heart belongs to Ruárc?"

She shook her head and rose from the bench. "No! I told you what happened. I don't even know a Jezebel! And I'm not Nasty Guy's girlfriend. He's gross, disgusting, nasty. I'd never."

"Ah, yes." Conell nodded and slipped his hands behind his back. "You grabbed a strange medallion, which magically brought you here from the place of parks, doctors and what words did you use? Ah, community service. A very imaginative story."

"But it did happen!"

Conell motioned to the dirty blanket. "We could bind her with some strips of cloth. We would still have a day's journey ahead of them."

Émer stepped between him and the girl. "Moji, I will not leave her in the hands of Ruárc and Toál. Still, we die tomorrow, why would the witch send a watcher now? And I do not think her eyes wander to Ruárc."

The girl pointed to Frigg. "If I were a spy, why would I help him? Would I honestly help if I belonged to that nasty thing? I mean, seriously! What is wrong with you?"

"Her words hold wisdom, Moji." Émer raised his eyebrows.

He pursed his lips. "And what if your eyes spy for the witch-queen and you convince me your heart beats pure and you betray me?"

The girl gritted her teeth. "I swear, if you don't take me with you, I will scream at the top of my lungs and tell the nasty guard everything."

Émer shrugged. "She has you in a net."

Conell growled and pushed Émer aside. "Our problems would flee if I broke your tiny neck."

The girl stumbled back. Anger rose in her young face. She stood on her toes and tried to meet his eyes. "Go ahead. Kill me now. I'd rather die than rot in this hellhole. Anyway, how do I know you're not just a bad dream?"

Conell's eyebrows rose. The cowering mouse was now a roaring kitten that looked and sounded like a little girl. The prince's rough fingers coiled around her small chin and drew her face towards his. "If you long to join us, I will take you with us. But if you betray me or my friends, I will break your neck and leave you to die alone. You will beg for Ruárc's arms."

Her face paled a deeper white and her brass voice became a small whisper. "I promise I won't betray you. Please. I just want to go home."

He dropped his arm. For a woman who was to be a spy, this one acted more as a frightened child. But the screams from Mother, the young maids and the children drowned out her innocuous whispered voice. He would not make the same mistake. "*Chuoha,* Émer and I both will have our eyes upon you."

With a nod, she plopped on the bench and wrung her trembling hands. "I promise I'll do whatever you want."

Conell exhaled a deep growling breath and leaned against the door. Every instinct begged him to abandon her to the mercy of the guards, but he had no choice. The fierceness in her blue eyes told the truth; the guards would know of their plans and none of them would leave this hell tonight.

He peered through the small, barred window at the deserted corridor. The prisoner in the cell across the hall yelled at him then dropped onto the bench and mumbled to himself.

"Captain, show her." Conell nodded towards the opposite wall that Émer had repaired.

He extracted two bricks. "Come here, Imogene Katherine Reazley."

"Please, call me Imie." She offered him a small smile. "It's what my friend calls me. And what is or are the *Atteek?*"

He gave her a small bow. "Lady Imie, the Attiyq is our God. He is holy, merciful and fair. He commands that the Maúl must care for the ill. I belong to the Maúl clan; you have no worries. See the large hole? We discovered it a few days ago when the guards put us in this cell. We found a loose brick, which led to a small tunnel. The previous prisoners must have dug it. We think it leads into the woods behind the prison, although we are not certain."

She peeked into the black hole. "How did they know about the tunnel?"

He shrugged. "King Broden made many tunnels which lie beneath the land. His soldiers used those years ago during the war with the Southern Lands. The prisoners may have known of them, and dug into it. They must have worked on it for a long time, but I do not know. The guards executed them before they could use it."

"Why didn't you guys use it earlier?" she asked.

Émer gave her a tight smile. "We have been in this cell for a few days; tomorrow is our day of execution. We must leave tonight."

"How do you know it's safe? And how did you find it? And where's the dirt?"

"She sounds like my sister," Émer said in his native tongue. "My Moji, I will let you answer this one."

Conell gave his captain a wry look and checked off the answers on his fingers. "Émer found a loose brick. The dirt lies in the main tunnel. And if you would prefer Ruárc's company…" He raised his hands and shrugged.

She shook her head; a small, withered leaf floated to the ground. "No, of course not. But how do you know which way to go?"

"You ask many questions for one who wishes to leave, *Chuoha*. We do not know, but as I said, we will leave you with Ruárc and Toál if you choose."

"No, I'll go. I'll do what you want."

"We leave tonight." Émer replaced the brick and stuffed dirt between the cracks. "Tomorrow the prince turns eighteen and it is also our execution date. We have no choice."

The girl looked back at the brick wall, then to the door. She bit her lip and avoided Conell's eyes.

Connell thought her words rang true regarding her innocence, but maybe he had stumbled into one of the queen's many snares and their lives would end before the sun rose. Paranoia teased him. Voices that only he heard whispered in the hallways. *"Traitor, murderer! How can you lead others when you betrayed so many?"*

"The guards will check each cell before retiring for the night." Conell checked the hall.

*Five boys and girls covered in blood gathered hands and skipped in a circle. Their childlike voices sang of a traitorous prince who left others to die. The children plopped onto the ground and disappeared into the floor; their laughter echoed along the corridor. The haunting past continued to torment him.*

Conell grabbed the blanket from the hay pile, shook it out and laid it over Frigg. "We will wait until the last sentry call to leave this hell," Conell said roughly. "The darkness will shield us. Betray me, woman, and you will rot in the forest."

She nodded, but kept her gaze on the floor.

Émer led her to the bench and handed her a plate filled with bread, fruits, a slab of beef and vegetables. "Here, eat."

Her stomach rumbled and she picked at the food. "How are you able to get this?"

The captain grinned. "The witch feeds us better than the other prisoners in hopes of them killing us before she can. The Moji is wise although I question his decisions. I believe we should feed others, while he has commanded us to eat, and to train our minds and bodies for this day. You must eat if you are to travel."

"Thank you." She studied the food on the plate. "Oh, please don't tell me the bugs and rats were also picking at your food."

Émer grinned. "No, My Lady, I keep them far from our food. Although the rats are quite tasty."

"They're what?"

He laughed. "I only poke you with a sword, My Lady."

"My Prince." Frigg licked his dry lips and his glazed eyes struggled to focus on Conell. "I will hold you back. Leave me here."

Conell wrinkled his brow and placed his hand on Frigg's shoulder. "No, my friend, I will not leave you here to die amongst the wolves. If I must, I will carry you to *Shes Cheez.*"

Imogene cocked her head at Émer and mouthed, *Shes Cheezse?*

Émer grinned at her. "Mother's Hills."

Conell frowned.

Her cheeks burned red and she looked away.

A hacking cough attacked Frigg. A deeper gray rushed over

his face as he rose onto his hands and knees.

Imogene placed her hands on his waist and pushed his hair from his face. "Try to take deep breaths."

He grasped her fingers as his lungs fought to expand.

"Now, let it out, slowly," she said.

He released his breath and the coughing ceased. She laid him back onto the surface and brought the blanket up to his shoulders. His eyes fluttered closed.

The prince laid his hand on the young man's arm. "Be strong, Frigg, by tomorrow we will be safe."

*But what of the girl?* Either his decision would become his worst mistake or a great blessing. Of course, trusting Jezebel became his worst mistake, *but would this be worse?*

Evil surrounds us. It eats into our souls, making us black as night. It weighs us down like chains wrapped around our necks. Who will save such a lost soul?

- From *The Chronicles of the King*,
Vol 3, Passage 6

*Imogene sat at the kitchen table; the sound of popping bacon and its thick, meaty smell drifted across the room. Aunt Laurie smiled at her, poured orange juice into three glasses, and sat one before Imogene and the other two before empty seats. Uncle Tim dropped onto the chair opposite her and sipped from one of the glasses. "Imogene. You better wake up before they leave you behind."*

Imogene's eyes popped open. Frigg's head nestled on her leg. The prince and Émer slid bricks from the prison wall and tossed them gently onto a pile on the floor. Distant sobbing replaced the screams from the halls and the other cells. Some poor soul left alone to die. A fist dug deep in her stomach. This had to be a bad nightmare.

She leaned the back of her head against the stoned wall. A dream of home. Like Dorothy trapped in Oz, but what if the dream was reality and this reality was a dream? She shook her head, too much philosophy.

The prince placed a brick onto the pile and wiped the dust from his hands. "You have awakened, Chuoha. I thought we would have to leave you behind."

Émer frowned.

Conell nodded towards the young man. "Check on Frigg."

She swallowed and clenched her fingers. *What was up with Conell's nasty attitude? What did she do to him?* Even here, people saw her as the nerd, hated by everyone. Maybe she should stay here? Those horrible men—Toál placed a knife against her throat after she tried to escape. Ruárc slid his callused hand up her shirt and touched her. A shudder slipped down her back. The thought of his rough hands made her sick. She tried to shove the chilling memory away.

*A skeleton's hand lay in the trail when Toál dragged her to the prison. It cracked under her foot. She shivered and wiped her foot against the floor. Horror movies always claimed one was cursed if they stepped on a dead body—and she was cursed.*

*Farther down the path, a body lay across the trail. Three arrows extended from the corpse's bloodied chest. The sight stole her breath and made her dizzy. The ground was dark red around him. The dead man's white eyes were locked as if enjoying blue sky. His mouth was open; a silent scream. The hot death stench that enveloped the green forest made her gag.*

*Toál laughed. "What is wrong, Princess? Have you not seen the glorious dead?" He yanked her over the bloated corpse. An arrow shaft snagged at her pant leg, making the body jerk. The arrow twanged. The bile rose in her throat and she vomited along the edge of the path.*

*Toál chuckled. "Poor little girl. Let me make you better." He placed his hands on her waist and pressed against her.*

*"Stop it!" She pushed him away.*

*He threw her down the path and into Hell. Crows sat on the branches* and scolded at the intruders who invaded their meal. A shudder's cold finger crossed her back.

Back to the present nightmare, this was God's punishment for being so stupid, for really thinking she could be one of the cool kids. Nerds always remain nerds no matter what, no matter where.

Once done with her, those brothers would toss her hands on the path and the crows would wait for their meal. The guards would turn her into a statistic on the late-night news. Some girl walking down the street, minding her own business and BAM! A freaky guy with a bushy beard, wearing an old-time army jacket rapes her and tosses her dead body in a field somewhere for the crows.

She shoved her shaking hands between her thighs and blinked back the tears. *Don't cry. Be smart. Do what Conell wants, look for your chance to get away and find the cops. Please, God, help me.*

She checked Frigg's wounds and placed her hand on his forehead. "The bleeding has stopped for now. He doesn't seem to have a fever, but I don't know if he'll make the trip."

"He has no choice." Conell kicked a brick into the pile of stones.

A large beetle scurried from under the rumble. A quiver rippled across her chest. *I hate bugs!* Her gaze refused all orders to avoid the two men and she wandered back to them.

Both men had removed their shirts and tight muscles covered their backs and arms that bulged with each toss of the rock. Conell's long silver dreadlocks floated against his sweaty back and Émer's scraggily hair fell in his purple eyes.

*Purple eyes? People had green, brown, blue, even black, but purple eyes?* Strange curling tattoos followed the curve of his jaw. The art looked like a vine with many branches. And Conell's eyes were a strange green, lime-colored. They looked like hot guys from a famous boy band. But these guys weren't singing and no one was cheering.

She would give anything to be in chemistry class right now, ignored by Kyle Peterson, the school quarterback—her secret crush—instead of sitting in this scary cell ignored by these two nuts. God only knew what Conell and Émer would do to her when they left the cell, but at least with these guys she'd have a fighting chance. Hopefully, help would be beyond this bizarre prison and in the park.

She pushed back wounded Frigg's hair from his eyes. The freckles on his face and red shoulder-length hair made him seem more like a fifteen-year-old kid who took care of the football team's equipment, as opposed to a prince's advisor.

How did these guys get into such a place as this? Émer had said that today was Conell's eighteenth birthday. The captain seemed older than Conell, maybe by a few years. And what did Émer mean when he called Conell a prince, himself a captain and Frigg an advisor? England had princes, and this place wasn't England. Who calls themselves Prince anymore? Well, except for Prince, the singer, she mused. And what about their clothing? Gray prison clothes? And the guards looked like something from the Renaissance Faire. Who dressed like that? Only those who are in Cosplay and this was far from Cosplay.

Imie started to think that maybe she was crazy. She needed to distance herself from these weirdoes as quickly as she could whether these people belonged to Buckingham Palace or not.

Émer broke through her thoughts. "Imogene, come, we go."

She rose to her feet. If the guards caught them escaping, they would die in short order. She took a deep breath and licked her dry lips.

Émer placed his hand on her shoulder. "Come, help me with Frigg. No harm will come to us."

They lifted the wounded man to his feet. Frigg's head rolled back and he blinked his eyes several times. "Captain Émer, where are we?"

"We are leaving this place and heading for home." Émer wrapped his arm around his friend.

Conell nudged Imogene away from Frigg and slipped his arm around his advisor's waist.

The wounded man's eyes rolled to the prince. "I am sorry, Your Highness. I will slow you…" His head rolled back and he **slumped** into Conell's arms.

Conell tightened his hold on him.

"Imie," Émer said, "take my place."

She slipped beside Frigg and slung his hand over her shoulder. Émer grabbed a torch off its holder and plunged into the dark tunnel. Conell took a step forward, dragging her and Frigg into the murky passage.

The passage immediately narrowed. "*Chuoha*," Conell said. "Go before us. Once the tunnel turns, assist me with Frigg."

She swallowed but nodded and stepped in front of them. Hopefully, Conell's attention lay with Frigg, and he wouldn't jump her from behind. If he wanted to kill someone, this was the perfect place to do it—slice her throat and toss her aside. Blood pooling under her body. No one would find her corpse in a cave especially if they bricked up the hole. Gone forever. Disappeared. She took a deep quivering breath, but it did nothing to quell her trembling.

The low ceiling brushed against her hair. She ducked and swiped at the crown of her head. Hopefully nothing big and black with eight legs had invaded her curls.

The walls narrowed. She forced her feet to follow Émer's light. One step at a time. The air became stale and her breathing quickened. She would die in here, suffocate. The ceiling eased lower and lower, squishing her like a bug.

Émer extended his arm. "Take my hand, Imie."

She grabbed his palm and squeezed his callused fingers.

"We are almost to the passage. There we will have more room," Émer called.

True to his word, the tunnel curved to the right. She reluctantly released Émer's hand and slung Frigg's arm over her shoulder. The ceiling grew a bit, but not much. The light from the torch caused shadows to snake and lunge across the cold stones. She blinked back her tears. This was almost too much—the hand, the dead man with staring eyes and the stench from the cells.

Community service looked great right now. She would pick up

the trash in all the parks in Illinois to get home again. *Did the supervisor call the cops and tell the judge she ran away? What if she did get home and the ticked-off magistrate sent her to Juvie Hall.*

A juvie record would destroy any chances of her attending The University of Chicago. This was her mess—a stupid plan to get a date with Kyle.

Ruárc and Toál would find the opening, brick it up and bury them alive. Kyle had forgotten her by now. He was probably snuggling with one of the big-breasted cheerleaders. He ignored her when the cops hauled them off to prison and he would ignore the two crazy guys who dragged her into the dark forest.

Her fingers dug into Frigg's wrist. The young man moaned. She looked over her shoulder, but blackness enshrouded the tunnel. Breathe in, breathe out, breathe in, breathe out. One step at a time. Oh please, don't brick up the opening!

*"Tamo Chuoha,"* came Conell's voice from the dark. "Keep calm, we are almost there. You can rest once we reach the forest."

She jumped. "Why do you call me, *Chuoha?*"

Conell chuckled. "You are a stranger to this land. Tamo means little and *Chuoha* means princess. How sad that we do not have a throne for you."

Émer snickered and coughed.

Imogene's mouth dropped open. "You mean you are calling me a princess, as in a spoiled-rotten princess? You're such a jerk!" If only she could kick him.

The dirt walls muffled his laugh. "Yes, Tamo Chuoha, but I was not the one who gave you the name, it was the *Mee* who named you."

"Me?" she asked.

"A dog, it is an insult to call one a dog," Émer said.

Imogene smiled. "A dog? Well, mee is worse than Chuoha."

"Yes, it is," Émer answered, "and I could call you Mee-Che, which means dog-droppings. And to hold up one's fist with the thumb facing to the side is more of an insult. It means you are an animal."

Imogene grinned. "The other guard was the mee-che. We have a gesture similar to yours. It's a bit different though."

Émer stopped and lifted the light. "Moji, I think we are here."

Conell leaned Frigg against her. Taking the torch, he shined it onto the ceiling. The light showed a small squared outline dug into the dirt ceiling. Émer shoved upwards on square. A soft thump sounded above them.

A chilled night breeze ruffled her curly hair and she filled her lungs with the fresh evening air. They weren't bricked in; soon she'd be outside and hopefully free.

Conell lowered Frigg to the ground and thrust the end of the torch into the dirt. "Stay with him, *Chuoha*, while we scan the woods. And remember my words."

Imogene sat on the ground and moved her hair aside. Frigg laid his head on her shoulder. The scary dark lurked beyond the torch light. It jabbed and slithered across the walls and floor as if toying with them. No soft footsteps came from the darkness. Maybe the guards didn't check the cells. Maybe.

Minutes ticked by. Had five minutes lapsed or five days? Maybe the arrogant prince thought Frigg wouldn't survive the travel and she was extra baggage thus leaving them to face the guards alone. Toál would find the tunnel, follow the light and find her and Frigg. Imogene thought of Ruárc's rough hands shoving her onto the bed. Maybe she should put out the torch. *And sit in the pitch dark?* Toál told the other guards that they could have whatever was left of her when he had finished. *How did I get into this mess?* A soft whisper escaped her lips, "Dear God, please help me."

"*Chuoha.*"

She jumped and squealed.

"Do not fear, *Chuoha*." The sound of crushing dirt came towards her. "It is I." Conell's strong face appeared in the light. "You are as a small mouse." He slipped past her and hauled Frigg to his feet.

A deep breath of relief escaped her. "I…I… thought you were gone."

"No, not today. Come, we have much ground to cover." He led them to the small hole and lifted Frigg up to Emer who pulled Frigg out.

Conell boosted her through the opening to Émer who gently drew her out of the hole.

She dropped to the ground. The cold air made her shiver. The same pitch black from the cave followed them and gave the tree silhouettes an appearance of possessed scarecrows waiting for their next meal. The cries of night animals drifted through the lonely forest. The moonlight filtered through a creepy, chilled fog that swirled around the branches and flowed to the ground like a ghostly waterfall.

Conell hauled his large frame through the hole and then hoisted Frigg over his shoulder.

"Are you sure you wish to carry him?" Émer asked.

Conell pushed past him. "My hand put us into Father's prison, I will get him out. We will move faster this way. We have at least five hours before the sun rises and the guards discover us missing. We can make Shes Cheez within six hours. We stay in the woods, avoid the hunting parties and the main roads."

"Aye, My Moji," Émer said softly. "But remember, we still must slip past the Jabba-Nott."

Imogene rose to her feet. "Wait, the guards said something about feeding my supervisor to a Jaba-thing when they found me. What is a Jaba-whatever?"

"A Jabba-Nott is a boar who feeds on men's flesh, Jezebel's favorite pet," Émer said.

"A man-eating boar? No, no, no, please, I don't want to do this." Imogene dropped her face into her palms. Someone wake me up!

Émer pulled her hands from her face. His dark head bobbed. "Imie, we have no choice. Do not fear. The Attiyq would punish me if I allowed harm to come to one who is ill. I will not allow it to harm you."

30

"Émer," Conell said. "I will lead; you keep an eye on our mysterious visitor."

Profane words sat on the tip of her tongue, but she swallowed them. It's best not to rock the boat, at least not yet. Émer took her hand and led her into the dark and foggy forest.

"Where is this Shes Cheez?" she asked.

"It is due south as the oza flies, My Lady," Émer said. "There are friends of Voobo-Maúl who will take us in and protect us."

Conell snorted. "Your trust lies in too many hands. Jezebel has her teeth in everyone's neck. We must reach the coast and leave this cursed place."

"You would rather trust pirates than your own people?" Émer asked.

Conell shifted Frigg's limp form. "Own people? They are no longer my people."

3

"Please have mercy upon us, My Queen!" Two trembling guards bowed with their faces to the floor before Queen Jezebel who sat on King Efuko's throne. Ruárc knelt beside them and lowered his head. The servants, keeping themselves in the shadows, scurried in and out of the murky throneroom. Fear swept across the palace over the prince's escape and the queen's wrath fell upon all those who faced her.

Jezebel rolled her eyes and looked to Argus, her personal

guard, who stood behind the King's throne. His dark orbs caught her angry face and he shrugged. She drew her attention back to the begging sentries.

A yawn escaped Argus's lips and he tucked his floor length white wings tighter around his body and folded his hands in front of him. Did Jezebel really think Conell would give up easily? The foolish woman again underestimated Conell's strength, believing the boy would die as easily as the other prisoners. She believed the young man to be a coward, but hidden inside him lay his father's strength, built from his forefathers—courage the woman should fear and respect. He stifled a chuckle. Jezebel was a fool.

"Explain to me how Conell and his friends escaped." Jezebel's long red nails drummed the throne's arm and she brushed her long black hair from her thin pale face.

The guard licked his dry lips. "My Lady, I do not know. It seems they found a tunnel and, well, escaped."

Jezebel's eyes questioned Argus who raised an eyebrow. Again, Jezebel played the fool.

She drew her red lips into a tight line. "What do you mean they found a tunnel? What tunnel?"

"I do not know, My Lady, it led to the woods." The guard's voice trembled. He licked his lips. His face fell.

Hope slid away from him and escaped through the cracks in the walls. Eagla rose from the floor as a phantom and wrapped her thin arms around the guard. Her long black sequin gown flowed over her thin curvy body. Argus placed his hand on the back of the throne and breathed in his child's fragrant wildflower scent. He grinned. Only he could see his beautiful children, his cherished secrets.

Eagla's long red hair floated on an invisible breeze as she glided to Argus and her cold fingers stroked his white feathers.

"Oh Master, how I have missed you." She kissed him passionately.

His toes tingled. Eagla drifted back to the guard and intertwined around the man. Her greatest talent, fear, entered through his eyes, ears, mouth and pores. The guard's face grew white, and his body shrunk before the wrath of the queen. Argus closed his eyes and smiled. Eagla was his delightful child.

Jezebel placed a fingertip against her lips; her other fingers cradled her jaw. "Argus, did you know about a tunnel?"

He shrugged. "Many tunnels cross the lands from the days of King Broden. They could have found one of them." He smothered a smile. Of course, the old king had made tunnels. The guards, the generals, and captains to the lowest of the king's men knew of the tunnels. The woman's shock proved her worthlessness.

She settled her anger back on the terrified guards. "You let them get away."

The guard's face went from pale to ghostly white. Argus grinned. Eagla squeezed the man's heart and smiled at it as a child discovering a new toy. Argus beamed with pride.

The guard's garbled words tumbled from his shaking lips. "My Lady, it was not our fault."

Ruárc raised his head and his steady eyes bore into hers. "If I may, My Queen, I overheard an interesting conversation from the prince and the others. You might find it useful. My brother, Toál, and I captured a strange girl in the woods near the prison. We threw her into the Moji's cell, hoping to keep her for ourselves since we were still on duty. She was to be our celebration after DeCapris's death." Ruárc grinned. "Anyway," he continued. "I heard her tell them she held a strange medallion and claimed it brought her here from another place. She did not know the prison or the prince and spoke strange words. The prince feared the girl was a spy sent by you. The captain claimed she was insane. I was called away and was unable to hear the rest. My brother and I will hunt them and bring them to you if you spare our lives. You know we are the best hunters in the land."

Argus straightened and his gaze fell upon Ruárc. "Describe the medallion."

"It was large with a purple stone in the center." Ruárc made a

34

circle with his index fingers and thumbs. "The prince said the writings were ancient."

Argus sucked in his breath. Could this item be what he sought these long years? He nodded. Fate placed him here for this time; to reclaim what once belonged to him. He struggled to keep his voice calm. "Where is this girl from?"

"I do not know, My Lord," Ruárc said. "I did not understand her words. Perhaps from the Northern Territories?"

Argus swallowed his excitement. For ages, he had heard stories of the Attiyq's Medallion, but it hid itself from everyone, including him, The Great Argus, leader of all men. Why it avoided *him* was a mystery. Was he not The Great One, higher than all mankind? Would it not be proud to hang around his neck to help him lead the lower beings scurrying across the planet? Did it not hear his heart cries? He would cherish it and use it for his and all mankind's glory. He paused. No, it would be for *his* glory and men would follow *him*. But why pick a weak female human and why now? Why not *him*? He shrugged. Soon it would be in his hands and the medallion would understand. It would agree and free him from the Attiyq's bondage and this useless woman. Yes, it would wait for him, The Great Argus, leader of all that is evil.

"Argus?" Jezebel asked. "Is something wrong?"

Argus leaned down to her. "My Queen, I suggest you take Ruárc's offer and track down the prince and his companions. The prince and his two friends are to die. Kill them quickly, but as for the girl, I would like to know where she is from and this strange medallion. Execute the guards for their stupidity, but use Ruárc and his brother."

Ruárc smiled and rose as his two companions' withered. Pleas of forgiveness fell on deaf ears.

Eagla giggled and rushed into Argus's arms. "Do not be long, My Master. I will be waiting for you." Her hand held onto his as she disappeared into the floor.

Argus's stomach rumbled. The two guards would taste good

this time of day.

"I give you my word, My Lady," Ruárc said. "I will find them."

Argus beckoned the queen's personal guards and pointed to the two men trembling at Jezebel's feet. One of the accused raced for the queen's personal doorway, but the queen's guards tackled him and dragged both screaming men from the throne room. The door slammed shut. The men's screams faded down the hallway.

"Ruárc," Jezebel said. "Spread the word amongst the hunting parties, travelers and the merchants, ten thousand *Ozefu* for the girl alive and the medallion, kill the others. But I want the girl and the medallion."

Ruárc bowed. "As you wish, My Queen. My brother and I will follow their trail. I promise you we will not fail." With his head held high, he strolled from the king's room.

"What are you thinking, my love?" Jezebel rose from her throne and her cold fingers brushed a strand of silver hair from Argus's face.

He kissed her fingertips. Her charms grew tiresome, the way she strove to seduce him. But who seduced whom? He cupped her face in his iced palm and whispered in her ear. "She may have the Attiyq's Medallion."

Jezebel's black eyes widened. "I have heard legends revolving around the medallion. It is said to have great powers."

"Yes, my love, great powers. The Attiyq's medallion can lead the wearer to great weapons no man can resist or stand against. No one. What does Conell know about the medallion?"

"Nothing, I kept these things from him. He is spoiled, arrogant, and rude, but I do not understand why he would bother with an insane girl. He cares for no one but himself."

Argus shrugged. "Nothing matters but the medallion. Nothing."

"How much farther?" Imogene planted her palms on her knees and squinted into the dark trees. Her long hair fell around her face. "We've been walking forever."

"We have been traveling four hours." Conell lowered Frigg onto the ground and stretched his arms over his head. "*Chuoha*, check Frigg. Émer, the Jabba-Nott's lair lies ahead. We must find weapons."

Imogene felt his forehead. "I think he has a fever, Prince Conell. He needs a warm place to rest or he might die."

Émer nodded to his left. Again, he used the foreign language. Émer kept glancing at her. He must know of her plans to escape, but the woods were still very dark. There had to be a better opportunity.

Conell squatted on the ground and studied the darkness. His green eyes looked into the black sky. "The night *Nool* has set, the sun will soon rise. The guards will be upon us quickly. Yet, the Jabba-Nott lies before us." Conell rubbed his chin. "I can only see one way out of this, Émer. You and Frigg go on, I will distract the Jabba-Nott, allowing you two to slip past it to safety."

Imogene tucked a strand of hair behind her ear. Conell failed to mention her; maybe she could slip away, make her way back towards the prison and find the park.

Her eyes took in the blackness smothering the once fresh green woods. Scenes from slasher films flickered in her mind. The stupid girls who ran off into the darkness with the killer close behind always ended up dead.

Émer crouched beside his friend. "Nay, My Lord. I will not disobey my father's last order. I will not leave you behind to die, but would rather taste death with you. We must find another way. And what of the girl?"

There goes Plan A; Plan B quickly formed in her head. Taking a deep breath and praying this would work, she took a step forward.

"I have a better idea." Her voice cracked. "I mean if you want to hear it. I saw it on TV once—a late-night movie. I like some of them, others are lame. Netflix has some cool shows though. Folks made them years ago in the seventies, old stuff."

Conell scowled at her and Émer gave her an impatient look.

She tugged at a curly strand of hair and refused to meet their strong faces. "Anyway, in the movie, the good guys lured the bad guys into another bad guy's lair and let the two groups kill each other. It was kind of gory, but it worked. Maybe you could lure the guards to the boar thing?"

Émer's eyebrows rose. "She says lure Jezebel's men to Jabba-Nott who will enjoy its human feast, while we slip past them both."

Conell rose and glowered at her. "Why would you help us?"

She clicked her tongue. "Because I'm nice, okay? I'll make my way back to the forest where Ruárc found me and find a phone or something. You don't want me here, I'll go now."

Émer spoke in the native tongue to the prince.

Conell shrugged. He crossed his arms over his chest and lifted his chin. "How do I know you will not lead the witch's men here?"

If he wasn't as big as a quarterback, she'd rip that egotistical chin right off his haughty face. Instead, she looked away. "I won't, I'll tell my aunt I was lost or something. No one needs to know this happened." *Stop babbling, go.*

She took a step into the woods, but Conell grabbed her arm.

"Please, I promise. I won't tell anyone about you."

His hand tightened around her bicep. "I am not letting you out of my sight until you either take your last breath or we arrive at the coast."

"You said, Émer and Frigg, not me. See ya, I'll be going." She tried to twist from his grasp.

He jerked her back. "Maybe I will use you as bait for the Jabba-Nott."

"You can't use me as a carrot. You may be a prince, but you're not mine." She yanked her throbbing arm from his grip.

He wrapped his fingers around her throat and dragged her forward. "Yes, I can."

The pressure increased, making her gag. This was her tomb, the scary dark far from home. *I won't see Momma or Aunt Laurie ever again. No marriage, no kids. Just a dark tomb, covered with hungry crows.* Tears rose in her eyes and she nodded with submission.

Conell threw her back. "Good, now we have an understanding. I will lure Jezebel's men to the beast, you three prepare to run."

*Oh God! They're going to kill me!* A thousand ants crawled inside her belly. She looked up with watering eyes. This is how it happens. A psycho steals a girl from her home and no one sees her again. Poof, vanished. *Is this what it feels like to disappear into thin air? Would it really hurt to die?*

Émer wedged himself between them. "I will go back and find the *mee*. Once I spot him, I will meet you one mile north of the beast's lure." Émer lifted his hands and spoke the foreign language to Conell.

Conell frowned and rolled his eyes, but nodded.

Émer gave her a small bow before trotting into the forest. "You are safe, My Lady."

The prince heaved Frigg over his shoulder. "Well, *Chuoha*, I am glad I did not leave you behind."

She resisted the urge to stick out her tongue.


Imogene squinted up at the stars. They seemed to have moved a bit across the sky, and according to last year's science class, at least an hour had passed since Captain Émer slipped into the woods. A yawn escaped her and she stretched her back against the tree trunk.

The moonlight spilled over into the small clearing and covered the trees in a silvery satin cloth. The cracking chirps of the crickets and an occasional hooting an owl eased across the dark expanse. For a split second, the nasty guy, the killer-pig, the dark and the two psychos disappeared.

A smile tugged at her mouth. The woods wouldn't be so bad if Kyle were here to protect and lead her to safety. His strong lips pressed against hers to chase away all fears. The strong hero would face the killer and chop him into pieces. Of course, as luck would have it, this romance scene included two lunatics running around with swords thinking they belonged in *Conan the Barbarian*. So much for starry-eyed movie themes.

Frigg's head rested in her lap. "Father, do not leave me."

"Hush now, go back to sleep." She stroked back his damp hair. His forehead grew hotter.

Conell stood facing the Jabba-Nott's hunting grounds. A deep growl and strange words came from his throat as he paced the small perimeter. His keen eyes searched the blackened forest for Émer. He looked like a crazy man—a guy who wouldn't let a prisoner escape. Imogene knew he would kill her sooner or later. She just wasn't sure how he would do it.

"Moji," came Émer's voice from the trees.

Imogene jumped. The leaves were undisturbed by Émer's feet, even the crickets seemed uninterested by his sudden presence.

"I thought you had lost your way." Conell crossed his arms over his chest.

Émer grinned as if Conell told an inside joke. The two men looked like dim statues as a cloud passed over the moon.

"They are three miles behind us," came Émer's soft voice. "But they move quickly, they will be here soon. We must make our way to the beast if we are to live."

Imogene chewed on her nail. Maybe this wasn't such a good idea.

Conell nodded and pulled Frigg to his feet. "Émer, you and *Chuoha* carry Frigg; I will lure the men to the Jabba-Nott."

Émer placed his hand on Conell's shoulder. "Nay, My Prince. You carry Frigg; I will lure the men to their deaths. I am faster and you are stronger. Do not argue; time is fleeting."

Conell shook his head, but he knew by his determined look that Émer had made up his mind. Conell reluctantly nodded and hauled Frigg over his shoulder. Émer trotted off into the woods. The prince yanked her to her feet and shoved her. "Try anything and I will kill you."

The burning tears threatened to fall. Imie had no other plans. The black tomb of trees enclosed around them as they stepped into the dimmed forest. The skeleton trees' finger-like branches snagged her hair and clothes. She'd be trapped in this dark wooden crypt forever. No search crew would find her bloodied corpse. Her body would be leftovers for the crows—no visitation, no tombstone, no burial, dying here alone in the scary dark forest far from home.

This might not be the end if she gave him what he wanted. *Stay alive for this moment, this second. Focus on this second. Nothing else matters but this second.* Morals, beliefs and the future slipped away. This second and keeping it alive mattered the most. A tear slipped down her cheek and she angrily swiped it away. No. That egotistic madman would fail in stealing her tears, the only thing she had left. This second is all that mattered, this second.

He led her to a tree and lowered Frigg to the ground. "Sit with him."

She nodded and sat, cradling Frigg's head in her lap.

"Child," Frigg said. "Get out of here while you can."

"Hush now." Her voice cracked. "You have to rest; we'll be safe soon."

"How is he?" Conell knelt beside them.

Her teary gaze locked onto the ground as her long hair hid her face, keeping her tears safe. "You need to get him to shelter. And he needs water. Please, let me go."

Conell surveyed the dark woods, and then his sharp eyes roamed back at them. "*Chuoha*, the Jabba-Nott is within the woods, Émer leads the soldiers here, you stay with Frigg, no matter what you hear, do you understand?"

She nodded and forced her bones to be still. He rose and disappeared into the black forest. A tremble raced through her. Maybe freedom did lie in the scary woods.

*Stay alive for this second,* she reminded herself.

The night grew quiet, broken by the crickets gossiping to one another. A crow cawed in the distance. Hopefully, they had forgotten about their free meal.

She looked down at Frigg. Without medical treatment, the young man would die. Conell had already stated his intentions. Only the three men would leave the woods alive. She thought about which would be worse—her allowing Frigg to die, or dying alone in the dark? A shooting star cut across the speckled night sky.

"Please help me get home," she whispered to whoever could be listening.

Frigg moaned. She pushed back his hair. *You have to make a decision. It's either you or him. Push him away and run. No one will blame you if you escape. They'll say you did the right thing.* She moved the young Frigg from her lap.

The sound of leaves crackling underfoot drifted through the air. A twig snapped. She jumped and slapped her hand over her mouth. Shouts of men grew closer. Her choices disappeared.

The guards were here.

She bowed over Frigg. Small pleas fell from her dry chapped lips. The guards' thumping boots crashed through the thicket. She pressed her lips together forcing down the rising screams.

"Moji!" came Émer's cry through the woods, "Over here!"

The guards' shouts followed.

Imogene held her breath and closed her eyes. The crickets stopped. There was quiet except for the thundering of her heart.

Then a sharp squeal cut the air. Men screamed. Bushes rustled. Boots beat on the path. The nocturnal birds shook the branches. The Jabba-Nott had found its human meal. The human screams pierced her bones.

This was immoral, sending people to their death. It was a stupid idea. She cried and rocked back and forth, chanting, "This isn't real, this isn't real."

"Imogene!" came a voice from the shadows. She yelped.

Conell emerged from the woods. He held a bloodied sword. "Get up. We have to leave. Now." He grabbed Frigg's arm and lifted him to his feet.

"Going somewhere, Moji Conell?" asked a voice behind him. He whirled and raised his sword.

Imogene squinted trying to see beyond the dark trees. A figure stepped into the moonlight. *Toál.* She gasped. He had come to take her back. This was never going to end.

Conell chuckled. "Toál. Ever since you threw me into the queen's hellhole, I have longed to feel my blade slip between your ribs."

"What if I give you something better? Your freedom. Give me

the girl and you can walk away. *Chuoha*, Ruárc gave me a message for you, he misses you as do I." He smacked a kiss.

She cringed. Toál would love to add her bones to the ones on the path.

Conell lowered his sword. "Why do you want her?"

"It is not I, but Queen Jezebel. Walk away, give the girl to me."

Imogene shook her head. "No, I don't want to go with him. Conell, please, please don't leave me, please. I can't go back to that horrible place. I'll do whatever you want, just please, don't." The stench of the cell filled her nose.

His eyes locked on her wet face as if reading her soul. He shifted his attention back to Toál. "Why does the queen want her? Does she spy for Jezebel?"

Toál laughed. "You are still foolish, DeCapris. Now, why would the queen send me here if the little bird worked for her? No, she is a prisoner. But the queen placed a large reward on this one, ten thousand *Ozefu*, alive. She gave orders to kill you and your friends, but I will let you go. I want the money and the girl more than I want you. Give her to me. And you live another day."

Conell's gaze dragged from Toál back to her.

How did this happen? A few hours ago, she picked up trash in the park. Aunt Laurie was waiting at home with a birthday cake with sixteen lit candles. Now, this animal bargained with a psycho to drag her back into hell. "God, please help me."

Conell nodded and held out his hand. "You offer much *Ozefu* for one small girl. I will give you my hand in a pact."

He actually agreed to Toál's offer! None of this was real. A bad dream, a nightmare caused by stress. *Oh, God, please make me wake up.* Words tumbled from her frozen lips. "Conell, please…I swear…I'm not working for her." Crows cawed in the distance.

Toál smiled and lowered his weapon. "You are wise, Moji."

The guard took a step forward and extended his hand but paused. His eyes lingered on Conell's outstretched hand then rose to his face.

Conell extracted his hand. "You do have the *Ozefu*, correct? I need the money in order to escape the queen. I will not give you the girl unless you give me what I want."

Toál shrugged. "Why would I lie to you, Moji? I only want the girl."

Conell's gaze roamed over her. "What will you do with her?"

"My brother and I wish to enjoy her for a while, then give her to the queen. Give her to me and I will allow you a few minutes of joy with her along with the *Ozefu*."

Conell raised his eyebrows and nodded. "You make a pleasurable bargain. One that I will enjoy."

Imogene shook in disbelief. Her nightmare was becoming more real.

Toál grinned and reached for Conell's outstretched hand. "It is a deal."

Conell jerked Toál towards him and plunged his sword into Toál's belly and through his back. "You are still a fool who dances with swords, Toál."

Toál gasped as he looked at the blade buried in his body. His lips moved, but his voice was frozen.

Conell grinned and yanked out the weapon. Toál dropped to his knees and fell on his face. Blood pooled under his torso.

The psycho prince stepped before her. His breath came in deep drags. Sternness sat in his hooded eyes. Blood dripped from the blade.

She screamed and staggered away. The insane killer's footsteps crunched the twigs. An arm wrapped around her waist. A hard body pressed against her back; a strong arm locking her in place. He planned to finish the job.

"Please, I swear to God I won't tell." The words were caught in her throat. The world spun. Her nails dug at his hands. "Oh, God, please don't kill me! I swear I'll do whatever you want."

He spun her around and held onto her arms. "Calm down, Imogene, I will not harm you. *Chuoha*, you are safe now."

"I swear I'll do whatever you want, please don't kill me." Her knees buckled; he steadied her.

"Calm down, I will not harm you. I know you are innocent."

Imogene pushed his hands away. "Let me go, please."

The copper reek of Toál's blood filled the air and covered Conell's hands and her forearms. A crow landed on the branch above the corpse and called to his brothers and sisters. Her stomach flopped. She whirled and vomited. Conell steadied her.

She shoved his hands off her waist. Words fell from her dry mouth. "Please let me go. I swear I won't tell anyone what I saw. Please."

"I cannot let you go into the woods alone." He reached for her.

She slapped his hand away and stepped from him. *Just get home; cling to the seconds. You know what he will do. Don't trust him.*

He grabbed her arm. "Come, we must keep moving."

"No. You killed that man." She wiggled her arm from his gasp.

He glanced back at the corpse. "I know. I am grieved you had to see him die. But I had no choice. Now we must leave. Please do not run, you will be lost in the woods."

Again, she shook her head. "Are you going to put me into a sex trade thing? I can't do that, please, let me go. Don't rape me, let me go." Her voice quivered and her legs refused to work.

Conell grimaced. "No, *Chuoha*, you are safe. I will not harm you."

She swiped away a tear. "You tried to kill me back there. You put your hands around my neck. You were going to give me to Toál. You said…"

His face wrinkled in pain. "I know, forgive me. I know you are not with Jezebel. I will not hand you over to him."

She stifled a sob. "What's with the change of heart?"

"Change of what?"

"Why are you doing this?" her voice peeped.

"Toál's words. The queen would never have put such a high reward on you if you stood by her side. You cannot stay here."

"Moji!" Émer jogged into the clearing. In one hand, he held a bloodied sword; in the other, a man's cape. His glaring purple eyes darkened into a deep violet in the soft moonlight at the sight of Toál's body. "Moji, my sword longed to kill him."

Bile rose in Imogene's throat, and she rubbed her forehead. These people were animals.

Conell grinned. "He offered you and me freedom for the girl. Fool. Thinking I would fall into his pit. Your sword will find Ruárc. The girl is not a spy of the witch. It seems Jezebel's eyes are on our young friend."

His black eyebrows rose. "Why?"

"I do not know, but she will travel with us. At least until we find a safe place for her." He spoke the strange language to Émer who nodded.

Émer's hand slipped into hers, but she yanked away and took a step back.

Conell again spoke to Émer, who extended his hand to her. "No, Imie, I could never do anything so vile. I am sorry we frightened you. And I have told you, the Attiyq demands I care for you. Please, come."

She was confused—so much violence and death. Weariness invaded her mind. This was too hard, and she slapped away his hand. "No, please, I want to go home. I want my mom."

"I swear upon the Attiyq, I will not harm you. I am a warrior of Voobo-Maúl, and I give you my sword, My Lady. I will take you home."

A loud grunt echoed from the forest, making her jump.

"Do not fear, I will protect you, My Lady." He draped the cape over her shoulders. "I do not want people to think you are a *Zuuho.*" Using water from Toál's water canteen, he wiped away the blood on her arms, then slipped his hand into hers and tugged.

At first, she resisted, but he wiggled her palm and she followed. Her feet fumbled; Émer steadied her. *Follow Émer. Home is too far away. Nothing else matters.* The cape smelled like a man's sweat. Some soldier had died in the cloak—eaten by a killer pig. A chill swept over her.

*Don't think about tomorrow, live for today.*

Conell hauled Frigg over his shoulder and stepped into the lead.

Her legs brushed against the dark ferns. The way home disappeared in the dark. The bright moonlight spilled over the trees and made them into skinless corpses.

"If I can find my way back to the park, then I can get home." Her fingertips rubbed her tight forehead as she mumbled. "I don't remember a Demon Forest anywhere near Peoria. I wish I wasn't so tired."

"Peoria?" Conell called over his shoulder. "*Chuoha*. This land is called *Ezasu*."

She stopped.

Émer tugged at her hand. "Come, Imie."

"*Ezasu*? No, we're in Peoria, Illinois, my home."

"No, Imie." Émer helped her over a log and her toe snagged on the wood. "Moji is right, this land is called *Ezasu*. To the south of us is *Uje Shoel*, Towering Peaks, then *Shes Cheez*."

"But how did I get here?" She rubbed the side of her neck. This delusion, coma, whatever it was overpowered everything, even the woods. All thoughts jumbled together in this Never, Never Land. Her thoughts were like a jigsaw puzzle scattered on the table.

"We will find a way to get your village once we arrive at the coast." Conell shifted Frigg's weight. He pointed up at the dark sky and spoke in his native tongue to the captain. Émer nodded.

"What did he say?" she asked wearily.

"He said we will follow the Ceq star at night to reach the southern coast. It points south."

"Like the North Star only it points to the north." Her gaze lifted to the dark sky, making her fingers tighten around Émer's grip.

The familiar patterns of Libra, the Little Dipper, even Scorpio slipped away from the black expanse as if they fled to their homes over Illinois. The stars now seemed to play a celestial game of tag. New dotted pictures covered the dark heavens. This wasn't real.

"My Lady?" he asked.

"My God," she whispered. "This can't be real."

"Imie?" Émer asked.

"No, you don't understand, I'm not here, I can't be here." Did someone pull a cruel trick? What if the door to the park was closed and locked? What if they left her behind to freeze or starve to death? *What if* … She tried to pull free from Émer.

Émer slipped his arm around her waist. "You are safe, Imie, do not fear."

"What if I'm dead?" she whispered.

"Your heart beats the same as mine, My Lady," he said. "We will find your village and your people. I will protect you."

But what if he disappeared like everything else? Her breath came out in deep gasps. "What if everyone disappears? I don't want to disappear."

Conell turned to her. "*Chuoha*, listen to me. It will be all right. Émer and I will not leave you and I will find a way to get you back to your village. Do you understand?"

She wrapped her arms around Émer's chest. *What if he can't? What if the guards dragged us back to the dungeon?*

Conell placed his hand on her shoulder. "*Chuoha*, calm down. As Émer has said, we will look after you and find your village. As you have Émer's sword, so you have mine. No one will harm you. Now be calmed."

Worries and fears fled his strong lime-green eyes and his firm face. He was a warm cave in a thunderstorm.

He smiled at her. She swallowed and nodded.

Émer pulled her forward, his arm still wrapped around her waist. "Do not fear, My Lady, I took the vow of the Voobo-Maúl, I will not break it."

She clung to his hand resting on her hip. *Voobo-Maúl, concentrate on Voobo-Maúl what ever that meant.* "Okay, I'll play, what's the Voobo-Maúl?"

"It means 'One-Who-Flies-on-the-Blade-of-a-Sword' or 'Sword-Flyer' in your tongue. I am the last of a great band of warriors. Jezebel killed the others."

"What happened to them? What if she finds you and Conell?"

"It happened a long time ago." Émer pushed aside a branch. "If we move ahead of her, she will not catch us."

The first fiery edges of the sun peeked from the horizon. Orange and red bursts of fire exploded across the sky and rose into the air as the sun emerged from the skyline. The men's eyes were locked on nature's performance.

"Father said sunrises were the Attiyq's way of starting over," Conell mumbled.

Émer's voice was soft and childlike. "I have missed these, My Moji."

Conell's gaze dropped to the ground as if to break the spell. "Émer, we cannot stop. The guards will be upon us soon."

"Aye, My Lord," Émer mumbled.

She moaned as they walked down the path. Conell led the way but looked over his shoulder several times, making her shudder.

"Émer." Imogene's voice was above a small whisper. "How do you know where we are going?" She looked for a scrap of normality. But in this crazy world, what was 'normal'? Émer and Conell seemed normal. Well, sort of.

"I know these woods, My Lady." Émer moved the hanging branches away. "The Voobo-Maúl held these woods before the rise of Jezebel and here we learned to wield our swords. Trust me." He pointed to the left. "Do you see that large rock?"

Imogene peered through the trunks of the trees. A boulder seven feet tall and four feet wide, protruded from the ground several feet from them. Strange markings peeked from under the ivy that covered the surface. Rusty swords protruded from the ground around the stone. "Yes, I see it."

"It is called the Maúl Stone. Here we carved the names of those who died in battle. We come here to remember their sacrifice. They died with their swords in their hands. We leave their weapons at the foot of the stone so the young will remember the dead."

She nodded. "We have something similar; it's called the Vietnam Wall in Washington, D.C."

"The Maúl Stone is a sacred place."

"So is the Wall."

He smiled at her.

"What are the markings on your face for?" She wiggled her finger in front of her cheek. "They look really cool."

He gave her a sad smile. "My father gave them to me when I completed the *Joem Lok*, my child training. He said the vines represent how I will grow into a warrior and how I will strangle my enemies in my grip. He was my *Gaevee*; my trainer and my voice before the elders. The lower ones here," he gestured to his jaw, "were given to me by a great warrior, who also trained me. And what is 'cool'?"

"Cool means they look impressive."

"Many Maúl markings covered my father's face. Each marking told a story of his battles and how he rose to become an elder. They looked *cool*."

She giggled. "Why do you have just the one?"

"It would be wise for us to make for *Uje Shoeli*," Conell said urging the group. "The beast will not leave his forest and hopefully, the mountains will hide us from Jezebel's eyes. Then we will reach *Shes Cheez*."

"Aye." Émer gave him a thankful smile.

A growling echoed through the dense trees. The birds squawked and dashed from the trees. The pig-thing had followed them. Émer whirled and grasped his sword. Conell slapped his hand over her mouth.

He hissed in her ear. "Do not scream or we will be found." Slowly, he pulled his hand away; she nodded.

"My Captain," Conell said, "we must move quickly. I do not wish to become food for the beast."

"Moji, I hear them!" Émer cocked his head.

"What's wrong?" Imogene yanked at Émer's sleeve.

"Who?" Conell asked.

Émer closed his eyes and his chest rose and fell in rhythm. "The guards. Four of them followed us through the woods." He opened his eyes. "They will be upon us soon, we cannot outrun them. We must face them, My Moji."

Imogene searched for the unseen enemy. Nothing stirred in the trees except the wind rattling the leaves and the morning birds announcing the sun's arrival. "How do you know this?"

The birds became quiet. The crickets stopped chirping.

Something lurked in the woods. Chills spread down her arms and she leaned closer to Émer.

"I heard them," the captain said.

She looked back at empty forest. "How can you hear them?"

He smiled and winked. "The Attiyq has gifted me."

A grin crossed Conell's lips. "Émer, I have an idea. Remember as children, we sought to hide from my father's eyes?" He lifted his eyes.

Émer's gaze followed his Moji's lifted face. "Aye, My Lord, the treetops! But how will we fight them from the trees?"

"We hide Frigg and the girl in the tree, while you and I once again set an ambush for the witch's slaves."

Émer chuckled. "Your father would be proud, Moji."

Conell pointed to the trees. "Imogene, you and Frigg will rest in those trees, while Émer and I set another ambush for the remaining soldiers."

Deception hides like a spider hiding from a fly. It waits until the last moment before sinking sharp teeth into its prey.

*– Writings of Jago,*
Son of Anu,
Leader of the Maúl Warriors.

## 5

Imogene's gaze followed the length of the branches reaching into the sky. "You're insane, I can't climb up there!"

"I will help you." Conell led her to a large oak tree and gently lowered Frigg to the ground.

Her wide brown eyes took in the myriad branches. "I can't."

"I am ready, Moji." The captain winked at the girl.

Conell hauled himself up to the lowest branch. *Mother's angry voice would travel over the castle lawns when he and his friends dangled from the branches. Mother would yell again if she saw him scrambling up one deep*

54

*in Yoem's Forest, but Mother's voice ceased on that bloody night. The 'What if's' traveled on the wind and blew their hot breath in his hair. Help the living, came Father's words. The accusing voices drifted away.*

Conell reached for Imogene. "Émer, help her."

He lifted her to Conell, who hauled her to the branch. She wrapped her legs around the limbs.

"*Chuoha*," he said. "I am going to the next branch and I will pull you up again, do you understand?"

She nodded. Conell inspected the many branches looming above. If she fainted or collapsed, her weight would drag them to a painful death. But there was no other way.

He held on to the branch above him, "I know you have gone through much, *Chuoha*, but soon we will reach the top and you may rest."

She gave him a long and discerning look. "How do I know you won't drop me?"

He grimaced and extended his hand. "*Chuoha*, trust me. I will not betray you. I have given you my word."

Imogene's small shaking hand slid into his palm and he helped her stand on the limb.

"We're so high," she said as her body swayed.

"Come, we are almost to the top. Do not look down."

Time slipped slowly by as they ascended the tree. Conell ignored the shooting pain in his muscles as he hoisted Imogene to the last branch. He moaned and stretched his throbbing arms. The lighted forest stretched to the gray prison buildings. Émer was correct; the four guards followed their trail. "I must go back and get Frigg. Do not fear, I promise I will not forsake you."

Émer climbed onto the branch with Frigg lying over his shoulders. "I decided to help you."

Conell gently lifted Frigg from the captain.

Émer winced and stretched his arms. "It has been too long since I have carried such a weight."

"You are aging, Captain," Conell said, grinning.

Émer grunted.

Imogene straddled the bough and pressed her back against the tree trunk. Conell sat Frigg in her arms.

Conell said, "I will come for you, I promise."

"Moji," she said. "This isn't a dream, is it?"

He touched her face and gave her a soft smile. "No, *Chuoha*, it is real." He followed Émer down the tree.

Both men reached the bottom branch and jumped onto the ground. Émer brushed away their footprints and sprinkled dirt and leaves around the tree. When they were done, the area looked untouched.

Conell chuckled. "You still have the power to amaze me. It is as if no one has touched this place. Are you sure you are not a true child of the *Eze*?"

Émer laughed. "No, My Moji, I am not of the fairies, but human such as you. My *Gaevee* taught me well."

Conell ignored the pain that ripped across his shoulders and back as he unsheathed his sword. "Lead the way, Captain."

Émer trotted down the trail to a path cut away from the dirt road, now covered with weeds and ferns. "Before the witch imprisoned us, trees fell across Yuh Road. I pray they still lie there. We can use the logs to ambush them."

The trees that hemmed the pathway created a cool green and brown corridor. A canopy of green lace stretched above them. Puddles of sunlight splotched the path.

Émer's eyes took in the green awning. "It has been years since I traveled the Maúl Road. I remember Father and me traveling with the merchants into the towns and villages. The Maúl guarded the merchants and they in exchange gave the Maúl their wares."

Conell frowned. "I am sorry that the Maúl are gone. And I am sorry I could not stop the witch from burning their scrolls."

"It is not your fault, Moji. I am thankful I was able to save some of father's scrolls. And I am thankful for Clemwyn." Émer smiled. "He was a good teacher and soldier. I learned much from him. I am still surprised he was able to read Father's scrolls and make out some of the teachings. Even in death, my father made him into a stronger soldier. He would have made a brave Maúl."

"Jezebel kept my hand from the sword, but Clemwyn placed the sword in my palm."

Émer chuckled. "All my life, I have wanted a scar on my face like his. I felt it made him look almost frightening, like a true warrior."

"When Jezebel ordered his execution my heart wept," Conell said.

"As did mine. My spirit was crushed when the witch burned Father's scrolls. Now, I have nothing. No training and no scrolls. How can I become Maúl without training? The blood of the Maúl races through my veins, but I cannot follow it. I cannot reach the level of elder warrior without the training. Perhaps this is where the Attiyq wishes for me to be. He has a plan; He knows my heart."

Conell held his tongue. It wasn't the Attiyq's hand that kept Émer from following his path, but Conell's stupidity. His thoughts haunted him mercilessly.

*"Here walks the traitor of Broden; he treads on the souls of the lost. His name will never be spoken, but keeps himself safe at all costs!" The creatures burst into laughter. Conell set his face and refused to look their way. A young TTisho, wearing a blood-covered silk and pearled gown, lay in the center of the road. She reached out a gloved hand; one of her fingers was missing and trails of red dripped off her arm. "Help me, My Moji," she whispered. Conell swallowed and walked past her.*

*"Forgive me, fair Afanen."*

*"Traitor!" Afanen hissed. "I trusted you!"*

Conell wiped away the sweat that broke out on his forehead. Once he and the others were free, he would listen to Afanen's accusations and all the other lost souls. Mother always said leave the past to the demons who rule it.

Émer laughed. "Do you remember the classes Lord Bach taught?" He stepped in front of Conell and pointed his finger at him.

"Now, Moji Conell." Émer lifted his voice to high squeal and made a pudgy face. "A prince must understand poetry and literature, otherwise, how will the kings beyond the borders accept you when you stand before their courts?"

Conell gave a soft chuckle. "Remember what Clemwyn used to say to Lord Bach when we would sneak from Lord Bach's classes and practice swords?"

Both men said together, "A strong warrior fights better with his sword while in the battle than quoting verses from the books." They laughed.

Conell gave his friend a soft smile. It seemed years since they last shared a joke. Jezebel's prison stole more than their youth. He peeked over his shoulder. *Thirteen-year-old Afanen had disappeared.*

"Once we reach the free lands," Émer said, "we must play a game of *Buvrems.*" He cupped his hands together and rolled an invisible ball along the ground. "I miss playing that game." He nudged Conell in the arm. "I always got the ball closest to the kkorr borr."

Conell suppressed a groan. *Buvrems*—their favorite childhood game. The once competitive sport of seeing which boy could get their larger ball or smaller ball closest to the kkorr borr had lost its joy since Father's death. Émer took the simple pastime as serious as sword fighting, even destroying the opponent's ball as it got closest to the kkorr borr. But for Conell, the rolling ball always materialized into Father's head lurching along the floor. The bloodied skull would stop in front of Conell and the mouth opened, saying, "Son, you betrayed me and the Maúl." He shivered and pressed back his tears, preferring the numbness.

"You always said it helped you to become Maúl," Conell said.

Émer's face twisted into a feign shock. "Yes, My Moji. All Maúl children play Buvrems and all of us win."

Conell gave the captain a sad smile. "I do not feel much like playing games anymore."

"You loved playing Buvrems, even disobeyed the teachers' orders not to play anymore."

"I know. I just cannot do it anymore. How much farther to the logs?"

"It is up ahead. My Moji, I thought once we escaped, you would be happy. But I see sadness in your eyes."

"It is nothing. I worry of the witch catching us."

They reached the two logs crossing the path. Émer pointed to the trees along the road "Moji, if you hide there and I, here, then we can attack and kill them as one. But first we must create a trail for them to follow."

Both men crossed the logs and followed the route for a ways. Émer surveyed the path behind them.

Conell followed his captain's gaze. "Where are they?"

Émer closed his eyes. "They are down the path. Moji. They wear the armor of the queen; they will have the advantage."

Both men brushed away their footprints as they crossed to the opposite sides of the roadway. Once in the forest, they eased back to the logs and crouched in the undergrowth. Soon the dull beating of boots on the dirt track drifted through the air.

Conell peered through the foliage and studied the enemy. The men wore armor shoulder pads, leather vests and pants. Only the squad's captain held a shield with the royal seal of a black horse's head, signifying his rank. Conell frowned. He nor Émer wore protection. This would not be easy. Each move must be marked and planned around the leather covering. Conell and Èmer would need to kill the captain and first guard quickly, thus confusing the remaining soldiers.

The queen's captain pointed at the footprints leading down the trail. His two men followed the tracks. The last remaining guard defended the path behind them.

Conell caressed the sword's hilt. The enemy had once sworn

allegiance to the Blood of Broden after Father's death to follow the House of DeCapris. Now, they stood by the witch's side. Betrayers of Broden and the House he built. Death would be a gentle punisher to the queen's traitors, but one he would enjoy.

Conell's gaze caught Émer hiding behind the trees. The guards bunched together. The company captain placed his hands on a log and heaved one leg over the fallen tree, while his comrade followed. The other two guarded the path.

One of men who guarded the road had a long bow and arrows slung over his shoulder. Conell raised his eyebrows. They could use those weapons. He nodded to Émer and both men rushed onto the path.

Émer stabbed the captain and slid his sword into the other sentry as they crossed the logs. Cries of death resonated through the forest.

The last of Jezebel's men drew their weapons and faced Conell. He licked his lips and forced away the knotting fear. The two men grinned at each other and took a step towards him.

Clemwyn's words rang in Conell's ears. *Do not allow the enemy to surround you, and show courage despite all fear.* Conell took a step back and tried to keep the men at bay.

Émer swung his legs over the log and drew the left swordsman from Conell.

Conell waited for the man to attack. Deep breaths calmed his nervous mind. *Watch your opponent,* Clemwyn had said—his voice coaching him. *Watch his arms and legs tense, his eyes narrow, his jaw clench. These small things will tell you more than his movements.*

The guard's arms tensed and his jaw twitched. Conell released his breath and waited.

The soldier charged. Conell ducked under the man's weapon. The man stumbled forward. Conell swung his sword at the back of the man's knees. The hard leather stopped the blade. The guard rolled forward and sprung to his feet. His elaborate armor was cumbersome and slowed his movements.

The man snarled and faced him. The impatience betrayed his bloodlust. Conell could use this to his advantage. He steadied his breath. *Let him come to you,* came Father's words. *Use the enemy's disadvantages as your weapon.* Impatience and impaired movements made a perfect combination.

This time the man stepped into the attack and brought his sword across the prince's chest. Conell brought up his free wrist, blocked the guard's swinging arm and thrust the blade into the guard's chest. He gasped and fell to the ground. Conell let out a sigh of relief and searched for Émer. His captain and the guard fought a few feet away. Émer's blade cut across the man's face. The man staggered back and Émer plunged his blade into the man's heart. He dropped onto the dirt trail.

Émer nodded to Conell. "Good, Moji. You remembered Clemwyn's teaching." The captain knelt beside each body and closed their dead eyes. "May the Great Attiyq have mercy upon you and forgive your sins." He cupped his hands together, raised them over his head and brought them down on both sides of his face.

Conell wiped the blood from his steel. "First, we strip the bodies; we will need their clothes if we are to travel to the seas. We can rinse off the blood once we reach the river."

He pulled the bow and quiver of arrows from the body and handed them to Émer. The captain slung the quiver over his shoulder. His strong fingers pulled back the bow and sighted down his arm. "This is a good one."

The two men undressed the corpses and jogged back to the tree that hid Imogene and Frigg. Conell scrambled up the limbs and reached the two hidden figures.

*Chuoha* gasped and clenched the branch. Frigg groaned and opened his eyes.

"Moji," Frigg gasped, "Where are we?"

Conell grasped his friend's shoulder. "We will soon reach freedom."

Frigg smiled weakly and his chilled body trembled.

The sunlight bounced off *Shioso Leo*'s flowing blue water which split the countryside. Crossing the River would be hard for Frigg and the girl. Jezebel would be protecting the only bridge and the orders remained: Kill everyone but the girl.

Time was slipping away. More sentries would pursue them once the queen discovered the guards failed. By now, all the hunters and travelers knew of the queen's high bounty so many would be pursuing the escapees. The fugitive group would have to cross at the river's shallow area and avoid all lanes of passage. Perhaps the Attiyq's hands would shield Conell from Jezebel's magic eyes.

Beyond the river, the gray and white peaks of *Uje Shoeli* reached for the sky like a child's fingers. Now that the air had become warm from the summer sun, Conell and the others could rest in the mountains for a day before moving towards the hills and onto the coast.

A lump formed in Conell's throat. Mother would have loved this warm afternoon with the mountains off in the distance. The red blossom field near the castle was Mother's favorite spot. Mother and Father were buried on a warm day like this one in that same blossom field.

*Mother had lain as if sleeping in the red velvet lined coffin. Seven-year-old Conell hoped to see her chest rise and fall, but it remained still. Mother hated the cold, so in order to keep her warm Conell laid her favorite dark-blue wool cloak over her slumbering form. Émer draped his arm over Conell's thin shoulders.*

*"Do you think it will keep her warm?" Conell asked.*

*Émer gave him a sad smile. "Yes, Moji, she will stay warm."*

*Conell buried his tears in Émer's chest.*

Mother's screams shattered Conell, but the guilt of knowing the blame laid at his feet diseased his soul. He should have told Father about the attack plans.

"Are you all right?" Imogene's pale face stared up at him.

He locked the guilt in a metal box. The sick girl, Émer and

Frigg now became the main priority. Lead the small group safely across the borders and to a ship that would sail to freedom. A hole would be Conell's kingdom, shame would be the throne, and a bottle of wine from the Southern Lands would be his queen. "Of course, *Chuoha*. It is time we leave this place. I need to help Frigg down first."

Émer climbed upon the branch. "I can get him; you help her." He stopped and his purple eyes absorbed the site of the distant mountains. A white thick fog settled onto the grey tops. It leaped and galloped over the ridge as if the vapor were one being—*Lozonj Moss*, or Living Mist, as the old ones called it. "Moji. How can we leave such beauty?"

Conell pointed to the *Lozonj Moss*. "Mother used to say that was the breath of God covering the lands."

"It looks so pretty," Imogene whispered.

"It is time we moved on, My Captain. If we do not leave, the witch will hunt us down." Conell hooked his fingers under Imogene's arm and helped her to stand. "We will go down the same way we came up, one branch at a time."

He climbed down to the below limb "All right, *Chuoha*, sit on the branch and slip down, I will catch you."

She whimpered, but Émer helped her to slide off and Conell steadied her on the branch. "That was quite easy, yes?"

A smile crept across her tired face. "I guess."

Bough to bough they traveled until their feet touched the ground. Émer dropped from the bottom branch as silent as a rain drop and lowered Frigg to the forest floor.

Frigg struggled to his feet. "I think I can walk."

"No." Conell heaved the young man over his shoulder and winced. "It will be easier and faster if I carry you."

"Émer, when I was up in the tree, I saw the river. Jezebel's men will be covering Eamon's Bridge as usual, but we can cross about ten miles downstream."

"Aye, Moji, I too saw it. It will be hard for Frigg and Imie, but I think we can make it." The captain gathered the bloodied clothes into a bundle and slung them over one shoulder and the bow and arrows over the other.

Émer once again took Imogene's hand and led them along the hidden Maúl paths. The group's speed slowed as the day grew hotter.

By mid-afternoon, Imogene dropped to her knees and rubbed her red and swollen eyes. "I'm sorry. I can't go any farther."

Émer handed the clothes and weapons to Conell. "Get on my back, Imie, I will carry you the rest of the way."

She moaned, but jumped onto his back. Émer matched Conell's pace. "I am worried, Moji, I fear the witch may have beaten us to the pass."

Conell shifted Frigg's weight. "The same thought entered my mind, but we cannot go back, nor can we cross into *Shez-Nool*. My father's domain belongs to the witch now."

Imogene yawned. "*Shez-Nool?*"

Émer bounced her up his back. "The territory of Ivory Moon. It is the king's castle, our home, now it belongs to her."

"Oh," Imogene said.

Before she could ask more questions, Conell said, "We must hurry. She might be waiting for us at the pass."

Émer nodded and trotted ahead; Conell wrinkled his nose. The captain loved to impress others.

Conell studied the girl as her head nestled on the captain's shoulder. *How could he be so cruel to one so innocent? She acted like a child, but was it just an act?* Father would have guarded the ill woman in the castle until he understood her motives. But they were running from the witch, away from the safety of the castle. What would King Broden have done? *What would Father do?*

Émer matched the prince's stride and used his native language. "You are quiet, My Moji."

"I was thinking of the girl. Do you really think her mind is ill or she is simply playing a part for Jezebel?"

64

Émer paused. "We have talked of this before. Based on her words, she must be ill. She does not follow the ways of *TTisho* nor Zuuho. Yet, all women in *Ezasu* fall into one or the other and she follows neither. She must be ill."

"But what of her clothes? She dresses as a man. Could she be running from someone, maybe be in hiding?" Conell asked.

"I do not have the answers you seek. She does not act as one in hiding, but one who lacks understanding. She is ill."

Frigg looked around Conell's shoulder. "But where will we take her? If Jezebel longs for her, then the girl may get us killed. It might be better to leave her with villagers in the mountains. She is not our responsibility."

"No," Conell said. "Father would never leave one behind who sought protection. Émer is right. I don't know why my distrust invades my mind," he shook his head attempting to remove the doubt. "She *is* my responsibility. And Ruárc will not cease until he has found her. I cannot hand her over to him. We know what he would do to her."

"I do not understand, Moji," Frigg said. "Why do you suddenly wish to cover her with your wings?"

Conell gritted his teeth and refused to meet Émer's questioning gaze. The black birds cried out *"If only, if only."*

"Because I am my father's son," Conell said. "Do not question me again." He paused gathering his emotions. "Émer, once we reach the Southern Lands, stay close to the girl. We will find a ship as quickly as possible and sail away. You will care for her if something happens to me. You are responsible for her, understand?"

Émer frowned at Frigg, who looked away.

The captain nodded. "Aye, My Moji."

"What made you believe in her innocence?" Frigg asked.

"Toál said the witch placed a reward over Imogene." Conell shifted Frigg's weight. "Ten thousand Ofezu."

"Such a large amount would make us happy for a long time," Frigg said.

"The Attiyq would disagree with you," Émer said. "You know He demands mercy. He would curse your life."

Frigg raised a finger. "Yet, even Gethin the Philosopher once said, 'Tis better to gather the grain in the summer than in the winter. For the winter cold eats a man's wages.'"

"And the Great One said, 'If you show mercy to others, I will show mercy to you.' And Frigg, you should also remember that the girl has shown you great mercy."

Frigg dropped his head.

Conell grunted. More babble regarding the Great Attiyq, the God who only cares little for the creatures crawling on the planet.

The one question he had avoided raised its ugly head: What if the ship captains refused to take them? Crossing the borders into the Southern Lands could mean their deaths. With Émer's Maúl Markings and Broden's mark on Conell, the Southerners would know the men's heritages as well as any ship captain. Separating from Frigg and the girl might be the only option. Frigg and Imogene would sail away safely on a ship, and Conell and Émer would meet their fate bestowed by the Southerners. The last of Broden and the last of Anu, perishing side-by-side. A fitting and brave death. One that Broden and Anu would bless.

"What do you think, Moji?" Frigg asked.

"What? I was not listening."

Émer chuckled. "You are always somewhere else."

"Émer," Conell said, choosing his words carefully. "Do you remember the story of Trou and Curre, the great Maúl warriors who saved a village by venturing into enemy territory while the others ran to safety?"

Émer gave him a quizzical look. "Yes, I remember, My Moji."

"If we must, you and I will be as Trou and Curre. And Frigg, you will take the girl to a ship and sail away. Do you understand? You will tell others that she is your sister and is under your

66

wing."

Conell held Émer's gaze. The captain gave his Moji a small smile. "Aye, My Moji."

"Yes, My Prince," Frigg said. "It will be as you have ordered."

The chatter filtered away. Hawks screeched overhead and small birds chirped in the trees. The wind rattled the leaves.

Conell scanned the path. The group had been walking for a while. He expected that the witch's guards would have shown up by now. The queen's men seemed to have disappeared. "What do you hear?"

Émer scowled. "Nothing."

"She would not give up easily, not for ten thousand Ofezu. Be on your guard, Émer, I fear we will walk into a snare."

"Our minds are alike. I thought the same." Émer straightened his back. "Forgive me, My Lady. But I must rest."

Imogene yawned as she slid off and rubbed her tired eyes. "Where are we? How long have we traveled?"

Émer leaned on his knees. "At least two hours and we are almost to the river."

Conell lowered Frigg to the ground and stretched his sore arms. "It was about this time when we ate the spiced meats from the Northern lands while on the castle balcony."

Frigg winced as he rubbed his neck and raised his shoulders. "Do not forget those fine breads. I wish we were there again."

Émer lifted his head and chuckled. "It seems a lifetime ago. I can hear the river; we are almost there."

Conell hauled Frigg over his shoulder. "As do I, so we must be close. Come."

Frigg stopped him. "Let me walk, Moji. I am feeling stronger. You must save your strength in case she is waiting for us."

"I can walk, too." Imogene slipped her arm around Frigg's waist and Émer led them through the trees.

Soon the soft sound of churning water drifted up from the riverbank and the musty smell of the river sat in the air.

"Moji," Émer said, "what now?"

"We make our way to the river and cross. There will be soldiers down by the bridge, but hopefully they will not think of checking the shallow part of the river."

Imogene placed her hand on Conell's arm. "But what if they are at the pass before us?"

"Then we run," he said. "Émer, stay with her and Frigg. I want to see what lies before us."

The captain nodded and Conell made his way between the trees and down a small embankment. The leaves crackled beneath him. The blue and white river came into view through the leaves.

He peered through the trees to the lifeless thin beach. Nothing stirred except for a lazy hawk circling in the sky. The river rambled past the forest and beyond it, gray mountains tops retreated into the clouds. A green pasture carpeted the countryside. The sweet smell of mountain air blanketed the land. Nature forgot the witch and preferred instead to lounge in her own serenity.

Conell shielded his eyes from the sun's brightness. Surely, Jezebel would have reached the pass by now.

Émer stepped beside him. "Moji, are you all right?"

"Yes, my friend, it is horribly quiet."

He nodded.

"Do you hear anything?" Conell asked.

"No. I hear nothing and the silence frightens me. Are you sure you wish to leave the girl with Frigg?" Émer whispered and gazed at him from the corner of his eyes. "Such a large amount would make him happy for a long time."

Conell nodded. "Frigg has always enjoyed luxuries. Do you not trust him? Do you really think he would trade her for the Ofezu?"

Émer shrugged. "I would feel better if she were with us."

"And if we go into the Southern Lands? Our markings tell a

story, the girl and Frigg have nothing. They would be safer away from us. Frigg has not betrayed us to the queen; he may not do so with the girl."

"I do not have the answers you seek, My Moji. I just question his heart."

Imogene and Frigg joined them.

"Wow! Who's that?" she asked, pointing to a monument of a strong man on a charging horse carved into the side of the mountain. The relief stood almost twelve stories high and ran the length of the mount. The firm-faced leader held a horn to his lips as if to give a sign to battle. A phantom wind blew his hair and clothes. The horse's legs disappeared into the stone. The man and beast looked like ghosts patrolling Ezasu.

"That is King Broden, the first King of Ezasu," Frigg said. "He is the greatest of our kings. This beach is called Broden's Beach. It was here where King Broden fought the enemies of the kingdom and won. Legends state that on nights when the wind blows hard, you can still hear the Horns of Broden calling for war. I can never be bored of this place."

"He looks so real," Imogene whispered. "It's scary, but beautiful."

Conell gazed crossed the vacant shore. "Yes, it is beautiful." He grinned at his captain. "We came here one year. Do you remember, Émer?"

Émer smiled. "I remember, My Moji. It was around your sixth birth-celebration. You fell into the water."

He chuckled. "And I remember you were frightened by a snake."

The captain's smile faded and his purple orbs probed the forest. "Moji! I was wrong, something approaches."

Conell's eyes followed Émer's gaze into the woods. "Human?"

He slowly shook his head. "No!"

The prince grabbed Frigg and tossed him over his shoulder, while Émer seized Imogene's small hand. They plunged into the cold river. A large black pig with bristled hair exploded from the trees and barreled towards them.

Conell pushed his way forward and struggled to stay afloat. Imogene tripped and fell face first into the water. Émer hauled her upright. The beast drove into the water.

"It is a wise King who refuses to take the hand of one who comes as an ally but hides a knife behind his back."

~ Told by King Ope, Sixth King of Ezasu
in the year 365 to his Captain of Guards
when the ambassador of the Northern Lands
attempted to lead the King
into a treaty that was not true.

The water splashed in Conell's face and blurred his vision.

Émer words shrilled over the water. "Run, My Lady!"

Imogene screamed as the boar plunged into the water. Émer unsheathed his blade and stood between her and the beast. The pig lunged at Émer.

"Émer, Imogene, run!" Frigg would drown if Conell dropped him in the water, yet the wild animal will kill Émer and Imogene if Conell wadded to the shore. Maybe he could reach the beach, drop Frigg and save the girl and Émer.

A shadow crossed the water, chilling the air. Conell raised his eyes.

A large man with massive feathered white wings—like a bird's—hovered over Imogene. Long white hair flowed behind the flying man like a floating cloud. White trousers and shirt billowed with each pulse of his massive wings. The hovering man gave the girl a crooked smile.

The flying creature plunged his sword into the Jabba-Nott's neck. Jezebel's pet stopped its charge and screeched. Its stubby legs collapsed and it sunk into the water. The front feet and snout bobbed above the surface.

Émer towed Imogene to the other shore. Conell staggered onto the beach and dropped to his knees. Frigg fell onto the sand. The Jabba-Nott shoved its head above the surface before disappearing into the river. The winged man vanished into the sunlight.

Conell placed his palms on his thighs. Men do not fly nor do birds resemble men. Yet, the Bird-Man killed Jezebel's pet. "Captain, what was that thing?"

Émer stood staring at the now empty sky. "A *Gazo*."

"A what?" Imogene sat and combed back her wet hair. The cape floated down stream.

Conell shook his head. "No, Gazos, along with the Attiyq, left us long ago."

"Then you tell me what we saw." Émer used his dry sleeve to wipe the moisture from his sword and slipped the weapon into his sheath.

Imogene wrung the water from the bottom of her shirt and smoothed out the wrinkles. "What's a *gazo*?"

"An angel of the Attiyq, I mean, the Ancient of Days." Émer gave the skies one last look before checking the bow and the arrows.

"Why would the Attiyq help us?" she asked.

"You ask a good question," Conell said.

Frigg struggled to sit up. "Because He has heard our prayers." He moaned and rubbed his face.

Imogene crawled to him and lifted the back of his shirt. His wounds began to bleed again.

Conell stood and brushed the sand from his pants. "The Attiyq has never helped us before, why would He offer His hands now?"

Émer shook his head and gestured to the mountain. "We need to be moving."

Imogene helped Frigg to his feet and slipped her arm around his waist. "Moji," she said. "We need to find a place to dry Frigg's wounds."

"We will find caves in the mountainside," Conell said. "Then we will rest. Émer, help me wash the guards' clothes."

Argus soared through the castle window and landed without a sound in the former queen's quarters. He slipped his large white wings around him and dropped to one knee behind the queen. "My Lady."

Queen Jezebel brushed her long black hair until it shined. Using a small dirty cosmetic brush, she carefully stained her white cheeks with red blush and puckered her colored ruby lips. Her beauty outshined her stupidity.

"It is done." He tightened his jaw. This game bored him.

"My pet is dead?"

"Of course, My Queen."

Jezebel released a long deep sigh and used an emery board to file her nails.

Argus struggled to not roll his eyes at the female's uselessness—even though she did keep his bed warm at night. But even the warm-bed games grew tiring and now this inept human sat like a baby dove in his palm. And one day, the strong hand would crush the infant bird. But only a true heir of Broden or a regent royalty could rule in the castle. Soon, however, the throne, land, and people would belong to him… again.

She gently laid the brush onto the table and caught his gaze in the mirror. Her tall, lean frame rose from the chair and bent over him. "You did well, Argus. My pet will understand his great sacrifice as all my servants do. Conell will not be easy to convince, he is stubborn and does not trust the Attiyq. The captain, on the other hand, maybe easier to manipulate. Be my angel of the Attiyq and bring me the girl; kill the others. But be careful."

He kissed her palm. "I am always careful, My Lady." His long wings opened and he flew from the window.

Conell watched as Imogene peeked into the cave that stretched back into the mountain. Its gaping mouth stood at least six feet high and a few feet wide. Moss covered the rocks that surrounded the cave and the daisies that grew around the entrance mouth gave the hollow an enchanted look. Conell brushed past her. The flying man seemed to know the girl; perhaps this young child act was pretense. If that was the case, the guards could take back what once belonged to them.

"It's awfully dark," she yawned.

"It will suffice us," he called over his shoulder. "We can build a fire here at the entrance. Émer, we will need food."

The captain flashed a boyish smile and adjusted his quiver. "Your wish is my command, My Moji." He gave a small salute before trotting into the woods.

Conell walked to the back of the cavern and ran his fingers

against the damp cool wall. Hopefully the cave did not intersect with Broden's tunnels. The girl lowered Frigg against the cave wall and sat beside him.

"How are you feeling?" she asked the younger man.

"I will survive," he whispered. "How are you?"

"Tired." She laid her hand on his forehead.

Conell walked to her and stood over them. "How is he?"

Dark circles sat under her droopy eyes and she yawned again. "He still has a bit of a fever, but I think he maybe getting better. I'm not sure."

Conell slipped from the cave and gathered wood from the forest floor. The girl pulled her legs to her chest, laid her head on her knees and her small eyes followed his movements. The large cave enveloped her small frame. He bit his lip as he gathered the twigs. Doubt and distrust seeped in. *What if Jezebel did send the girl to follow them and the guards slit their throats as they slept? Why did the bird-man smile at the girl? What does the Chuoha know?*

He made his way back to the entrance of the cave and knelt. Father and he had sat at the entrance of a cavern like this one years ago and made a fire together. *Put the smaller pieces of wood on the bottom with the dried leaves*, Father had said. *Clap the flint stones together.* A smile lingered on Conell's lips. Father could start a fire within seconds, while it still took him a while to create a flame. He blew on the small blaze until it caught the wood. Within minutes a fire burned.

She smiled. "Where did you learn how to make a fire?"

"From my father."

"Oh," was all she could say. A blush covered her cheeks and she gently laid out the guards' clothes before the small fire and helped Frigg move closer to the flames. "Oh, that feels better."

She gave Conell a small smile. "Happy birthday."

He fanned the blaze with his hand. "Happy what?"

"Happy birthday. Émer said you turned eighteen the other day…so…happy birthday. It's what we say when someone turns a year on the day they were born."

He nodded and shared her smile. "And happy birthday to you."

"We had a wonderful birthday, didn't we? Chased by a couple of crazy guards, a man-eating boar and now hiding in a cave. Yippee." She twirled her finger and twisted her lips. "Happy birthday to us."

Conell chuckled. "It will get better, you will see."

"I hope so. You don't think that was an angel back there?"

Maybe the girl was innocent. The "angel's" eyes did not hold sympathy or kindness for Imogene, but instead darkness slipped from the creature's face and threatened to devour the sunlight. The air grew cold when his wings flapped over their heads. Even the sun buried its face behind a cloud. He rubbed his eyes. These thoughts exhausted his already tired mind. A small sigh escaped the girl.

He pushed the judgments aside. "I do not know, but *E Vajie* has always ignored my pleas."

"I don't know either," she said. "But maybe God decided now was a good time."

Conell grimaced.

She bit her lip and looked away.

He chuckled. "Tell me about this medallion you found."

"Oh, yes I forgot about it," she said.

Frigg grimaced as he moved closer to the pair. "You found a medallion? Can I see it?"

She pulled the item from around her neck and handed it to Conell. "I found it in a bush, or more like it found me. It's a little heavy, though. It might be made of pure gold. I thought of selling it. Getting money to run away to New York takes a lot of money and that's where Mom lives. She's a famous model, at least that's what she says. Anyway, I've never seen her in magazines or on TV, so I'm really not for sure what she's doing. But she says she travels all over the world and…"

The babbling words drifted past him as the light grabbed the purple jewel turning the hue from shades of deep purple to light pink. The gold winked in the sunlight. The script must be the words of Broden, the first language of Ezasu. Only the old priests could read it and most of them died years ago. How did she find this?

Frigg looked over Conell's shoulder. "My Moji, what is it?"

"A very old medallion, perhaps before King Broden. I cannot decipher the writing, nor have I seen anything like this. But it maybe the reason why the witch pursues us."

"For the medallion?"

"Perhaps. Perhaps not," Conell said.

"But what was it doing in the park?" Imogene asked. "I mean, obviously, it belongs in Never-Never Land, so who or what brought it to my land?"

Conell grinned at her insanity. Émer was right; the girl's mind had fled. Why would Jezebel use a damaged girl to do her bidding? Such a being would not last long in the clutches of Ruárc or the queen. "I do not know how it came to your land. But it does not matter now." He gave it back to her. "And we need to do something about you." He rose to his feet and pulled a dagger from his belt.

Imogene gasped and pressed her back against the rock wall. Frigg raised his eyebrows.

"The guards are seeking three men and a woman, not four men," Conell said. "I need to cut your hair."

She jumped to her feet and brushed her hand over her unbrushed hair. "No, not my hair!"

"Would you rather face the witch?"

"No. But you don't understand. The girls at school tease me about how I dress; if they see me with short hair, they'll never stop."

He spun her around and cut away her silky ringlets. "Forgive me, *Chuoha*. I do not wish to destroy your golden locks, but I have no choice. As of now you are *Zuuho*, not *TTisho*, so you must become a man."

"What? That doesn't even make sense!"

Pieces of blond curls drifted to the ground and she wiped away the tears. Once done, he stepped back and brushed the hair from his hands. Yellow tresses lay in piles at her feet.

"Now you are one of us." He tossed her a light brown shirt and dark brown britches. "Step into the dark and change your clothes. We will do the same here."

She flung an angry glare at him and trudged deeper into the cave. Strange angry words exploded across the expanse.

He shook his head and furrowed his brow at Frigg, who shrugged. "Who can understand women, My Lord?"

"I do not know how Father survived. It is only hair."

Frigg chuckled. "Women are strange creatures, My Lord."

Conell slipped out of the prison clothes and kicked the rank garments aside. The dead guard's clothes smelled like sweat and dirt, but it was better than the stench of the jail. The reek from the confined cell clung to his skin. A week's worth of hot baths with scented oil might erase the smell.

A smile tugged at his face. To lounge in a soaking tub would be a great luxury. Watching the pretty Ladies-in-Waiting strolling under the trees would be another. At this point, a clean creek and bar of unscented soap would be an extravagance. He knelt and helped Frigg into his other clothes.

"I'm done, can I come out now?" she called.

"Aye." Conell ripped strips from his prison clothes and handed them to Frigg. "You need to cover it."

Frigg frowned but took the bandage and carefully covered the tattooed Sign of Broden, a long filled-in sword facing downwards with diamond-tipped ends, and the words *Ezasu, dhes sihv lei* carved on Conell's bicep. Frigg's fingers tugged at the dressing, careful not to touch the sacred sign.

Conell looked down his arm. "Trust me, My Friend. It will be safer if we cover it."

Imogene joined them and tossed her old clothes to the side. "Are you hurt?"

He looked up at her. "No. Frigg covers the Sign of Broden,

the symbol of my kingship."

"Your *what*? Oh, cool tattoo."

Conell's eyes grew wide as her fingertips traveled over the sacred mark. No one dared touch the king's symbol without his permission. The younger man tied off the rags and gave his prince an amused glance.

"I'd like to get one one day. A nice heart." She made a symbol of a heart with her index fingers and thumbs. "Or something cute, maybe a kitten. Not something gross like a skull—on my ankle, not my arm. But I can't until I turn eighteen, Mom said, when I'm an adult." She huffed, "Like I'm not one now. And what do those strange words mean?"

Frigg chuckled. "Ezasu, just and true." He sat on the cave floor and stiffly stretched his arms over his head. "She does sound like the captain's sister."

Conell decided to let the innocent slight pass and gave the girl a look-over. A grin broke over his face and he tugged at her pants. "Your clothes are quite large, My Lady."

She giggled and slipped a finger through a hole in the shirt. "I'm sure. What do we do about the holes? It's gross knowing some guy died in these."

"We will not think of the holes. And the dead do not need garments," Conell said.

He used his knife to rip a long strip from his old grey pants and pulled her trousers to her stomach. A smile played on his lips. "You have a lovely waist, *Chuoha*."

Her cheeks burned. "Thanks. Sometimes I think if I were skinnier, I'd be prettier."

Conell's eyebrows rose as he slipped the belt into the first side loop. "You are pretty, *Chuoha*, why do you think I cut your hair? As a lovely woman, you are a danger to us, but as a homely man, no one will bother us."

Her blush deepened. "Um, thank you."

"He is right, Imogene," Frigg said. "Plus, the merchants in the streets may try to buy a lovely girl, but they will not buy a young man."

Conell stopped. A large bruise covered her stomach. His eyebrows knitted together as he rubbed his fingertips over the black and blue surface. Her stomach twitched.

"What happened," he asked.

"Toál hit me when he took me to the prison. I panicked and jabbed him the ribs, then ran. He caught me and punched me." She wrapped her arms over her chest. "Ruárc, um, touched me. Toál, he…"

His gaze rose from the homemade belt. "He touched you?"

"Yeah, you know, *touched* me. Toál, he…did *things* to me." Her head lowered and a shiver ran through her body. "Never mind."

He lifted her fear-covered face. "You mean, touched you wrongly?"

"Yeah. I mean, you know…bad." She shrugged.

Conell sneered and cursed. "He will not touch you again, I promise. As for Toál, he will not do things to you ever again."

"A man lay outside the complex." Her frightened eyes met his. "Three arrows stuck out of his chest. He was dead. So much blood. I got sick and Toál, he came up behind me and put his… on my waist. He…um, did things. I just want this to stop."

That explained her frightened behavior in the forest. "Toál cannot hurt you anymore, so put this out of your mind. As for the man. He was Eamon, a friend of mine."

"Oh," she mumbled. "I'm so sorry."

He threaded the belt through the belt loops. "The guards hauled him from the compound and told him to run, then hunted him. Ruárc killed him." The dull sound of the arrows plunging into Eamon's chest and his dying screams still haunted Conell. He blinked the vision away. "The *mee* made us watch from the gates."

"Oh, my God. That's horrible. Why doesn't someone shut

that place down?"

Who would shut that place down? Father would burn the building to the ground, yet his son runs away. He slipped the belt through the last loop and tied the ends together.

She licked her lips. "Do you, do you think he's still out there? Ruárc, I mean. What if he finds me?"

Conell suppressed a shiver. Toál's haunting words lingered. *My brother and I wish to enjoy her for a while.* Ruárc, the best tracker in Ezazu, would delight in avenging Toál's death, and enjoy the queen's bounty and her escaped possession. Once done, he would toss the tainted Imogene at Jezebel's feet. The now *Zuuho*-child would become the witch's slave until her strength drained away and this innocent girl's life ended in the Slave Runner's hands as a paid joiner, dead before her twenty-first birth celebration. Who would tell her mother in the far-away village of New York?

He shoved away the horrid image and could not meet her gaze. Another ghost to prowl his dreams. "No, *Toma Chuoha.* I am sure he now sits in the belly of the Jabba-Nott. You stay with us and I will keep you safe." He pulled the shirt over her pants. "There. Now you are a boy. We must abandon our names if we are to reach the ports."

"Well," she said, "I could be, um…"

"Aidan," Conell said.

"That's nice, what does it mean?" she asked.

He knelt beside the fire and stroked it. "It was my uncle's name. But he is dead now."

Conell shuddered, his memories horrid.

*Aunt Breen's slender arms were wrapped around the five-year-old Pata's body; a Barbarian's thick spear pinned mother and daughter to the ground. Uncle Aidan's corpse laid over them with arrows protruding from his strong back. The family's blood flowed down the stairwell. The bloodied faces of the five murdered chambermaids peeked into the cave and laughed.*

*"Here sits the Coward of Broden;*

*A lovely lady on his arm;*

*Little does she know;*

*The souls that he did harm."*

*Pata peeked around them. "Conney, why did you leave me?" Bloody tears ran down her ghostly-pale face and light shined through the hole in her small chest.*

Conell focused on the fire, then quickly rose to his feet and his trembling hands snapped a twig. Pata and the phantoms disappeared, but their wails boomed in his mind.

"Oh. I'm so sorry," was all Imogene could muster

"And you shall call me Cahal," he said roughly. "Émer will be Nevan and Frigg, you will be -"

"Pol, in honor of my father." A small smile inched its way across his freckled cheeks.

"Aye, Pol." Conell gave him a sad and understanding nod. "So, *Chuoha*. Can you remember our new names?"

"I'm Aidan, you're Cahal, and Émer is Nevan."

He nodded. "And Frigg?"

"Pol." She smiled. "Aren't you supposed to call me Aidan? I mean *Chuoha* may not work. You're calling me, a supposed boy, and a princess."

"She has you in a net, My Moji," Frigg said, grinning.

Conell bowed. "That she does. As you wish, Lord Aidan."

The girl covered her mouth and giggled.

"I have our food." Émer stood at the cave's mouth and held two dead white long-haired rabbits by the ears. "I found *jados*. We feast tonight. And I found vegetables." He tossed the rabbits to Frigg, then dug into a bag tied to his waist and produced carrots and potatoes. "I found *avozaie an oshuie*."

She stroked the soft fur and peered at the tiny face hidden under the white hair. "Wow! It's got such soft fur. I've never seen a rabbit like this one. They're so cute. I hate eating them."

Émer smiled at her. "I will dry the skins for you, Imie."

Imogene took the vegetables from Émer. "So we're having *avozaie*, carrots, and *oshuie*, potatoes, with *jado*, rabbit."

A smile inched across Émer's face. "Very good, Lady

Imogene."

Conell scowled. The girl was going to get them all killed if she continued acting as one who rebelled against the queen. "You will never use the forbidden tongue again. We do not know who listens to us. You will speak in the queen's tongue."

She blinked twice. "Well, you use it."

Émer gathered up the food. "Do not fret, My Lady. Moji is wise when he says to not use the forbidden tongue. The queen commands us to use her tongue. We do not fear her commands, but it will be safer for you to use the queen's language."

"Why can't you use your language?" Imogene asked.

Émer shrugged. "It was her command that we learn her language when she took the Moji's throne. She made all children and adults learn her tongue, saying it brought unity to the people. Although it never did." He studied her face. "You cut your hair."

"Oh, yes, Conell, I mean Cahal, cut it so I could blend in."

"Cahal?" Émer's arched his eyebrows. "It seems much has happened since I left. Imie, your clothes seem too large."

"My name's not Imie anymore. Cahal has changed it to Aidan. I'm supposed to be a boy." She winked and flipped up her collar with her thumbs, then rocked back and forth on her heels.

The captain made a sweeping bow. "I am pleased to make your acquaintance, Lord Cahal. And what a lovely boy you make. Have we changed names, My Lord?"

"Yes, Émer," Conell said, "I felt we would be safer if we left our names behind. I am Cahal, you are Nevan, and Frigg is Pol. Aiden, you have already met."

"Nevan, an interesting name."

After dinner, Frigg fell asleep on the chilled dirt flooring. Émer threw the rabbit bones into the woods and Conell burned their old clothing.

Imogene stood at the entrance of the cave as the sun slowly lowered over the clouding horizon. Her beams peeked through the layers of clouds and raced to the earth. The clouds reflected the sun's rays and became a canvas of burnt orange and yellow spreading across the skies.

Conell cut off a piece of cooked rabbit and studied the girl. Where did she come from? What is this place called New York? And the village of Peoria was nowhere in Ezazu. The ways of the Zuuho were far from the girl as if from a nurse's training, but the ways of TTisho seemed out of Imogene's understanding. She did not act as one from the Southern Lands nor the Lands of the Barbarians. An escaped slave from the Northern Territories? If so, then how did she survive such hardship?

The thirteen-year-old Maúl warriors that were sent into the Northern Territories as the Maúl initiation who came back alive told tales of large orange skinned warriors who dressed in animal hides and carried round shields and large swords.

Conell grinned. Émer was so disappointed when he came home from his travels, but not as an escaped slave, but as one who was untouched. Children escaping the slavery were quickly elevated to warrior status, while Émer had to endure more training. Maybe this girl was an escaped slave? But she did not speak as one. But if the children could barely survive, how did she survive? Could the slavery and travels damage her mind? Would it be wise to leave her with Frigg? Or would he trade her to the Slave Runners for the queen's bounty? Ruárc longed to find the child and make her his own.

He made his way to the mouth of the cave. "What are you thinking, *Chuoha?*"

She startled. "I was thinking about home and my mom."

"Your mother lives in the place you spoke of, New York."

84

"Yes." The sun's painted etchings arched across the dark blue sky. "It's so beautiful here." She leaned against the cave's wall and slipped her hands behind her back. "Why is that woman after you?"

Conell slowly chewed the meat, while his gaze drifted into the woods. "It is a story I wish to avoid."

"I have plenty of time," she said, smiling.

He snorted. "If you wish. After my thirteenth-birth-year, the queen accused me of a crime I did not commit and threw me into *Ioole Chaj*, then stole my throne. My parents died when I was only seven years of age."

"Émer," Conell said. "You said friends of the Maúl lived in the mountains. Where are they?"

"To the south in the hills, My Lord. But I do remember a small village very close to here. It is called," he rubbed his chin. "*Eced Shiaku,* Hidden Village. It is very remote, but they are very hospitable. It should be about three miles from here?"

"Good, we will leave tomorrow for Eced Shiaku," Conell said.

The warm breezes ruffled Ruárc's hair and cooled his sweating body. It caressed the trees of *Yoem Eoko* like a mother soothing a frightened child. With the boar beast dead, everyone could move safely through the woods, but Ruárc did not rejoice and ignored the gentle breezes. Instead, he used a thin piece of wood to cover Toál's body with dirt, and then drove Toál's sword into the earthly tomb. "May the mighty sun god, Ookéza, lead you to your new destiny, My Brother." Mother's heart would break at the news of Toál's demise.

Argus knew Ookéza demanded his dead be buried within two days of death or their tortured souls would roam forever on the planet. Yet, the demon waited for two days to inform Ruárc. Ookéza led Ruárc to the body today, just as the sun was setting. He growled and broke the wood over his knee. Argus would pay. "Thank you, Ookéza, for leading me to my brother's body. Thank you for taking care of my brother."

He smoothed the dirt covering Toál. "I know this is not what you wanted, Brother. I know you longed for the hero's burial, to be buried on top of your enemies on the battlefield, but this is all I can do. Rest in peace and do not haunt me." He chuckled; Toál would.

Ruárc wiped the sweat from his face. Toál had been lying face down in a mud puddle when Ruárc found him—his precious blood mixing with the dirt. He shivered. Toál was the stronger of the two men and protected the older brother from bullies. Ruárc should have stopped the Moji's sword. According to Mother, big brothers are to shelter the younger ones. Ruárc failed.

Argus had grinned as he retold how Moji killed Toál. The demon did nothing to assist the young man. The demon's words still set a chill over Ruárc.

"The queen never ordered it," Argus had said.

He roughly rubbed the sides of his cheeks three times and bowed before the fresh grave. "Ookéza, I pray you give my sword swiftness and my feet strength so that I may feel DeCapris blood running through my fingers. Help me to avenge my brother. And give me Argus, the coward. Let my brother rest in peace. Let it be so."

The girl's soft face appeared in his mind with the cleanness of her skin and the flowery fragrance of her long swirling hair. A smile covered his thin lips. "And my god, give me the girl." He followed their trail until Ookéza rested for the evening.

It is not by man's strength which allows him to move a mountain, nor by the strength of many animals. It is by faith in the Attiyq's hand that the mountains move.

– Words of the Attiyq

It was the first day of creation. The bright Ezasu sun rose over the mountains and burst her bright columns through the forest. Everything looked clean and new; it had to be the beginning of the world. Conell smiled.

Five years passed since he saw the forest bright with life. The scent of pine, dew and grass lingered around him and a gentle breeze played in his hair. The same spring smell drifted through the castle windows years ago.

Mother would insist on taking down the heavy draperies covering the windows when the warm spring air invaded the lands. The whole castle smelled of fresh morning dew mixed with perfume of pine and spring flowers.

The forest looked endless when compared to the small prison cell. Every green field in Ezasu called out and the trees branches motioned for climbers. But running and climbing had to wait. Jezebel would pursue them until she died. To have the child of Efazu alive meant Broden's throne still belonged to the DeCapris family. She would be a servant to the king as long as Conell was alive.

Imogene moaned and her eyes flickered open. Last night, Émer had made her a bed of pine branches and leaves, claiming a TTisho must have proper sleeping quarters. Conell smiled. The manners of the king's courts ran strong in the strange girl. Instead of rejecting the captain's kind gesture, she graciously accepted it. For a TTisho who refuses the Arashi of the Maúl brings shame to all. Mother would have been pleased with this TTisho as would the Maúl tribe. Imogene rose and ran her fingers through her short hair. A sour look crossed her small features.

"You are awake," said Frigg. "Were you having a *shucko*, I mean, a nightmare?"

She stretched her arms. "Yeah, but I'm okay now. I was hoping you all were just a dream and I'd be home again."

Frigg offered her a playful grin "My apologies, My Lady. We are as real as the sun rising."

Émer poked at a large fish cooking over the fire. "Ah, Imie, I have prepared fish for us to eat. We also feast on berries."

She rose from her bed and yawned. "Oh, it's too early for fish. How 'bout some eggs?"

"Forgive me, but the birds seem to be guarding them this morning," he said with a sly grin.

A blush covered her cheeks and she gave him a tight smile. "Fish will be fine."

Conell kicked dirt onto the fire. "Eat quickly. We will leave soon. Frigg, are you able to walk?"

The young man nodded. "I'll be ready, My Moji."

"Good," Conell continued. "We will make our way through the mountains, then to Eced Shiaku. We will stay in the village until Frigg heals, then we will make our way to the ports."

"Where will we go then?" Imogene asked.

Émer offered her a hunk of cooked fish. She smiled at him and bounced the hot meat from hand to hand.

Conell cut off a chunk of blackened fish. "To the Southern Lands then across the seas. Perhaps Jezebel's eyes will look elsewhere and she will give up her hunt."

Émer wrinkled his brow. "Do you really think the witch will let us be? My Moji, you and I both know she will pursue us to where the sun rises. We cannot escape her."

"We can try," he said as he rose to his feet.

The sun stood overhead when they reached the mountain pass. The white covered peaks of *Uje Shoel* towered like guards lining the road to the castle and a white misty blanket enshrouded the mountaintops. Conell leaned back his head as the wind caressed his cheeks. It felt good to walk in the sunshine and allow the grass to tickle his ankles.

Imogene helped Frigg as they walked ahead of him and Émer led the small group. Still, there was no sign of Jezebel's army. The group kept off the main trails and there was no sound of human movement amongst the trees. The lowest of the queen's guards could track them, unless the queen had other plans.

"The witch might send someone new, someone no one would expect," Conell said. His hand gripped his sword.

"Émer," called the girl. "We have no coats. Won't we freeze if we go into the mountains?"

"We will be safe," Émer said. "We will stay near the base of the mountains."

The girl stopped and stared at the green and gray walls rising on either side of them like a sloping stoned forest while a small clear stream gurgled at their feet. The light dusting of grass and moss covering the valley floor and sides like a rug crunched under their feet. Small *otogi* sat on the rocks and clucked at them.

Conell followed her gaze up the sides of the gorge. A longing to lie in the sparse meadow and spend the day staring at the verdant mountains filled his heart. To lie and sleep for hours as the breeze cradled him and the warm sun became his blanket. A cool green scent sat on the air unlike the stench of the prison. He breathed it in and enjoyed each aroma. The grassy mountain range seemed to stretch into the horizon. Behind them, the white covered mountaintops peeked over the lush ridge. Imogene stretched her neck upwards and even stood on her toes. It was obvious she was unable to see the end of the emerald range from here.

"*Chuoha*, keep up with Émer!" Conell barked. Jezebel wouldn't stop to admire the mountains; neither would they.

She wrinkled her nose at him. A rock tumbled down the side of the hill. Imogene shielded her eyes from the sun. "What are those chicken-like things up there?"

Conell stepped beside her and followed her gaze. "They are called *otogi*."

"They look like tiny brown chickens with brown hair sticking out of their heads. Look at their little eyes. They're so cute. Can we catch one?" she asked.

Conell forced a serious look on his face. "They will bite you. They have been known to remove a man's finger. So I would ask that we leave them alone."

She peered back at them. "Are you serious? They're too tiny to bite anyone."

He pulled her away. A larger male *otogi* raised its brown wings and squawked at them as if to scare the intruders.

Émer looked over his shoulder and smiled at her. "Are you enjoying the view, Imie?" he asked.

"Oh, yes! It's stunning! The mountains are breathtaking. And I love the chicken-things. *I doubt* they bite."

The captain laughed. "I pray you will only see the parts blessed by the Attiyq." He stopped and motioned to the prince. "My Moji, the village is over this ridge."

Connell nodded. "We will now use our other names. Remember, no one is to know I am a prince and that Jezebel's eyes seek us. Émer, what must we do to enter the village?"

Émer rubbed his chin. "If I remember correctly, for the elders to welcome us, we must bring them a gift of meat or fruits or vegetables. Imie, we will tell them you are twelve-years old and not yet a man. We will not have to explain your *Mim Eho* or Fire Hunt."

"Fire Hunt?" she asked.

Frigg moaned as he sat on the ground. "It is what young men must do to prove their manhood when they become thirteen. They must spend a week alone in the wilderness and come back alive. I endured it as did the captain and the prince."

Émer nodded. "It will also explain why you have no sword. The boy receives his sword when he returns alive to the village."

Connell shielded his eyes from the brightness of the sun. "Captain, we need to find some meat. The sun will be setting soon and we will not endure the evening cold."


It took most of the afternoon, but Émer found his prey. He placed the large buck over Conell's shoulders. The two men followed their trail back to the girl and Frigg.

"It is strange," Émer said. "It is not hunting season. The buck should have been easier to find. It's as if someone or something chased them from the forest."

"I agree," Conell said. "I think it is best if we reach this village."

The sun began to set when they made their way back to their small group.

Imogene peered at the animal. "Wow! He's huge."

"We will get a wonderful reception with this animal," Frigg

said, smiling.

Imogene helped him to his feet and slipped her arm around his waist.

"Émer," Conell said, "Since you understand the village, you will lead us, then Frigg, Imogene and I will take the rear. *Chuoha*, help Frigg, but stay beside him. The others will think you are a boy. The eldest takes the lead while the next eldest takes the rear, followed by one who is younger. The youngest boy is in the center. Remember we traveled through the mountains to get to Shea Village. Do not speak of Jezebel, the past or the coast, remember our story."

The others nodded and followed Émer through the mountain passage. The valley became wider and the path led over the rocky ridge down into a small clearing.

Émer raised his arm and they gathered around him. Thin spirals of smoke rose lazily into the evening sky from chimneys. The small wooden homes with straw roofs circled a larger wooden building in the center. Children ran around the outskirts of the community, and a few adults squatted on the ground in front of the homes. The small field of dead stalks lay on the far side as the sun slowly set.

Imogene dragged her gaze to Émer. "I thought folks planted in the spring and picked the crops in the fall?"

"They do," Conell said.

Frigg nodded to the dried crops. "Then why are they dead?"

"We proceed with caution." Conell took a step down the ridge staircase.

The small group picked their way down the dirt incline to the settlement's borders.

"Captain," Conell said, "Do you notice something strange?"

Émer nodded. "Aye, my Moji. It is frighteningly quiet for a village. There are no guards defending the village."

"Give me the buck and you watch the rear. This does not seem right."

Émer did as suggested.

The path weaved down the hill and through the woods. An old woman sat on the edge of the road. Her leathery, thin fingers lifted her empty wooden bowl and she nodded. Imogene smiled and placed a piece of dried meat in the beggar's dish. A small smile crossed the woman's thin lips and she mumbled a response as she chewed the tough meat.

"Please don't tell me this is the guard," Imogene said.

Émer knelt before the old woman and spoke in his native tongue. Her gaze dropped to the ground and she whispered a reply. He patted her shoulder and rose. "She said the witch sends her troops each year to take their crops. This year the elders refused, so the witch cursed the crops and her soldiers stole what the villagers had collected in the summer. The warriors of the village tried to hunt meat, but the witch cast a spell and chased away the animals. If they try to leave, the witch's men will hunt them down."

Conell bowed before the old woman and dropped the large animal at her feet. "Accept this as our gift to your children."

Her eyes lit up. She stood and hobbled into the village. Within minutes, a group of men approached them. Swords hung at their sides with bows and arrows slung over their large shoulders. Each man's chest was covered in thick layers of brown leather and strappings covered their calves and large forearms. These were the warriors of the village, the ones who decide travelers' fates. Conell's group would either die on the spot or be welcomed into the village.

Conell scanned the men and the town for the queen's cursed banner, a blue flag with a black rearing horse that trampled the Sword of Broden. He leaned into Émer. "I do not see the queen's sign."

The captain nodded. "Perhaps they do not follow her?"

Conell and his captain stepped in front of Frigg and Imogene, but kept their hands close to their weapons.

The leader raised his sword. "You are from the queen. We have told her our wishes. What do you want here? What business do you bring?"

Conell bowed. "We mean you no harm; we are men separated from our legion. We are only seeking rest for the evening. Please accept our gift."

"How do I know you do not mean to trick us?"

An elderly voice rang out from the crowd. "Let him be, Aeron! This man means us no harm. Accept his gift."

The group parted as an old man stepped forward. A robe made of woven purple material rested on his thin slumped shoulders and feathers stuck in his shoulder-length grey hair. A gray beard covered his chin. Wrinkles surrounded his laughing brown eyes. Despite his slim figure, his arms were muscled.

"But Aho," Aeron said. "They wear the queen's symbol."

The Aho smiled and patted Aeron's shoulder. "They are not as they seem. They come in peace."

Conell bowed. "Greeting, Aho. You are correct. We mean no harm and are making our way to the sea. Please accept this gift."

The old man smiled and nodded. "Thank you, stranger. We accept." He lifted his hands into the air and Émer and Frigg dropped to their knees. Imogene copied the reverence. Conell lowered his head, refusing to give *great and mighty* God any respect.

"May the Attiyq bless you for your generosity," the priest said. "And repay you in His own time tenfold."

Everyone cupped their hands and brought them over their heads. Their fingers trailed down the sides of their faces. Imogene tried to follow along. Once done, they rose.

The old man grinned. "You speak the forbidden tongue. You know it is against Her Lady's orders. And you do not protest my prayer as the queen now commands we do not pray to the Attiyq."

Conell smiled. "You are wise, Aho. No, we do not serve the queen, but only wish to pass through the valley unharmed and undetected. I do not see her banner waving over your village."

The Aho's eyes beamed. "We too do not serve the queen. Her banner sits close to the ground near the elders' meeting hall. It keeps her somewhat happy. The Attiyq told me that you come in peace, so we accept you in peace."

"I am known as Cahal, this is Naven, Pol and Aidan. As you see, we have brought you a gift and seek shelter for the night. A lion injured Pol and he needs attention."

The priest nodded. "I am called Cián son of Owian of the Eced Shiaku, priest of this village. Of course, the Attiyq demand we take in strangers. Please, come and we will feast on your gift."

Conell stepped beside Cián and the older men came behind them, followed by Frigg, Imogene and Émer. The younger men took the deer into the woods to process it and the women followed with the children running ahead of them.

"What just happened?" Imogene whispered to Émer.

"The Aho gave us a blessing," Émer said. "In order to accept it, we go onto one knee. You did well, Imie. Stay close to me and do as I do."

The priest gestured to a small wooden building the size of a bedroom and opened the deer-skinned flap. "Your injured friend can find rest here."

Chattering children tugged at Imogene's and Émer's tunics. Imogene slipped her arm over a girl's shoulder and tossed the girl's long brown hair. The child looked up at Imogene and grinned. The priest gently shooed the children away.

Conell bowed slightly. "Thank you, Cián. Aidan, stay with him and care for him."

Imogene's small brow furrowed, but Conell nodded to the door. He ignored the unspoken protest and followed the priest. Émer held back the flap and Imogene helped Frigg into the hut.

Cián led Conell and Émer to a larger wooden building. As promised, a very small blue flag hung lifeless a few inches from the ground as if forgotten. A young man in his early twenties with shaggy brown hair held open the cloth door. Émer and

Conell allowed the priest and the elders to enter into the large meeting room first.

The elders took their assigned wooden chairs, each seat backing carved with elaborate details dictating the clan's victories in war handed down from generations. The seats surrounded a burning fire centered in a raised stoned fire pit. The white smoke rose lazily up to a hole in the roof. Cián took a larger seat and picked up a wooden staff engraved with swirls from the bottom to a carved head of a man at the top.

Behind Cián's seat, hung Broden's banner, a large yellow flag with Broden's sword facing downward sewn in the center of a white square.

A twinge of guilt bit at Conell's heart. Broden's flag was a death sentence to all who followed the king's lineage. These people were very brave to remain faithful to the deceased king and now the prince was abandoning the devoted villagers to the sword.

The priest extended the staff to Conell, who placed his hand on the carved head. "Tell us what you seek."

Conell bowed. "We are seeking shelter for the night and healing attention to Pol. We traveled from Lorccan and are making our way to the seas. May we stay?"

Cián nodded his thanks. "Of course you may stay with us. You have saved the village from the queen's wrath."

Émer extended his arm. Cián placed the staff head into Émer's open palm. "Aho Cián, please tell us why the witch has placed a curse on the village."

An anger crossed Cián's face. "Each year the witch demands most of our crops. Our children starve, while she and her courts eat to their fill. This year, the elders refused her demands and kept the crops for our children. She sent an envoy, but he left with pockets emptied. Later, she sent the spell. A great darkness covered the land for a day and a half. Along with the darkness, the animals disappeared and the crops shriveled."

"Great Aho," Émer said. "When did this happen?"

"Two days ago. We eat dried meat, but it is now gone. I prayed to the Attiyq and He has answered our prayers by sending you. But this will not last long. We need the spell to lift and the queen destroyed."

Conell frowned at the dirt floor. No power in Ezasu could lift the queen's evil spells and no hand could destroy her. The old man chased butterflies. "No one can stop her or lift this spell. You must leave this village and hide in the mountains."

A gray-haired elder spread his bony arms. Despite his age, his strong voice rang across the room. "We will not be chased from our homes. This village is our village, we will die here. We will not leave this place. The Attiyq has provided us with this meal, He will provide more."

The men nodded and mumbled their agreement.

A large man with a gray speckled beard stood. "We will send out hunting parties and the Attiyq's hands will guide us."

Conell pursed his lips. The entire village will starve by the end of the season. The Attiyq refused to help the villagers. The *Great God* will not extend His hands now.

Cián gave him a small smile. "What a shame you do not trust the Attiyq."

Conell shook his head. "I do not trust Him, Aho. Trusting in children's stories will kill your people.'

Émer jabbed Conell in the ribs.

Cián laughed. "I am glad I do not believe this way. Come. You are weary and you must see to your friends."

Émer and Conell bowed before the Aho and then exited the building. Mumbles came from the elders inside.

Émer grabbed Conell's arm. "Moji, you had no right to speak those words to the great Aho. He is a good man who has given us shelter."

He yanked his arm free. "You know how I feel about the Attiyq. I cannot tell them to follow wives' tales. These people will die and you know this. You have seen Jezebel's spells and her evil books. She is a child of Satan, born of his hellish seed. She will not stop until these people are dead."

Émer grabbed his prince's upper arm. "You know what you must do, Moji."

Conell broke Émer's grip and marched to Imogene's hut. "I will not discuss this with you. I have told you my decision."

"You can lead them," Émer called behind him.

Conell threw back the curtain door and burst into the room. "I will not listen!"

Émer stood in the doorway with his arms crossed over his chest. "My Moji, how can you reject them?"

Imogene rose from the side of the bed. "What happened?"

Frigg lay on his stomach and tried to look over his shoulder. Imogene gently laid him back onto the bed.

Émer glowered at Conell as the young captain stepped into the room. "Each year the villagers must give most of their food to the queen's soldiers or she will kill them. We must help them."

Conell glowered at his captain. "And what would you want me to do? You and I alone can fight. Imogene knows nothing of the sword and Frigg is wounded. How can we fight against her?"

The young captain took three strong steps into the room. "Lead them. Remove her from your rightful throne."

He held up his hand. "You wish for me to fight against the witch with mountain farmers? Impossible. Jezebel is too strong."

"The Attiyq will guide you."

Conell snorted. "The Attiyq has kept His face and His hands from me."

Imogene squeezed a cloth saturated with yellow liquid into a bowl and dabbed the cloth onto Frigg's back. "He's right, Prince Conell. It's not fair that these people starve to death."

He crossed his arms over his chest and cocked his head. "And what am I to do?"

"What would your father do?" Émer asked. Conell only growled and shoved past.

Conell ambled down the dark path. Stars thrown against a black canvas twinkled above him and seemed to say w*hat would Father do?* Conell Bearech DeCapris was the son of Efuko Einri, but he was not the king. The king fought for the throne and protected those he loved. The son, on the other hand, betrayed those he loved and fled from the enemy. Efuko would not hesitate to lead the villagers into battle and the small army would grow as Efuko gathered the people. The ragtag militia would probably destroy Jezebel. But he was Conell, the traitor to Broden and Father, who spent five years in Jezebel's prison and now ran away.

"It is a cold night, is it not?" came a voice behind him. Cián stood behind him, a blanket wrapped over his old shoulders.

"Yes, Aho, it is getting cold. The winter season approaches."

The tiny star-flies buzzed around them, their blue-green bottoms flashing with ethereal light.

The old man cocked his head. "It is hard to decide what lies in your heart and what lies in your mind, is it not Moji Conell?"

Conell blinked twice. "You know who I am?"

Cián chuckled and nodded. "You have your father's face. King Efuko was a great man." The old man joined Conell on the path.

"Everyone wishes for me to walk down his path," Conell said.

Cián gestured ahead of them. "It is hard to follow the path of a dead man."

Conell nodded. "Everyone demands I take back my throne, yet I cannot save myself."

"You wish to leave and hide?"

Conell sat on a log, rested his elbows on his knees and

entwined his dangling fingers. "What else am I to do? My captain thinks I should fight the witch, lead your men into battle and take back my throne. What he asks is impossible."

Cián nodded as he sat beside Conell. "You are right. It would be impossible for you to take back what the witch stole. You would require help."

"Help will not come from this village or from anyone living in Esazu. The witch has convinced them to stand against me and my father's house."

Cián swatted away a mosquito. "Help can come in many packages and sizes. The girl, for instance. You think it is coincidence she is here with you?"

Conell caught the old man's gaze. "You know about her?"

He nodded. "Yes. The Attiyq revealed her identity to me once I laid my eyes on her. The Attiyq has seen your plight and sent her here to help you, if you will allow it. She admires you greatly and feels safe by your side."

"How can the small one help me? She is frightened of the dark and has lost her mind."

"Trust her and the Attiyq. Both are on your side."

Conell sighed and straightened. "No one stands on my side. You will have to find a leader from somewhere else. I am not the one who would free you."

"You will continue south?"

He nodded. "Yes, to the Southern Lands. I hope the witch will let us live in peace."

"And your people?"

"They stopped being my people a long time ago," he snarled.

"Including me and my clans?"

He pressed his elbows into his thighs and rubbed his forehead. "I know Father would fight. But I have no training, no skills, no one follows my lead and Father's soldiers now follow the queen. Forgive me, but what am I to do?"

"Your hope is flimsy like the mist blanketing the land in the morning and is killed by the hot sun. Your father would not believe in such hope."

"I cannot fight one as strong as the witch. She rules everyone within her hand. Hope burned in my father's heart, but it flees from me."

The old man picked at his yellow teeth. "And if she pursues you? What will you do?"

Jezebel's eyes roamed over the lands and heard men's whispered words. The queen's sword sought out the enemy and showed no mercy. Conell would have to lead his small party quickly and cover much ground. Maybe Jezebel would not follow or she may toy with them like a dog with a dying bird. "I do not know. I hope she bores of this chase and lets us be."

"Then you must run and hide. But do you think fleeing to the Lands of the South will be far enough to hide from her ever-seeing eyes? And are you willing to take a young girl to the Forbidden Lands? The Southerners rarely allow others into their lands. What if they capture you? They will not be gentle with you or her."

"If we will stay close to the Fainebo Sea, we should be safe," Conell said. "I will have to find a captain willing to take her and Frigg aboard his ship. Émer and I will face whatever fate in the Southern Lands. I know we cannot fight her."

Conell kept his gaze on the ground. "My father tried for many years to create a treaty between Ezasu and the Southern Lands, but they refused Father's hand. I know what this could mean. They would kill Frigg, hand Émer and the girl to the Barbarians and torture me until I die. But if we stay, the witch will find us and do the same. So which path do I take? The girl and Frigg must escape to the seas. Maybe they will find peace."

Cián chuckled and shook his head. He placed his withered hands on his knees and slowly rose from the log. "The last of Broden and the last of Anu, dying in enemy hands. It is frightening to think of losing both of you. Again with the misty hope. All right, I cannot make you stay. I will let my people know you will leave tomorrow morning. But first, join in our feast tonight."

"Wait." Conell grabbed the old man's arm. "I am in debt of your help. The witch's eyes are on the girl and I fear she will take her. Please care for her. You are right when you said taking her across the border is foolish."

The old man slowly nodded his head and lowered onto the log. "Why does the witch want her?"

"The Attiyq has not revealed this to you?"

He grinned. His front teeth were missing. "Sometimes He makes me ask."

"Her men tried to take the girl a few days ago. I do not know why they want her." He shrugged. "Perhaps of the strange medallion she has found."

"A medallion? Where did she find it?"

"You will have to ask her. But we have no time, Aho. Please, keep her under your wings."

"We have time; let us see about this medallion." He rose with a cracking of his old limbs and shuffled down the path to the village.

Conell clicked his tongue, yet knew the village laws forbid one to argue with an elder. It could mean danger for the girl.

The hearty, rich aroma of cooked deer meat floated down the pathway and made Conell's mouth water, along with the delicate scent of cooked vegetables and warm soft bread. The soft twangs of stringed instruments and the pounding of drums echoed across the valley. The people gathered in the center of the village and danced in a large circle, twirling in and out. The children skipped around them and sang the praises of the Attiyq.

A young curvy woman with long brown hair and large smile tried to place a flowered wreath around Conell's neck, but he gently moved her from his path. His eyes followed the curve of her body as she strolled away. She was very pretty and any other time, he would have obliged her wishes.

Conell weaved his way through the small crowd and followed

the old man to the guest hut. He held back the cloth door for the Aho.

Imogene smiled at them as she held a bowl of meaty smelling broth to Frigg's lips. The young red-haired man tried to rise from the bed, but Imogene gently pressed him back into the pillows.

Émer rose from his seat at a small table and led Cián to his chair. The old priest settled back and took a deep sigh. Émer sat on the edge of a chair opposite the revered man. Conell leaned against the wall near Frigg's bed and crossed his large arms over his chest.

"Oh, you're back," she said as she helped Frigg drink from a cup.

Conell nodded to the priest. "Imogene, show him your medallion."

"My name is Ai-dan." She raised her eyebrows up and down.

"He knows all about you, Imogene," Conell said. "Now show the priest the medallion."

She put the bowl on the nearby nightstand and pulled the medallion from around her neck.

The old man squinted at the gold trinket and examined it. He gazed at her from under his black eyelashes. "Child, where did you find this?"

She sat on the edge of the bed and told him the strange events that led her to Ezasu. The old man nodded his head and repeated, "Mmm," over and over. His old lips pursed into a tight line and his old eyes grew sharp and clear. Conell kept his tongue in check. The old priest wasted valuable time.

Cián looked at him from the corner of his eyes. "What you think is a waste of valuable time, Moji, is really your salvation."

Conell coughed. "How did you know?"

Cián chuckled as he squinted at the item lying in his palm. "You have much to learn, Young Prince."

Émer leaned forward. "What do you see in the medallion,

great Aho?"

The priest scooted the chair forward and took Imogene's hand. "My child, you must trust Him to reveal to you His secrets."

Her eyes moved from Conell and back at the priest. "Trust whom?"

He smiled. "The Attiyq. He wishes to use you and that is why He gave you the medallion. He chose you to be His handmaiden."

She tugged her fingers from his grip and held up her hands. "Okay, but I don't know who He is or what He is or where He is."

"I will help you, Imie," Émer said.

Imogene gave her friend a small smile. "Cian, you must be wrong. I mean, why would the Attiyq want to use me? I mess up all the time and the other kids think I'm weird. Why me?"

The old man's face creased as a smile spread across his thin lips. "He uses whom He uses. He sees things we cannot see. Do not question Him, Child."

Imogene shrugged her shoulders and gestured. "You're not making any sense."

Cián gazed at Conell. "You cannot escape Jezebel, she will hunt you down. She cannot completely claim your father's throne if you are alive. She will kill you and your companions."

"How do you know this?" Conell asked.

"I know her and I remember your father." Darkness covered his wrinkled face. "He was a good man, strong and fierce, but gentle and kind. She hated him, hated his power and his reign over the land. She longed to rule the peasants, but he would not allow it. So, she killed him. She wanted to kill you also but was unable. The peasants expected you to be the king, so killing you would have meant her downfall. Instead, she waited until you could give the kingdom to her, and then your blood would flow."

Conell rubbed the bridge of his nose. "I did not hand it to her, she simply took it." He pressed his left fingertips against his temple. "So what would you have me do?"

"You must fight her," the priest said. "The girl holds the secret to your own salvation; it is through her that you will find what you need to defeat the witch."

Conell stared at Imogene's pale face then back at the priest. The old man had lost his mind. "How do you know this?"

The old man leaned forward. "Keep the girl close to you, for the witch longs for her. If she captures Imogene, then you will die with her."

Whiteness fell over Imogene's features. Émer jumped up and gently rubbed her back.

Conell silently cursed. Now more than ever, fear wrapped around Imogene's heart. She dreaded Ruárc. "I do not understand your words. I still believe we must flee to the borders and away from here."

The old man stopped picking his beard and held up one finger. "If you are to survive, you must allow the girl to lead you to your salvation."

"And how does she do this great deed?" Conell asked.

"That is up to her."

Imogene's frantic eyes grew wide as river rocks. "I don't know what to do."

Cián's old foggy eyes focused on her. "My child, all you must do is trust the Attiyq to lead you. He will tell you what the medallion says and how to find the Moji's salvation."

She twisted her fingers. "But you know so much more than me, why can't you read it? You can help him. I can't. I can't help anyone."

The old man smiled. "Because He has chosen you, not me."

None of Cián's words made any sense and if Conell followed them, his friends would die. Fighting Jezebel was hopeless; the witch was too strong. "I do not believe you speak sane words. You have frightened the girl and what you ask can never come to pass. Can she stay with you?"

"I have told you," Cián said. "The Attiyq revealed this to me. And no, we cannot let her stay. We already sit in the queen's hand. She will crush us if she finds the girl here. Plus, you need her. Trust the Attiyq and trust her."

He shook his head and placed his hand on her trembling shoulder. "*Chuoha*, I give you my word, I will get you home to your mother in New York. But now, we must run to the borders. Once we reach the borders, then you will not leave Émer's side. For now, give me the medallion. I feel you will be safer if it hangs from my neck."

Thieves come into the house during the evening bells. They know the darkness hides them. Guard your houses well, for no one knows the day or the time of the thief.

~ From *The Chronicles of the King*, Volume 10, Passage 5, by King Alun, Tenth King of Ezasu in the year 500.

Ruárc bowed deeply and gave homage to Ookéza as the sun god slipped away to sleep in his dark home. He kneeled and rubbed two flint stones over the small stack of sticks and leaves. A spark erupted the kindling, but his eyes were focused on the south. Moji's trail led to the *Uje Shoeli*. The prince always stayed pure to his habits. Not to mention the girl's small footprints were like tracks in the snow.

He finally took a small package from his satchel. His fingers brushed over the blue velvet cloth covering the small wooden box. Ookéza's demanded his followers respect his vows, including this one, an act Ruárc wished he could avoid. But Ookéza's will be done. He carefully lifted out the thin, steel stick with a pointed end and the small blue ink jar and laid the instruments on the ground.

"May Ookéza's face always shine on you, my brother.
May his hands cradle you to his bosom.
May your home be in the sky with his children, the stars.
And may your feats here allow you to become his child,
Shining in the night sky, leading your people.
…leading me."

He rolled up his sleeve and then dipped the end of the stick into the ink jar. Tenderly, he scratched Toál's name and death date into his forearm, ignoring the nipping pain. This was for the boy he should have protected; a memory mark in honor of the one he loved. Every warrior in his clan scratched the name of dead loved ones on their body. A sacred ceremony. Memories flooded his mind of a small boy always following Ruárc and his friends. Regret from chasing the boy away filled his heart. If only the two had stayed together the night the Moji escaped, Ruárc could have saved Toál from the sword. But Toál insisted the two separate to cover more ground—a deadly mistake.

A tear formed in his eye and he quickly wiped it away. Toál scoffed at weeping calling it a weakness. He placed the instruments back into his bag. Who would print Ruárc's name on their arm if he died? No one. There was none to honor the name of Ruárc.

He threw another log on the campfire. The prince and his band headed for the mountains, perhaps hiding in the caves. If he were Conell, he would travel to the Southern lands. People rarely ventured into the far south, except the merchants bringing back exotic treasures. Crossing the Southern Lands would be risky, but desperation pushed the coward prince. Southerners seldom allowed intruders into their lands, but no one guarded the borders. The prince and his group could survive for a while, if the people did not find them. He rubbed his chin. If he were the prince, he would find a ship to take them away from Ezasu.

110

The Maúl captain was another issue. Émer could be a problem. Despite Ruárc's mocking, a great fear clutched his heart each time Émer stood before him. The captain was the fastest swordsman in all Ezasu. Ruárc was a great hunter and tracker, but the sword was his greatest weakness. How to separate the girl from the men?

He would have to leave at first light to find them. Once they reached the seas, they would disappear. The traitors' path lay a day ahead of him and if they reached the mountains, their feet could take them anywhere. Ookéza forbid his followers from traveling at night, but gave favor in the day. In the morning, he would join his friends in the mountains and together they would find and kill the prince and the captain. He licked his lips. He was determined that the girl would be his.

As stars above him, Ookéza's children stepped out from their black caves and twinkled and played in the dark sky as their father slept. The spawns of the sun god understood sibling love and cheered for his victory. Even now, they whispered to their father of Ruárc's task. Ookeza nodded and spoke kind words to his offspring. "Yes," the deity would say. "We will see that justice is done."

Ruárc narrowed his eyes. Conell's blood did not flow as Broden's once did and as it did in the kings of his line. Instead, the prince acted like a spoiled dog. Ruárc yearned to bathe in the Moji's blood.

A younger Conell and Émer sat in the king's garden and called him and Toál. Women danced with swords as the two brothers practiced their swordsmanship. When Ruárc traveled to his *Mim Eho*, the brat prince stood at the castle gates and cried, "The son of Rua will never see home again, but a rabbit will eat him." But he did come back, much to Conell's disappointment.

Of course, the queen doted over the prized child after the attack on the castle and the death of his parents. The brat had horses and special rooms dedicated to his greatness. The precious offspring would walk down the halls of the castle and the servants bowed as the prince walked by.

Ruárc sulked and tossed a log into the fire. The sparks burst into the night air. The brothers huddled together in the guard's tower during the winter as the iced wind wiped up the tower stairs and they slept on the tower balcony during the heat of the summer. Ookeza heard Ruárc and Toál's prayers and gave them the greatest privilege of tossing his royal highness into prison with the rats and lice.

He picked the dirt from his nails and a smile crossed his lips. Ookeza also sent him a gift. *Chuoha.* Her skin was soft like a rose petal and she smelled like clean linen. He picked at his front teeth. *Now why did the witch want a worthless piece of jewelry and a strange girl? And where did it and she come from?* He asked a few people in the kingdom, those considered wise, but no one could give him an answer. It was one of the witch's secrets.

His eyebrows rose. Maybe if he found the medallion before Argus, he could use it as leverage against Jezebel. Maybe it contained great powers. Maybe he could be king. "Being king would be nice and the girl could be my *Zuuho*-queen. Ookeza, I want Jezebel as my dog who eats my table leftovers. And Argus. Oh, my god, help me to stuff that demon and place him over my mantel."

Imogene lay on the thin cot and studied the morning sunbeams hitting the dirt floor. Villagers walked past her small hut; their morning-hoarse voices intermingled with the sunrise birds. A smile crossed her lips. The celebration last night was like a senior party at the beach and lasted late into the evening. After the music died down and the children went to bed, the young women led Imogene to the creek, while Conell, Émer, and the other men went farther down the bank.

The moonbeams reflected off the water's surface and the crickets chirped loudly. A gentle breeze caressed the tree branches and rattled the leaves. The women gingerly stepped into the pure river water, splashing and giggling while washing with Jasmine-scented soaps. She sniffed her skin. The flowery scent still lingered. *I wonder if anyone else will notice.*

Imogene and her new girlfriends gossiped, and the girls asked about her home and her family, and of course, the handsome men who traveled with her. They giggled and shared their true-heart loves. *Gencie,* the man who holds a woman's heart as tenderly as the wind holds the rose. A blush covered Imogene's face as she told them about her *gencie,* Kyle, who lived back home and that she hoped one day to marry him.

At the midnight hour, the women trudged back to the village. The stars shined brightly above them as if tossed there by an invisible hand.

A peace existed in the darkness. It hid her from everyone and everything; she was for an instant blessedly invisible. Free from the cheerleaders who relentlessly teased her. Free from bullies who pushed her down in the hallways. Free from a crazy witch who hunted her and henchmen who groped her.

She laid in freedom's arms, strong men looking out for her and nestled in a cute and charming village—safe from wack-a-doodle nut jobs. She stretched her arms over her head and her smile broadened.

But one day, this charming paradise would disappear and she would be tossed into the throngs of the high school bullies; the ones who tortured the nerdy girl who traveled with a prince and a Maúl captain of the guards. Imogene missed her world, but she loved the acceptance she had here in Ezasu. She was important here. She was noticed. Yes, the fear of death was ever present here, but the fear of rejection was a part of her previous existence.

She leaned her head back against the headrest. No word from the Attiyq. *Come in, Attiyq. Can you hear me, Major Tom?* No answer. Not a peep. Maybe the Attiyq saw her as useless as the popular girls saw her? Maybe Conell was right. The Attiyq was a fairy tale. No voices in the dark, no messages in a bottle, no genie in a lamp. The only sound she heard was the wind rattling the wooden hut and night animals. Maybe He changed His mind and decided not to use her. She wasn't as smart as Émer or as wise as Cián.

She yawned and rubbed the sleep from her eyes. A small lizard scurried across the ceiling. Émer amazed her. He knew the sixty-six books of the Attiyq and what each one meant to man. But when he prayed, he heard silence—a one-way connection so to speak. Sure, strange things happened, contacts made with others who helped him, he picked up on things quickly. Weird things. Yet, rarely did others hear a booming voice or messages scrawled in the dust.

Maybe He kept silent when others sought Him or maybe the priest was wrong. Maybe Conell was right. Maybe they should make their way to the borders. But what if the crazy queen forced her to stay here? What if the door leading home remained closed? At least a good witch helped Dorothy in *The Wizard of Oz*. Her help came in the package of a silent Attiyq who may not even exist.

Someone tapped on the doorframe. "Yes." She tugged the blanket around her chest.

Émer stuck his head in the room. "You are up, Imie. Come, for we leave soon."

She nodded. Émer winked at her and dropped the door flap.

A smile rose on her lips. Even through this whole mess, Émer still had faith in her and the Attiyq. "He will speak to you, Imie," he said. If only she obtained such faith.

She pushed the covers away, grateful for last night's stream bath, and dressed in the fresh green pants and a brown tunic laying on the chair. The rabbit vest also lay with her clothes. A girl from the village spent the afternoon stitching Émer's rabbit skins into a warm vest. A smile rose on her lips as she ran her fingers over it. No one in school would do something this kind. She folded her vest and placed it into her supply bag.

Sitting on the edge of the bed, she pulled her socks and tennis shoes. Now, for the hair. Conell's free haircut still irked her. It was short and seemed to have a mind of its own. No matter how much she wet it down, brushed it or played with it, it was still short and wild. Her reflection in the small mirror showed a pale-faced girl with very short blond hair.

She squeezed her cheeks. Her punishment for not stashing foundation and blush in her pockets. "Note to self, always put makeup in your pockets." She had to run around looking natural. Her short locks mocked her and did as they pleased—their revenge for cutting them. If only she had some hair gel.

She leaned her palms on the basin table and lowered her head. "Please just wake up, wake up." The ants invaded her stomach again. The "what-ifs" lined the path like a crazy homecoming parade. *What if* the queen found her? *What if* Ruárc was still alive? *What if* she couldn't get home? *What if* she died? *What if* the guys died?

*What if* Ruárc found her? A shiver wiggled its way down her back. That madman had a sword and God knows what else. All she had was, well, a rabbit vest. He certainly wasn't happy that Toál was dead and the others escaped. But maybe Ruárc was dead? Maybe he gave up looking for them? She nodded. Yes, anyone would get tired of trouncing in the woods day and night. But *what if* he didn't die or give up? *What if* he found their trail? *What if? What if. What if?*

"Come on," she said to the girl in the mirror. "Pull yourself together. You got three hot guys waving swords over their heads, looking out for you. Think of this as a wild adventure. Any kid in high school would kill to be here."

"They can take my place any time," the reflection said. "And *what if* you're wrong?"

"What if I'm wrong?" she asked. "You don't have a plan, no weapons, and no escape plan. What if you're wrong? I can't be wrong. I have to be right." She pressed her fingers against her lips. "Oh, God, let me be right, please!" She stepped outside.

Émer and Conell wore brown pants and green long-sleeved tunics similar to her clothing. But both men also sported the leather vests and bands on their legs and arms they took from the dead guards. Their pants seemed thicker than hers and they stuffed the pant legs into short leather boots. Their swords hung at their sides and Émer's bow and arrows slung over his shoulder.

Conell's clean silver dreadlocks hung down his back and Émer's clean face showed off his strange markings. She smiled. The men looked quite dashing like the characters from *Lord of the Rings* and she looked like *Orphan Annie*.

Conell glowered and covered his chest with his large arms. Great. The sun rose an hour ago and already something new had upset him. This would make for a long day.

"Okay," she said, stepping beside them, "Let's do this."

Conell glanced down at her. "There has been a change of plans." He nodded to Cián. "The priest insists on traveling with us. I do not believe this is a good idea, but it seems my words fall on deaf ears." He fixed his frown on Émer, who grinned back at him. "Insanity surrounds us. The priest said the Attiyq commanded him to accompany us."

Imogene winced. Cián hears from the Attiyq, but she hears the rustling of the wind.

"It is best if you eat now," Conell said, uncrossing his arms.

She pointed to his sword strapped to his side. "Can I have a sword or something?"

His gaze followed her finger. He raised his eyebrows. "Do you know how to use one?"

"No," she said, sheepishly.

"Then no. You cannot have a sword unless you can use it. You may hurt one of us."

*What if I'm wrong?* "But I don't have anything."

Conell gave her a small smile. "We will look after you."

*But what if you're wrong?*

Frigg stepped from his hut and hobbled to his prince. "My Moji, I am ready to follow you."

Conell's stern face softened and he placed a hand on Frigg's shoulder. "Nay, My Friend, you will not follow me this time. I want you to stay with the villagers. You are no use to me wounded."

The younger man's freckled face fell. "But you cannot leave me behind. I am much stronger now. The liquid the girl used on my wounds strengthened me. I will make it with you."

He shook his head. "No, Frigg, you must stay here."

"Oh, but he can accompany you, Prince Conell." The villagers gathered around the Aho and some of the children grabbed his fingers. "You will need many weapons. The young man can use a sword. Also, you must protect the girl. Let him come with you."

Conell moaned and rolled his eyes. "And the Attiyq has told you this?"

He smiled and shook his head. "No, my experience told me."

Imogene dropped her gaze. These brave men willing to risk everything, and here she was, Miss Nerd, scared of her own shadow, while listening to the wind blow the leaves with no gel, foundation, or weapons.

She made her way to the community table. Last night, the women smoked the deer meat over a wooden fire and made it into a type of jerky. There wasn't a lot of meat strips left and the villagers needed it more than she. Instead, she grabbed a strip of the dried meat and a few berries to eat on the road. Émer was quite the hunter; he could find something on the trail.

She added the clean cloths at the end of the table to use as bandages. Mentally she made a list and picked up the needed supplies: salve the villagers used for wounds, extra salve for Frigg's injuries, clean water in her water canteen, and a hunting knife for cutting bandages. She smiled. These should hold them for a while. The men were still crowded together when she rejoined them.

"It is time," the Aho said.

His people gathered around him and dropped to one knee. Imogene followed. He raised his hands, his palms facing them and said more strange words. Another blessing for the villagers. Hopefully one for her.

"Attiyq," Imogene whispered. "If You can hear me, then help me. And protect me."

Cián spread his arms over their heads. "My Children, I must

leave you now, but know the Attiyq will always be with you and will never leave your side. Trust in Him and He will never forsake you. Know that I will lift you up in prayer and you will always be in my heart."

A gray-haired woman with a humped back wiped a tear from her eye. She cried out strange words to the Aho. The people mumbled a response and nodded their heads. The children gathered around the old man and he placed his palm on each of their heads and blessed them. The small faces looked up at him with sunny, yet sad smiles.

The small crowd parted as the elders stepped forward. The oldest man carried a long narrow sword. He bowed before the priest and said something in his tongue. Cián bowed and repeated the words.

The younger elders came forward and handed him small things to take on the road: a canteen, a knife, two rocks—perhaps flint— biscuits wrapped in cloth, some cheese, and a small book. He gave each person a kiss on the cheek and slipped the items into his pockets.

A young woman with long dark hair followed the men. She shook out a green cape and slipped it over his shoulders and fastened the snap. Her fingers brushed away invisible dust on the cloak and then she kissed his cheek. He smiled at her and touched her face. "Take care, Uncle," she said.

Imogene looked away. Visions of Aunt Laurie and Uncle Tim danced in her head.

"Aho," Imogene said, "what about the people? How will they eat?"

Cian's sad gaze drifted over the villagers. "The Attiyq supplied us with enough food for a day. He will supply for tomorrow. Already a few men have killed some rabbits in the mountains this morning. It seems the people's faith in the Attiyq is stronger than the demon's power. If they leave, the queen will find them. It is best if they stay here."

Émer grasped her hand. "Imie, stay close to us."

She forced a smile across her lips. "Of course."

The children grabbed sticks and battled one another, each pretending to be the priest. She longed to stay with the villagers, but she was the mighty "Oracle" of the Attiyq, who may or may not exist.

Émer, again, led the group south to the ocean. Along the route, Émer hunted for game and told Imogene more of the Attiyq. Cián would nod and filled in any gaps.

Frigg limped beside them but said little. The young man's face had faded from a pale pink to ashen-white during the day and his shoulders slumped. He should have stayed in the village.

Conell trailed behind and ignored everyone. It wasn't until the sun began to set in west when they stopped for the evening.

Imogene collapsed on the ground and pulled off her sneakers. Blisters had popped up on the back of her heels sometime during the day. She rubbed some ointment over them and wrapped her ankle with the bandages. Émer made a fire, while Conell cleaned the small white turkey Émer had caught earlier in day. At least it wasn't a rabbit.

"How far did we walk?" Imogene asked as Frigg slowly lowered himself to the ground and stretched his arms over his head. Dark circles sat under his eyes.

Émer took supplies from his bag. "Maybe a few miles. We still have two day's journey before reaching Shes Chez."

She suppressed a moan. Once done with her wounds, she examined Frigg's back and took his pulse. "How are you feeling?"

He gave her a small smile. "I am fine."

"You don't look fine. Maybe you should have stayed back in the village." She unwrapped the dirty bandages from his torso.

The wounds had stopped bleeding, but the blue and black bruises still crossed his back. She smoothed the ointment over the gashes. He flinched, but said nothing. Once done, she rewrapped his chest and lowered his shirt.

"Thank you," he said as he eased himself back down.

The last rays of the sun slipped under the horizon. Cián sat beside her. His dark eyes focused on the campfire.

"Penny for your thoughts?" she asked him.

"A *what* for my thoughts?" The firelight bounced off his wrinkled cheeks.

"It means what are you thinking?"

"Ah. The Attiyq is warning me to be careful. Evil lies in the hands of those who claim to be allies."

She tossed the used bandage onto the fire. "Okay, so why does He talk to you instead of me?"

"Because you do not listen to Him." He pointed to his ear. "He spoke to you all day, yet your ears are closed to Him."

"How do I open my ears?" she asked, shrugging a shoulder.

"When you hear Him, then your ears will be opened."

She rolled her eyes. "Whatever."

Conell sat on the ground next to Imogene and extended his legs. "So, Aho, how many times does this Attiyq speak to you?"

Cián lifted his dark gaze to the prince. "Many times. You do not believe in the Attiyq, do you, Moji?"

He shrugged. "He abandoned me years ago in the prison. Why must I extend my hand to Him?"

"You used your experiences to explain away the Great One. Your words make little sense." Cián pulled his cloak around his shoulders, then pulled a blanket from a backpack and slipped it around Imogene. She gave him a smile of thanks and lifted the blanket up her back.

"Experiences told me He does not see or hear my cries." A haunting look covered Conell's young face. He brought in his legs and crossed them. "I truly believed in Him, but then the witch tricked me. I trusted in my people and the witch, and as a result, my friends and I were thrown into prison." His finger drummed against his chest. "I escaped with no help from the Attiyq."

Cián asked, "Why did you let me come along?"

He pursed his lips. "Émer's complaining rubbed against my ears."

"Ah." The old man tapped his chin. "Do you continually give into others?"

Conell shook his head and looked away.

Cián lifted his shining face to the star-filled sky. "The Attiyq says, He has been with you through these trials. His hands have led you to the girl and to this place and soon He will reveal His secrets to her."

"And He has," said a deep male voice from the darkness.

Émer and Conell jumped to their feet and grabbed their swords.

"Who are you?" Conell demanded. "Show yourself."

A man stepped from the woods and stood in the perimeter of the small camp. The light from the campfire silhouetted his large frame and long feathery wings spilled down from his shoulders. Imogene rubbed her eyes. He seemed more like a vision than a real person.

"I am your friend, Prince Conell. Do not fear me." The stranger's voice was deep and commanding like a cannon boom echoing in a valley.

The man stepped into the fire light. His long white hair lay over his broad shoulders and his snow-white wings trailed to the ground. The angel looked strong enough to lift a mini van with one hand.

"Hey, he's the guy from the river," Imogene said.

Émer lowered his weapon. "Attiyq be praised! My Moji, he is the angel who saved us."

The angel smiled and gave a polite nod. "Yes, Captain Émer, I was the one. I was sent by the Attiyq to protect you and guide you. I am known as Argus."

Conell extended his sword. "How do we know He sent you?"

"You must trust me." Argus's tight smile spread across his thin face.

Imogene shivered. The angel seemed like a knight when he flew over the river. But in person, this being seemed more like a fast-talking car salesman, almost too slick. His voice was hypnotizing. *But what if the Attiyq speaks through him and I missed it?*

"And you," Argus smiled at her, "are known as Imogene

Katherine Reazley of a far way land called Illinois. You are as beautiful as your name."

She looked behind her, before turning back to him. A small grin crept onto her face. "How do you know me?

He took a step towards her, but Conell moved in front of him and slipped his sword under Argus's chin. "Stay away from her."

The angel held up his palms and lifted his eyebrows. "Please, My Prince, I mean no harm. I was sent to guide the girl into God's wisdom."

"Cián," Imogene asked. "Is this what you meant by hearing from Him?"

The priest gestured to the angel. "Moji, let him be. I wish to hear what he has to say."

"Thank you," Argus said.

Conell lowered the sword but stayed between Argus and Imogene.

"The Great One has heard Émer's and the priest's prayers. I was sent to help the girl reveal the medallion's hidden words and to lead her home. I am also to help you, Prince Conell, to find rest from the one who pursues you. You do wish for me to help her, do you not?"

Imogene took a step towards him. "You can take me home?"

Argus nodded. "We can leave now if you wish."

Conell crossed his arms over his chest. "Let me speak your words. You say you are a messenger from the Attiyq and He sent you to grant our wishes. Why now? And you ignore my questions. How do I know *He* sent you?"

Argus cocked his head and smiled sweetly.

Coldness washed over Imogene. Her blood felt like an iced slushy in her veins. Her nightmare from the other night swept over her. A handsome and dashing angel wrapped his muscled arms around her waist and kissed her neck. Romantic words spilled from his warm lips. The being was like a character from a Manga and she was lost between the pages. The striking creature's hand entwined with her own and he led the charming damsel dressed in a pale blue gown across a red and blue flower covered field.

The ground rumbled and lurched. The dirt collapsed and the sides of the pit plummeted into the earth. She screamed and lost her grip on the angel. The Manga hero's wings burst open. Instead of flying her to safety, he dragged her towards the fire pit that rose from the bottom of the crater and tossed her into the blaze. The flares splashed her face and burned her eyes and body. His laughter rolled as her scorching hands reached up to him.

The same handsome angel from her dream now stood here in the fire light. What if he dragged her into hell? What if he was as evil as in her dream? What if he was good and her dream was, as Dickens had said, "… an undigested bit of beef, a blot of mustard, a crumb of cheese, a fragment of an underdone potato."

His eyes shifted to her; she dropped her gaze and shivered.

Argus nodded to the young red-haired advisor. "Your companion is wounded, is he not?"

Conell's eyes became thin slits. "Yes, he is."

Argus eyed the wounded man. "How do you feel now, Frigg?"

Frigg wiggled and stretched his back. "I do not hurt anymore."

Conell motioned to Imogene. "Check him."

She made her way to him and lifted the back of his shirt. Her small hands maneuvered him into the fire light. A gasp escaped her. "His wounds! They're gone."

Frigg smiled at the angel. "Thank you."

Argus gave a small, gallant nod.

Conell kept his sword raised as he stepped back to Imogene and peered over her shoulder.

"Yes, they are," Conell said. "You healed Frigg. Am I now to fall and worship you?"

Darkness covered the angel's face. "You are a stubborn man. I healed him to prove to you the Attiyq has sent me. Will you now push aside His hands?"

Conell looked to the priest. "You claim to hear from Him, what is He saying?"

The old man made a face and shrugged. "Nothing. Perhaps He has gone to bed."

Conell frowned. "For now, the girl stays with me. Leave us; I will speak to you again in the morning."

Argus smiled at Imogene. "Until the morning."

He spread his great wings and rose in the black sky.

Conell slipped his sword into its sheath. "Émer, we will take turns guarding the camp. I will take the first watch, you take the second, Frigg third, and Cián will take the last."

The men nodded. The group slowly settled around the camp. Conell sat beside Émer and spoke to him in his native tongue. Émer noticed Imogene staring at him and winked at her, then speared the turkey carcass and placed it over the fire. Soon the familiar smell of cooked meat filled the air. The scent brought her back to "normal" again. But what was normal? Normal left the day that stupid medallion grabbed her.

Once cooked, Émer cut off chunks of hot meat and gave a piece to everyone. Conell grew quiet during the small meal only grunting a yes or no to their questions. He seemed lost in some far-off world. She pulled off a small piece of meat and slipped it into her mouth.

Émer, as if sensing his prince's irritable mood, moved beside Cián and spoke in their native tongue. Their soft voices and odd words calmed her nerves. Frigg moved closer and asked a few questions using the same strange language. Cián smiled and used a thin bone to pick at his teeth.

She placed the meat against her lips and slowly chewed. The strange incidents with the angel felt strange and wrong. His insistence to take her away and showing up at the right times and the right places. "Everything," she whispered. She rubbed her forehead and yawned. Wooziness enveloped her mind and jumbled her thoughts like a vegetable stew. A chill spread over her as if unseen eyes were on them, on her. She looked around but saw no one. Émer seemed not to notice and kept talking to the others. It must be from the walking. She stretched out on the ground and her eyes closed.

Argus sat cocooned in his dark magic on the upper branch of the tree that overlooked Conell's small party. Imogene's insecurities tasted sweet like blossom nectar and her fear smelled like summer rain. Breaking her strong soul would be difficult, but the great Argus was up to the challenge. How many other young women had the god of Ezasu broken? Thousands. He flicked his hand. The naïve child's heart lay open like a deer carcass. A longing for acceptance and love filled Imogene's heart, useless things that he could manipulate. He nodded. Give the girl a smile and she would lead him to the Attiyq's legendary weapons—heaven's gates would fling open. The heroic Argus would seize God's throne and annihilate the Heavenly Leader.

She sensed him and twisted to see who hunted her.

*Yes, my love, sense your master's presence.* Argus closed his eyes. Eagla leaned her soft head on his shoulder and caressed him with gentle hands.

"My Lord and Master, what is your bidding?"

He kissed his devotee. "You are my favorite of all my slaves."

Eagla smiled. "I know."

"Do not let the girl go." He kissed her again.

The shapely brown-haired follower floated down and enveloped the teenaged girl. A grin slowly crossed his handsome face. His spells squeezed Imogene like a snake. She would crack, as would Prince Conell DeCapris, son of Broden. Already Argus laid claim to the young man who would snap like thin glass. The outraged prince who kept his mouth shut while the king's foolish mistakes betrayed the kingdom. Argus smiled at the irony of it all. Humans were so pathetic.

Brón's slim arms still embraced the prince as she had done for years. Her beautiful songs slipped into DeCapris's ears and twisted his once childlike heart into a massive mud pit of regret, ripe for destruction.

Argus hummed along to Brón's hymn. She blew him a kiss and he smacked his lips. Long red hair framed Brón's thin pale face and her curved body always set a chill through him. She was lovely and her songs of Conell's shame sent tingles down his arms, but all of his children were lovely and amazing.

Brón giggled and snuggled closer to Conell DeCapris, who now followed the destructive footsteps of his father. The young man winced.

The hands of time wove together Argus's beautiful tapestry. His chess pieces stood in their places and would soon crumble like a sandcastle. Ezasu would belong to him again. A satyr king and an angry prince paved the road for the great Argus. How he loved the thoughtless decisions made by humans, the cursed Attiyq's cherished dolls.

He chewed on the inside of his cheek and studied the young Maúl Captain. Now *he* could become a problem. The last of the hated Mául. How he despised Anu, the Mául's first inept leader. Argus's fist would grind Anu's last warrior into dust and the cursed clan would disappear forever. A perfect justice. He lifted his chin and smirked.

And why not? After what Anu and Broden did to him centuries ago, the pests deserved it. The blights of the Attiyq would suffer his fiery breath. They would tremble at the feet of the great God who could do nothing, but sob in despair. Soon Broden and Anu would mourn their actions done to the great Argus centuries ago. They would pay with the lives of their children. He breathed in deeply as the joy of vengence flowed through him.

His eyes focused back on the last Mául and tapped his finger against his jaw. The question was how to destroy this one last annoying insect. If he could separate Émer from his beloved God…The Attiyq's warriors guarded him day and night. He rubbed his chin.

Argus's child, Amhras, slithered like a snake up the tree and across the branch. He laid his handsome head on Argus's arm and stroked his father's feathers.

"Father," Amhras whispered in Argus's ear. "You know it breaks my heart to see you in such pain. Give him to me, allow me to bring you comfort. I will pull him from his God and destroy him. I will not fail you, Father. Once I am done, the man who troubles you will doubt his God."

Argus caressed his son's firm face. "Yes, My Loyal Son, you may have him."

Amhras squealed with joy, kissed his father, and slipped away.

"Use Conell's fears and his secret against the one he called his brother. Amhras nodded. Yes, his answer lay before him. Make the captain suffer as Anu made Argus suffer. With the men destroyed, he would own the girl and the medallion.

Argus frowned and crossed his arms over his chest. How could Anu and Broden do something so dreadful, so shocking, so horrific to a majestic creature as himself? Their heirs would suffer along with the Attiyq.

Brón lifted tearing eyes to her father and wept. "Father, you know I love you, please remember how much I care."

He spat the words from his mind. He wanted to rule. Once the people realized their mistake in worshiping the Attiyq, they would revere him. He shrugged. Yes, millions of people would die, but think of the honor the survivors would bestow on him. And his seer, Imogene. His grin expanded. Cián would scream for mercy, but Argus would show none. The priest would pay for his intrusions.

Cián's eyes slowly rose and captured him as if he heard Argus's unspoken words. The old man's lips moved. Brón threw back her red head and screamed a wail unheard by the humans. It echoed off the mountains and shook the trees. Eagla whimpered and raced to hide in the woods.

Argus cringed and gritted his teeth as a slight stinging morphed into white-hot pokers that dug into his head and torso. He clenched his stomach and locked his screams inside. The searing pain ripped the breath from his lungs. His vision blurred.

The words of the Attiyq! The cursed Attiyq. The betraying beast who forever stood before him and stole what once belonged to him. Rank, rancid, fetid animal!

Argus, the great leader, handsome knight, the brave conqueror, defender of the unholy, Prince of Darkness, forced to grovel at the feet of the Attiyq's servant. Argus snarled and gasped. Cián and his religious ways disgusted him. Once he possessed the girl and the medallion, he would dig out the old man's heart and roast it over a fire for his dinner. He rose into the sky and disappeared, leaving Brón behind to sob in her suffering.

Conell tossed fresh wood on the morning fire. Imogene lay asleep in her blankets, Cián left to pray, while Émer and Frigg hunted for breakfast. He rubbed his chin and jabbed the wood deeper into the flames.

These past days confused and haunted him. Argus saved them at the river and claimed he could take the girl home. *But why now and here? Why did the angel or the Attiyq not save Emon from Ruárc's arrow? Or save mother from the barbarian's sword?* He poked at the fire. Years ago, Conell longed for the Attiyq's help, but He kept His hands behind His back and His ears shut off from Conell's cries. The Great God would rather sit while His people perish as opposed to sending chariots of fire to help him.

Again the night air chilled in Argus's presence as if a frost covered the grass. The same finger slid down his back when he held his sword against Argus's throat. The so-called angel's eyes became pools of darkness. His voice was like the screeching of the crow.

128

Conell shivered and pulled the blanket over his shoulders. After Argus left, the air warmed again. He was coming back today to take the girl. He pulled out his sword and sharpened it. He would be ready.

The void of voices made Conell twitchy. It was this same silence, an unheard accusing voice that followed the attack on the castle years ago. Father always said the quiet was when a man faced his sins. Conell's transgressions danced around the fire and the birds' songs chanted his crimes.

A haunting gathered in his mind like a thunderstorm as ghosts from the past planted their roots. He shivered as the past rose up from the smoke. The bloodied faces threw back their heads and wailed the same screams night after night and stole his sleep.

*Émer, a ten-year-old boy, slowly opened the closet door from where the boys hid during the attack on the castle and peeked around the doorway. A seven-year-old Conell hiding his face; holding his breath. Waiting for the yells from the barbarians. Émer giving him a small smile, gently helped Conell to his feet. They stepped from the safety of the closet.*

Conell closed his eyes tight and shivered before the warm campfire. A bird screeched overhead and he jumped.

*Émer lead him through quiet, bloodied halls. The silence pressed into their ears, but was broken by the moaning wind. Their footsteps crunched like thunder on the stoned tiles. Weeping drifted down the corridor from Father's study. Three-year-old Frigg whimpered and cowered under Father's desk. Émer coaxed him out and Frigg clung to him. They stepped out into the gory hall.*

*The young Maúl warrior held the shocked Frigg in one arm, told the boy to look only at him. Conell clung to Émer who buried Conell's face in his stomach and covered Conell's eyes with his hand, but he saw through Émer's fingers. His tears ran down Émer's hand.*

*Everyone was ripped open like stuffed animals—friends, teachers, mentors, even the old cook who yelled at him for stealing apples before dinner and the young maids who gossiped over the Lords and Ladies. Father's captain-of-the-guards hung from his neck—Broden's banner used as a rope. Maúl warriors and the guards clenched their swords with white, bloody fingers. The elders covered the corpses of the children. Their lifeless white orbs fixed on him as he walked by them. Accusing him. Lying in pools of blood. The thick red ooze mingled in the cracks of the stoned floors and blotted the grey and white stones with crimson stains.*

*Father. Mother. Conell pushed those images from his mind.*

*The young Maúl walked passed the torn bodies of his father and clan. Émer lips pursed and tears danced in his purple eyes. Young Emer swallowed his pain and led them out of the castle.*

Conell choked back the lump in his throat and mopped the sweat from his face. A shiver ran over him. If only he had told his father the words that would protect him, but the boy remained silent. Always silent.

And still silent to this day. Was it any wonder that the same silence now accused him?

The girl's stirring chased away his haunting and she spread out her fingers on the ground. He cocked his head as the past drifted away like the smoke from the fire. He was thankful for the memories to leave him.

She slowly opened one eye before opening the other and moaned. "I'm still here, aren't I?"

He forced a smile on his face. "Yes, *Chuoha*, you are still in Ezasu."

She tugged the blanket over her shoulders, sat up and ran her fingers through her short hair. "Where are the others?"

"Cián is praying, and Émer and Frigg are finding breakfast."

"Rabbit? Again?"

"I do not know. Perhaps."

"I would give anything for an Egg McMuffin."

"A what?" he said, furrowing his brow.

She giggled, and shook her head. "Never mind. It's the best food in my world."

"Ah. Well, I will see to getting you home, then you can eat this…" he twirled his fingers, "Egg thing."

"It's a deal." She held out her hands to the fire's heat. "So, what do you think? I mean, about the angel?"

"I do not trust his words."

She nodded. "I don't know. I'm so sorry, Prince Conell, but I can't hear from the Attiyq. I don't know what He's trying to say. I want to believe Argus, he did heal Frigg. I mean, what if he can help me to read the medallion and get me home? I don't want to stay here."

Conell tossed leaves into the fire. The same chill from last night spread down his back. "I know, *Chuoha*, I know you long to go home. But I do not know if this is the right way. Something is wrong. I think it would be best if you stayed close to me."

She suppressed a small smile. "But if he has the way home, maybe I should go with him?"

"Give it time, *Chuoha*. We do not need to hurry."

"Moji, I want to trust him, but…I don't know about all of this, I mean, he gives me the creeps."

Conell caught her gaze. "Creeps?"

"It's like when he's here, I can't think what's right or what's wrong, but I don't, I mean, I want to go with him, but I don't know. I can't shake this bad feeling. He creeps me out, scares me." She flicked her fingers. "Maybe I'm tired."

The fear inched its way across her small face.

Cián stepped from the trees and made his way to the fire. "Imogene, you are up. Did you sleep well?"

Émer and Frigg followed the old man. Frigg carried a dead rabbit by its ears and blackberries in a cloth.

"Yes, thank you." Imogene rose and cupped her hand under Frigg's cloth and took some of the berries. "Did you hear from the Attiyq?"

"I did. He was not in a talkative mood today. I did most of the speaking."

Conell snickered. He grabbed a few berries from Imogene and tossed them in his mouth. "Maybe the Great and Mighty God is still in bed?"

Émer glared at his prince. He grabbed the dead rabbit from Frigg, made his way from the campfire, knelt and began to skin the animal. "My Moji, please have some respect for the Attiyq."

Cián rubbed his hands together over the fire. "When do we eat and has your angel friend not revisited us?"

"We eat when Émer cooks the rabbit." Conell rose to his feet. "And the angel is not my friend."

"Really?" asked the old man. "You do not trust him?"

"No. I trust those I call friends."

"Your words spear my heart, Prince Conell." Argus landed gently on the ground and tucked his wings behind him. The wind made his feathers vibrate. He stepped in front of Imogene and smiled at her. "And you." His voice was deep and soothing. "My lovely Oracle, the Attiyq has asked me to take you home, if you choose to go." He lifted her hand and kissed the back of her fingers.

She gave him a small shy smile and ran her fingers through her curling blond hair.

The air instantly chilled. Conell pushed Imogene behind him and raised his sword to Argus.

The angel took a step back and his white eyebrows rose like a large tree looming a small weed. "I do not think I am speaking to you, Moji Conell."

"*I* am speaking to you; you will not take her anywhere. I do not trust the Attiyq and I do not trust you."

She placed her hand on Conell's arm. "I'm not for sure. I mean, Cián said I was to read the medallion for you. Maybe I should stay here for a while longer?"

The angel's smile avoided his eyes. His dark orbs caught Imogene like a spider's web. His words were deep and soft as if he spoke from a padded tunnel. "But you know your mother misses you. Have you already forgotten her, child?"

"My mother?" She rubbed her forehead and weaved against Conell. "Momma misses me?" Her voice was soft and weak.

"Yes, she does, my dear." Argus's smooth tones embraced her mind. "Take my hand. Let me help you."

Her small hand slowly reached for his outstretched palm, a claw made of bleached drift wood.

"Enough!" Conell grabbed Imogene's wrist and led her to a rock. He gently sat her down and knelt in front of her. "You will not go with him until I can understand his motives. Until that time, you will stay with me, understand?"

Whiteness coated her small face and her bright eyes glazed over. She lifted her head. "Momma."

"Your mother will still be there." Conell moved her face back to his and pressed his fingertips against the large vein in her neck. Her heart raced. She blinked twice as if trying to find him.

*He creeps me out.*

The darkness crept up behind him. Chilling his bones. Death's orbs drilling into his back. Pinpricks danced up and down his arms. He slowly faced the demon.

Argus sneered. Dark, red eyes encased in the angel's face tightened around Conell like a snake. They squeezed Clemwyn's teachings from his mind. Father's words drifted away. Talon hands pulled him into black pits and held his head under water. He was unable to breathe. His heart tasted the sting of Argus's blade. He could see Mother's blood pooling into the cracks of the castle floor.

He knelt before Imogene and held her small pale face in his trembling hands. Her eyes glazed over. As if a demon stole her soul. "Stay with me, *Chuoha*." His voice shook; he coughed and cursed silently.

*Never show fear to your enemy.*

"Moji." She rubbed the bridge of her nose and weaved towards him, almost tumbling from the rock. He held her against him.

"You truly do not trust me, do you Prince Conell?" came Argus's stabbing tones.

The girl's eyes were glazed and hazy. She looked lost, unable to find her way back to him. He closed his eyes and took a deep breath. *Fight this!* But the fear held him in vise. Father had said, "Do not show the enemy your fear." *Fight!*

He faced the angel.

His heart thundered in his ears. The wetness from his palm made the blade hilt slippery as trails of sweat dripped down his back. He pressed the air from his lungs. "No, I do not trust you. You appear out of the sky and then demand to take her away. What spell have you put on her?"

"What a shame." Argus's blood-red eyes rose to Conell like a snake gobbling up a small bird. "What a foolish prince. One who keeps his secrets close to his heart," the angel smirked.

Conell blinked twice and shivered. A fist grew in his throat. Argus's trap tightened around Conell's lungs. He winced. Trails of moisture trickled from his hand onto his blade. The creature's murky presence captured him. It was suffocating. Like Émer's rabbit. Conell took a deep shaking breath. Imogene moaned. Frigg's sharp words drifted past him.

"Stop this now." The Aho stepped between the two men.

The lingering darkness fled. The chill lessened. Argus took a step back and lowered his gaze.

Cián looked from Conell to Argus. "There is no need to raise the swords."

Conell closed his eyes and forced his hand still. The fear vanished. It was over. He breathed deeply. *Yet, what did he mean by secrets? What did this thing know?*

"Prince Conell," Argus said. "Why do you suddenly care?"

"I have explained my reasons." He shoved the old man aside. He stumbled, but Frigg caught him.

Conell crossed his arms over his chest with his eyes focused on Argus. The dark pools vanished and in its place, an angry face. The large tree dwarfed into a swaying reed. Conell now towered over

Argus, the small weed. "Now, answer my question, why do you want her?"

Frigg stepped in front of Conell. "Forgive me, My Prince, but perhaps it is better if the angel takes Imogene to her home. It will be a matter of time before Queen Jezebel finds us and *her*."

"I have made my decision. The girl stays here with me." Conell moved Frigg from him and stepped before Argus. "And you will stay away from her."

Frigg grabbed Conell's arm. "My Prince, I have never questioned your decisions before, but now I must question this one. Where will you take her? Across the sea with us? Then where? She does not belong here. Let her go home to her village and her people. If she is ill, then they can care for her more than we can."

Conell gave him a sharp look and yanked away his arm.

Imogene shakily rose from the rock. "I'll stay here for a bit longer. It's okay."

Argus's eyes rested on her and her legs buckled. She plopped on the rock and placed her fingertips on her forehead. Conell stepped in front of her and blocked Argus's view.

"Captain Émer," Argus said. "You have been silent. Tell us what you think of the prince's decision."

Émer's eyes flickered from his prince to the angel, then he continued skinning the carcass. "I do not question my Moji's orders."

"If she dies then her blood will be upon your head. I must leave for the Attiyq is summoning me. But I will be back for your answer." He rose into the sky and disappeared across the horizon.

Conell knelt in front of Imogene and gave her a small shake. "*Chuoha*, can you hear me?"

The same whiteness covered her face and her hands trembled. "Moji?"

Émer knelt beside them. "Moji, what is wrong with her?"

"I do not know," he said. "I think Argus has put a spell on her."

"What kind of spell?" Émer asked.

She rubbed her temples. "I'm just tired."

Émer lifted his canteen to her mouth. "Imie, drink."

She drank deeply and forced a smile. "I'm okay, now."

Her hands shook. ...As did Conell's.

Argus landed softly in the queen's courtyard. The dead and gnarled trees spotted the yard like tumors and the dead grass crunched under his boots. The beauty of the former queen's patio died when she passed away. No matter how hard Jezebel worked at the plants, they wilted under her cold touch. He grinned. A woman so useless even the plants gave up on her.

The queen's white fingers caressed a fragile branch. The twig snapped. "So, Conell again stands in my way."

He dropped to one knee. "Forgive me, My Queen, but he will not let me have her. DeCapris is stubborn. It seems a priest has joined the group. Cián, Son of Owian of the Eced Shiaku."

Jezebel's hand froze over the dead twig. "Cián? Are you sure?"

"Yes, My Queen. It seems he is still alive. And he is more powerful now." He winced.

Another dead stem broke and fell to the ground under her chilled touch. "I thought the old man was surely dead."

"No, he lives to bother us another day. I also heard Cián say the Attiyq wishes to reveal His secrets to her. She can tell us where the Attiyq's great weapons are hidden. I tried to convince her to come with me, even cast my spell upon her, but again, Conell and the priest stand in my way." As did Broden and Anu. He spit on the ground.

"Reveal His secrets? Why reveal to a small, insignificant girl? I raised Conell to be selfish and conceited, a perfect puppet in my hands, and yet somehow he has gained a conscience. Perhaps he is more like his father than I first thought."

He rose and stroked her hair. "I have others ways in which I can get the girl, do not worry, My Lady." He kissed her and her body melted against him.

"And if you cannot?"

He pulled his face from her neck and his eyebrows rose. "If I cannot? Is that the way you see me?"

She lowered her gaze. "Of course, not. Do what you must."

"You worry too much, My Lady," he said, kissing her again.

Conell threw the bones from their dinner into the fire. Imogene lay curled up in her blankets. All day she leaned on Cian's arm as they made their way across the fields. Each time they met this strange angel, Imogene's strength slipped away. It had to be a spell of some kind. Conell would have to be more careful.

*Afanen's image sat across the fire reminding the prince of his abandonment. She lifted her bloody head. "So you will save her and let me die?"*

He walked away and readjusted his weapon trying to avoid the memory, but the haunting continued.

*Afanen hummed a strange tune that sent shivers down his spine.*

He let out a deep breath and focused on the creature from this morning. *How could this thing, this "angel" be of the Attiyq?* Yes, the beings were strong and fierce, but not this fierce. From what he remembered, the beings were kind and gentle. The spell Argus had placed on her was not gentle. He licked his lips. Hopefully the strange creature would not visit tonight.

*Afanen giggled. "Secrets? You have so many, My Moji. How do you keep track of them?"*

The sun began to set and another long, dark evening faced him. Frigg pulled a blanket around his shoulders. "Moji, I think you are being selfish. She wants to go home, and yet you make her stay. The girl is ill. She could come from the Northern Territories or the Southern areas, maybe across the seas or the Eastern Borders. We will never find her home, but the angel can. Why make her stay?"

Conell walked back to the fire and knelt next to Cián. "What do you truly think, *Aho*? Is the angel from the Attiyq?"

The priest shrugged. "What I think makes no difference." He stretched out on the ground and placed his hands under his head. "You are the leader, not me." He gave Conell a long, concerning look. "You need to stop listening to the voices of the past."

Conell cocked his head wondering if the priest knew of tortured conscience.

Émer dragged a sharpening stone over the blade of his sword then picked up a rag and polished the metal. "What does the Attiyq say?"

Cián raised his head to the darkening sky. "Nothing, His tongue is silent."

Émer slipped his sword back into its sheath. "That is odd. Surely the Attiyq would tell *you* something regarding Argus. Why does He remain silent?"

"Perhaps," Frigg said. "He is testing your faith."

"And perhaps the angel is lying," Conell said. "Something… happened." Clemwyn's words whispered in his mind. *Do not show fear to your men.* "I felt something from Argus. Something evil. I cannot let her go with him. Did anyone else sense or see something?"

Émer reached behind him and grabbed the quiver. Pulling out the arrows, he dipped the ends into mud. "What kind of *something*?"

"Evil, cold, something morbid?" Conell asked.

Émer looked up from his task and shook his head.

Frigg shrugged. "No, Moji. All I saw were you and Argus

arguing."

Cián narrowed his eyes. "What did you feel, son?"

Imogene gasped and sat upright. "Conell!"

"What is it, *Chuoha*?" Conell asked.

"I think I heard something." She rose onto her hands and knees and scanned the woods.

Conell said to Émer, "Is something out there?"

He shook his head a little confused and made his way to Imogene. He knelt beside and peered into the trees. "What did you hear?"

The girl leaned back on her haunches. "I don't know. A voice, whispering to me."

The priest leaned towards her. "What did it say, child?"

"That I'm supposed to stay here with Prince Conell."

Conell cocked his head and narrowed his eyes. "Are you sure?"

She nodded and lay back on the ground. "But I don't know who or what it was. Maybe I'm tired."

Cián gave her a knowing smile. "Or maybe you heard from the Attiyq, child."

"But how do I know who is whom and who is me?" she asked.

Émer covered her with the blanket. "Not to worry. Sleep now, we will discuss this tomorrow. You need your rest."

She grinned at him and pulled the covering to her chin.

Cián pointed to the girl. "There is your answer; she is to stay with you."

Imogene opened her eyes hoping to see the white ceiling in her baby-blue bedroom and the poster of Harry Styles on her wall. She sighed as she saw the sunbeams cutting through the trees. She moaned and put her hand over her eyes. Still trapped in the Great

Land of Oz and her strange companions strolled right along with her. Maybe if she tapped her heels three times, something would happen. *Don't be stupid.* Dew that smelled of pine drifted in the air. She liked the scent, but she'd avoid camping for the next ten years.

Cián shook out his blanket. "Ah, our young oracle awakens."

Imogene squinted at the bright sunbeams cutting into the woods and gave him a soft grin. "Good morning, Aho. I don't know if I'm still an oracle."

"Now your ears are open, My child," Cián cut off a piece of cooked wild chicken and chewed it slowly.

Her stomach churned. What she would do for some plain toast and butter. He used the chicken bone to point at her. She suppressed a face.

"What else does He say?" he asked.

She sighed and rubbed her eyes. "Nothing. How do I know who is me and who is Him?"

"What do you feel inside?"

"Sort of happy like, like I found a pair of two-hundred-dollar shoes for twenty bucks," she said.

Émer handed her a piece of cooked chicken. She resisted a grimace, took it from him and gave him a tired smile.

The Aho cocked his head and nodded. "Well, um, that same feeling of shoes will follow the Attiyq."

"He seems, well, nice." She forced the chicken down to her rumbling stomach.

"Humph!" Conell threw a blanket on the ground. "He has never been nice to me. Finish eating, we leave soon."

She rolled her eyes, but grinned at the old man. He winked back at her and rolled up his blanket. After a quick breakfast of cooked chicken, the group headed south for Mother's Hills.

The cool mountain air stayed behind and in its place, heat rose from the ground. The land became uneven and twice Imogene stumbled. Émer took the lead and Imogene leaned on Cián's arm. Conell and Frigg took the rear and talked softy in their native tongue.

Eventually, they passed through a small grove and emerged into a meadow covered in red and blue flowers.

Imogene pulled her blanket from her pack and spread out it on the rough grass. "We'll have a picnic here."

Émer gave Conell an amused look. "A picnic would be nice, Imie." Émer sat on the blanket and gave the others sharp looks.

Conell grimaced. His captain pursed his lips and nodded sternly to the blanket. Conell rolled his eyes, but sat down. The others joined them.

She pulled dried rabbit and apples Frigg had picked earlier in the day from her bag and gave it to her friends. The men passed amused looks at each other. *Warriors taking time to have a picnic* they seemed to say. Their ancestors were laughing.

After eating, Émer lay on the blanket and watched the floating clouds. Imogene couldn't resist and lay beside him.

She pointed to the sky. "Doesn't that cloud look like an elephant?"

"An elephant?" Émer gave her a puzzled look. "My Lady, what is an elephant?"

She giggled. "See the long thing coming out of its face? That's its trunk; it's like a long nose. And see how big the body is and the legs? That's what an elephant looks like."

Émer erupted with laughter. "An animal with a nose that long? Come now, Imie, you poke me with a sword."

She laughed with him. "My mom and I used to do this. We'd lie on the ground and pick out pictures in the clouds. We did it every summer."

He gazed at the billows. "It sounds magical. My mother said the *cruid*s, clouds, were the Angels' chariots and they rode them in and out of the Attiyq's throne room. But tell me more of your mother?"

"She went to New York a few years ago. She used to call almost every day, but now she sends me cards and a few gifts. When I get home, I'm going to run away to New York and find my mom."

"How far is this New York?"

"Far, really far." She studied the sky. "If we were to walk, it would take us a year to get there."

"Imie, what other pictures do you see?"

She pointed to the sky, but Émer's attention refocused on the trees.

"Émer?" she asked.

Conell eyes followed Émer's gaze and tossed away a small stick. "How many?"

Émer's hand gripped the hilt of his sword. "I am not sure." He studied the sky and shrugged. "I think maybe a few? They have followed us all morning."

"Is someone out there?" Imogene started to rise.

Émer gently pushed her back to the ground. "It is best if the prey stays still."

"Émer," she whispered.

"Shhh, tell me what you see in the sky, Imie."

But this time the clouds no longer appeared as cute animals, but like clawed knives.

Frigg peered into the woods. "My Lord, shall I go investigate?"

Conell picked a blue flower and sucked out the pollen. "No, let them come to us. Aho, can you use your sword?"

"Yes."

The prince nodded. "Stay with Imogene; Frigg, you and Émer are with me. If we must separate, then Aho, you take her to Shea Shiaku, Nestled Village, beyond those hills. Émer says he has friends there who will help you."

Imogene licked her lips. Her nerves showed themselves.

The captain smiled at her. "It will be all right. No worries, Imie. I was hoping to have some exercise."

"I don't know if I'm ready for this," she whispered. "I'm scared."

He patted her hand. "Stay here, let them come to us. They want us to separate, destroy us one by one. We can defeat them if we stay together. It is not a single stick that defeats the enemy, but a club made of many sticks. Moji, I hear maybe five men, could be more beyond the trees."

Conell lay out upon the grass and placed his hands under his head. "Stay with our plan."

Émer slipped his callused hand into Imogene's and gave it a quick squeeze. He jumped to his feet and shuffled the supplies. His quick eyes took in the woods. "There are seven, My Moji." His deep purple eyes caught his Moji's gaze. The captain sneered. "They are *Upeshi*."

"*Upeshi*?" Imogene asked.

"Barbarians from the west," Émer said. "My sword has longed to taste their blood. They killed my father and my people years ago."

"Careful, Émer," Conell said. "Do not let revenge blind you. Imogene, do not let their appearance frighten you."

She whimpered. According to the *Conan the Barbarian* shows, they chopped off people's heads, not to mention what they did to young girls who were alone and did stupid things like spray paint the school in order to catch a guy's eye. Why did she have to pick up that stupid necklace? *Go back in time and find yourself and tell yourself to stop. Avoid the stupid bush and make this madness go away.*

Cián made his way to her side and lowered his old body to the ground. "Do not fret, child. The Attiyq will guard us."

She nodded and gave him a small smile.

Émer squatted on the ground. "They are circling us. Imie, stay close to the ground."

She closed her eyes and said a prayer to the Attiyq.

The enemy comes like a beam of light, taking the innocent away. They are never seen again.

~ King Catrin, year 555
written in the *Manual of the Warrior*
after the Battle against the Southern Lands.

Seven men emerged from the treeline like ghosts in a vampire movie. They raced across the flower-covered grass; their hide-covered feet crushed the small floras. Red and black swirling tattoos covered their bald heads, faces and bodies. Small horns surrounded in white paint protruded from their foreheads and animal skins covered around their groins. They raised long curved swords over their heads and screamed like madmen.

Émer grabbed his bow and launched an arrow into the air. It hit one of the tattooed men. Conell jumped up and pulled his sword from its sheath and grounded his feet. Émer tossed away the bow and grabbed his sword. Frigg also drew his sword and planted his legs. Cián rose, yanked Imogene up and shoved her behind him.

Two of the warriors broke off and attacked Conell, while three raced for Émer and Frigg.

The last *Upeshi* darted for Cián. Imogene stumbled back and tried to catch her breath. The barbarian's wide eyes fixed on her and his crazed screams echoed in her ears. He licked his lips and took a step towards her. Cián thrust him back with his shoulder.

She searched for Conell.

Two barbarians rushed him. Conell swung his sword upwards to the first man, but he jumped back. The second man thrust his sword at Conell and he blocked it with his own blade. The prince slipped between the two men. One of the wild men swung his sword at Conell, but he countered the swing and pushed one man into the other. The two barbarians gathered their footings. One swung again at Conell. He stopped the upward swing and kicked the man in the stomach. He doubled over and staggered back.

Conell danced away from the other man, who raised his sword to the prince's chest. Conell again, stopped the attack and punched the man in the face with the hilt of his sword. The man stumbled back and Conell thrust his blade into the barbarian's stomach.

His partner growled and jumped to his feet. The madman charged Conell and screamed strange words. Conell slipped past him and whirled around the man, shoving his sword into the man's back. His back arched as he let out a scream. He staggered, then toppled to the ground.

Her stomach flopped. The charging barbarians' blood spilled onto her blanket. The flowers now lay squashed underfoot. Death came quickly here.

Conell raced to help Émer, but Émer stabbed the last of his attackers in the stomach. The man staggered. His knees buckled and he fell beside his friend.

This looked like some sick Renaissance scene, but the enemy

died instead of jumping up and taking a bow. The coppery stench clinging to the air was nauseating and the sound of pinging swords filled the air. She covered her nose with the back of her hand. Someone grabbed Imogene's wrist. She squealed.

Ruárc smiled. "I missed you, *Chuoha*." She screamed and slapped his face with her free hand. He grabbed her by the back of her neck and raised his sword to her belly. "Do it again, Little Bird, and you will taste my blade."

Her eyes dropped to the sword hovering inches from her stomach. She raised her eyes to his blood-lust face. Surely, he wouldn't do it, he wouldn't stab her. "Leave me alone."

Cián plunged his sword into the *Upeshi*'s belly. The old man faced Ruárc. "Let her be!"

Ruárc threw Imogene to the ground. The tip of his blade pointed at her face. "Do not make me hunt for you."

She scooted back from him and found herself shaking her head. Cián circled Ruárc and drew him away from her.

"You are an old man." Ruárc waved his sword in the priest's face. "Do you really think you can beat someone younger and faster?"

Her eyes clung to the old man. He was too old to fight Ruárc.

"Imogene!" said a voice beside her.

She looked up to see fingers outstretched. The hand connected to an arm covered in a billowy sleeve which led to an angel's handsome face silhouetted by the sun.

"Argus."

He shoved his hand closer to her face. "Take my hand."

Long fingers. White. Cold.

His silky commanding tones drowned out the battle cries. "I will take you from here. Trust me, Imogene, take my hand."

The fog rolled over her mind like an ocean's wave. The shouts faded. Her heart stampeded. *What did the Attiyq say?*

Conell's gaze locked on her from across the field. His mouth opened. His eyes grew wide. He shouted, "Imogene!"

Argus's lips moved.

Her hand rose and her fingers slipped into his cold palm. His strong grip crushed her hand hurting her.

Conell raced to help Frigg as his friend shoved the other man back, but the *Upeshi* punched Frigg in the face. He stumbled back and fell to the ground. The man grinned and raised his weapon over the young Frigg. Conell came up behind the *Upeshi* and thrust his blade between the man's shoulder blades. The *Upeshi* shrieked and dropped to his knees.

A scream drew Conell's attention. Ruárc pushed Imogene away and swung his sword at the priest, but the old man waltzed around the younger guard and taunted him with his sword. Ruárc growled and jumped at him again, but Cián met each swing.

Conell shook his head. The crazy old man was playing with Ruárc. His gaze drifted back to Imogene. A man with wings stood over her—Argus. The angel held out his hand and he spoke to her. Argus's head slowly swiveled towards Conell, and he sneered. A chill enveloped Conell. Imogene's eyes locked on his, but drifted back to Argus. Her hand slowly slipped into Argus's palm.

There was a flash and they were gone.

"*Imogene!*" Conell raced across the field to the spot where she once sat. "Émer! Argus has the girl!" He raised his blade to Ruárc's face. "Drop your sword, *mee!*"

Ruárc's jaw dropped open and he released his weapon and raised his hands.

Émer and Frigg raced across the field and joined Conell.

"What happened?" Émer asked.

Conell's gaze searched the grove, then the sky. He should have stayed by her side; he should have been in Cian's place. "Argus took Imogene."

Émer placed his hand on Conell's shoulder. "But this is good, My Moji. He will take her home, where she belongs. She is safe now."

Conell brushed off his captain's grip. Time repeated itself. He failed to save Father, Mother, and his unborn sibling due to a childish argument with Father and now he failed to save the girl. He would not let an innocent die. Not again. Not ever.

Evil lay in Argus's eyes, but Conell hoped the demon would leave them alone. Cián's words repeated in his mind.

Cián tossed Ruárc to the ground and placed the point of his sword against the guard's neck. "Where is she?"

Ruárc's eyes grew as large as the moon rising from the earth's edge. "How am I supposed to know?"

"I think you know," the old man said. "Take us to her and I will let you live. If you refuse, then I turn you over to Moji Conell."

The guard's gaze darted from the priest to Conell. "My Prince, I tell you the truth; I do not know where he took the girl."

Conell's eyes narrowed. He knelt before the trembling man. "Either you tell me, or you will join your friends as food for the birds."

Ruárc held up his hands. "All right, all right! But you must promise to protect me, or she will kill me. Promise!"

Cián pushed on the sword and blood trickled down Ruárc's throat.

"Stop!" Ruárc gasped. "Argus works with Jezebel. The witch has the girl. She cast a spell on the demon which allows him to travel on the wind."

Conell rose; his breath ripped from his lungs. Jezebel has Imogene. His legs became like flimsy weeds and he grabbed Émer's shoulder. Imogene could die tomorrow or tonight. Jezebel would not be gentle with the girl.

Conell grabbed Ruárc by his throat and dragged him to his feet. His grip tightened around Ruárc's throat and his eyes bulged. "*Mee!* Where is she?" He shook the frightened guard and his head bounced back and forth.

Ruárc gagged. "Castle!"

Conell moved his fingers to the back of Ruárc's neck and he

drew back his sword.

Ruárc raised his hands. "No! My Prince, please! I can take you into the castle."

His hand tightened on the sword's hilt. "I know the corridors of the castle, remember? It was my home."

"Wait! Those secret ways no longer exist. The queen destroyed them after she imprisoned you. Please, spare my life."

Cián grabbed Conell's arm. "He has a point, Moji. We need a way into the castle. Then you can kill him."

"And what did you plan to with Imogene?" Émer asked.

Ruárc shrugged a shoulder and a small smile appeared on his face. "She is young, I am old. I only wanted her for a while."

Conell's hand tightened around Ruárc's throat and his fingers pressed into the guard's chubby neck. "If you come near her again, I will carve out your heart. Do you understand?"

Ruárc's eyes bulged and his tongue slipped from his mouth. He nodded.

"You will take us into the castle and to her cell. If you refuse, my sword will find its way into your throat."

Again, he nodded. Conell threw him to the ground.

The bright sun from the field disappeared and a dim light filled the area. Imogene blinked as her eyes adjusted to the soft glow. It seemed like a room. She blinked again and gasped.

Light blue, gold and dirty white mosaics clambered halfway up the twenty-foot walls. White paint covered the rest of the surface, along with tapestries of a dark-haired man charging on a wild horse into a bloody battle. He looked like the same man carved on the mountainside. King Broden maybe? A large blue flag centered with a large horse rearing over a small golden sword hung beside the tapestry.

Her gaze followed the walls up to a gloomy three-tiered ceiling. The first layer was adorned in a thick silver layer with swirling dark circles. The second lined in dull gold, the third layer had a large lackluster gold inlaid disc sitting in the center of the ceiling, gobbled up by murky shadows. Rich blue and sterile white tiles covered the floors.

A hand gently placed on her shoulder made her jump. Argus stepped beside her and smiled down at her, but his smile didn't reach his dark hidden eyes. He gripped her arm and led her forward. They walked past tall wide windows placed in the stoned wall. She paused and admired the green fields below. The warmth from the sun fled the room. Instead, a chill covered her bones.

Despite the warm sun shining on the fields, a gloom sat in the room. Shadows oozed across the walls like serpents as if the light feared the dark and preferred to stay outside, safe from harm.

Argus's hand slipped to her elbow and he guided her through the dimly lit hallway.

The stench of the candles suffocated her in a perfumed grip. The wax sizzled as it fell to the sterile floor. Dancing phantoms covered the walls like gangrene.

She tried to tug her arm from his strong grasp. "Argus, I needed to stay with Conell."

His rich cold voice echoed along with his strong footsteps. "You are safe with me, My Lady. I will not allow harm to come to you."

He walked her past rooms with gaping mouths that longed to be fed. Unseen foes crouched in the darkness and waited for their victims. She shivered. In one of the rooms, a marbled fireplace gripped a wall. The firebox embraced the charred bones of past trees.

*What did the Attiyq say? Something about Conell.* She tried to remember.

Ahead of them, two mosaic covered arches opened into a dining room. Two hanging candle-chandeliers hung within the arches. The brightly burning candles looked like a deranged, angry man's eyes glaring at her. Glowering. Warning. She knew she needed to leave. She looked behind her and tried to pull away.

Argus stopped and slowly kissed each of her fingertips. His eyes rose under his lashes. His lips brushed her palm.

Goosebumps spread across her arms. A smile played on her lips.

"Do you wish to leave me this soon, My Lady?" His voice was smooth and soft.

Her knees melted beneath her. She shook her head. "No."

His hand moved to the small of her back and he led her forward.

They passed into the dining room. The burning eyes within the arches studied her as if she were an intruder. She knew she wasn't supposed to be here, but she couldn't remember where she was supposed to be.

She looked back into the hall. The darkness conquered the hallway. It slithered along the walls. It raced before them and attacked the light coming in from the open windows and from the burning candles.

A shiver raced down her back and into her legs. She looked up at Argus. His stern countenance seemed like stone as he led her into dark. She knew she would be lost forever.

But this was Argus, the angel whom the Attiyq promised to send to take her home. She paused. She had to do something. She was supposed stay with someone. *Who was it?* She rubbed her forehead. Wooziness chased the name away.

Argus slipped his hand into hers and she followed him into the darkness.

They reached a raised mahogany platform with three steps encasing it. A heavy velvet red tapestry sagged behind the ethereal stage. A wooden canopy hovered over it.

She squinted at the words inscribed above, but couldn't understand them. Two high back wood chairs with elaborate artwork guarded the platform. The blue flag with the horse hung on the wall behind the chairs and similar blue flags were draped around the room. But still, the sunlight refused to enter through the windows.

The darkness reigned here like a gargoyle leaning sitting on their roof to over see the castle.

A woman with black hair flowing off her shoulders sat on the left throne. The candlelight bounced off the tiny beads sewn into her silver V-neck gown.

He bowed before her. The woman smiled at both of them.

"Imogene," Argus said. "May I introduce Queen Jezebel."

A wise man considers other's
words before trusting him.
– Proverb from King Broden

10

Imogene's eyes grew wide. "Jezebel!" She yanked her hand from Argus and stumbled away from the witch.

Argus led her back to the queen.

"Do not be frightened, Child." Jezebel's voice was pitifully gentle. "No one here will harm you. And I do apologize for Toál's horrible behavior. I sent him to bring you back, not hurt you."

The hair on Imogene's neck rose. "I'm sorry, I don't understand."

The queen's lips curved into a tight smile.

Imogene swallowed and leaned into Argus.

Argus gave her a lopsided grin.

His strong arm looped around her waist pulled her closer. "Imogene, do you really think I would take you someplace that led to danger? Is that what angels do?"

She shook her head. Her skull was heavy like lead and she laid it on the angel's chest. The strange fog washed away all logic. *What did the Attiyq say?*

The queen rose from her throne. "You must be hungry after your hard ordeal." Jezebel's dark gaze stabbed Argus. He reached up to take her hand, but she brushed past him.

The queen led the couple to the dining room with the strange chandeliers that resembled an angry man's eyes. Blazing orbs glowered down at her.

Argus led her to a long dark-wooden table with large claw-like feet that dug into the scuffed wooden floor. He took a candle from the hall and lit the tapers on the table. The shadows raced along the floorboards, upset at the intrusion.

The queen clapped her hands and three teenaged male servants dressed in gray pants and tunics entered the room. Each young man carried a tray full of fresh apples, pears and grapes, breads, steaming broccoli and peas, cooked turkey and slabs of broiled roasts. They kept their tired gazes to the ground and set the food platters on the table.

A skinny girl, no older than Imogene, wearing a plain sleeveless grey dress and long brown hair pulled into a ponytail carried a large wooden box into the room. She placed the container on the table and pulled out dishes and utensils and set them at three places: one in the center of the table and the other two to the left.

Argus's eyes lingered on the girl. She lifted her gaze for a second then focused on her task. Her hands shook. When they had set the table, the four servants bowed before the queen and scurried from the room.

The deep rich scent of the cooked meat filled the air, followed by the warm yeasty aroma of cooked bread. Imogene's stomach growled.

Jezebel smiled and led the small party to the table. "You are hungry."

Argus pulled out the ornate center chair for his queen and helped her to sit. Imogene began to pull out the smaller chair farthest from the queen, but Argus stopped her.

"Here, let me." He pulled out the seat and helped her to sit, then slipped into the chair between the two women.

He squeezed Imogene's arm. "It will be all right, Imogene."

The female servant with the brown ponytail entered the room. She bowed before the queen, then cut off a slab of roast, scooped some vegetables and placed them on the queen's plate.

Argus's sharp black eyes roamed over the girl as she served him. Her hands slightly trembled and she dropped the vegetables on the table. She bit her lip as she scooped them up and dropped them into her pocket.

Lastly, the girl served Imogene who smiled at the servant. The young server gave Imogene a small sad grin.

Imogene took her fork and poked at the food. There wasn't any rabbit. She suppressed a chuckle.

The queen nodded, and the girl scurried from the room.

Jezebel cut her meat and stabbed it with her fork. "It pleases me that my servant, Argus, was able to rescue you, Lady Imogene. We have been quite worried about you. And I do wish to apologize for my guards treating you roughly. By the time we realized you were not an enemy, Conell had taken you."

Imogene poked the firm cooked broccoli with her fork. Maybe if she ate something, she'd feel better. Eating fruits, vegetables and light carbs were better than wild game. Conell did what? "What do you mean Conell had taken me? I went with him."

Jezebel patted her blood-red lips with a milky-white napkin. "Did he tell you I framed him for a murder?" Imogene nodded.

"He will say anything to get what he wants," Argus said.

Imogene cut the broccoli with her fork. "Meaning...?"

He caught her gaze. "You cannot trust that scoundrel. He lied to you, Imogene. Conell killed an innocent family which was why the queen imprisoned him. After his parents died in a raid on the castle, he fell into a fit of rage. It was quite horrible."

Imogene moved the peas around with her utensil. A voice deep inside of her whispered words which inched up to her mind; the fog devoured them. "What do you mean, he killed a family?"

Jezebel chewed her food and placed the sharp knife on the edge of her plate. "Well, as Argus said, after Conell's *Mim Eho*, he became proud and cruel, thinking everyone needed to follow his rule. He saw himself as the king, yet had not taken the throne. A man refused to follow him, so Conell killed his family in a fit of rage. There were, let me see, three children, is that right, Argus?"

He nodded. "He killed them all. I caught him and the queen sentenced him to death. You are lucky I found you alive. And now I wish to protect you from him."

The tines of Argus's fork scraped against the plate as he stabbed the meat. Blood oozed onto the porcelain as he brought the fork to his mouth.

Imogene's stomach soured. "Why?" Who did the voice say to stay with? Was it Argus? Is that why she was here?

He slowly chewed. "Because I am the queen's guard, and it is my duty to protect the weak and innocent." He shoved more into his mouth. Red juice dribbled down his chin. He wiped it away with his finger.

Jezebel pointed her fork at Imogene. "Child, eat."

The blood spread across Imogene's plate and blended with the vegetables. She made a face. Argus tapped Imogene's plate with his knife.

Imogene poked at the meat with her fork and then reluctantly ate it. The chef cooked it rare, the way she liked it, with lots of fat. Her stomach rumbled as she chewed. She closed her eyes and allowed the tender flavors to melt in her mouth. Her fear dripped away with each swallow. The green vegetables snapped under her fork. The warm soft bread dripped with butter, which ran down her arm and she licked it off.

Jezebel raised her eyebrows. "We use napkins, dear."

She grabbed her small hand towel and mopped up her greasy mess. Before long, her plate was empty. She enjoyed the meal, but she missed Émer's burnt rabbit. What were her friends doing? Wasn't there a fight somewhere? A chill spread over her and she rubbed her arms. The fog wrapped around her mind. Their faces faded.

Jezebel folded her napkin and sat it next to her plate. "So child, you are a mystery to us. What village do you come from?"

Imogene placed her fork on her plate and gave a side glance to the queen. "Well, um, it's a little far from here. It's in a place called Illinois."

The queen's eyebrow rose. "No matter. I am sure my Argus will do to your mother what he did to mine. Is that not right, my love?" She placed her hand over Argus's fingers and gave him a sly grin.

Imogene took a breath, but the fog ate the woman's words. She rubbed her temples.

Argus's cold finger traced Imogene's cheek. "You are tired. Allow me to escort you to your bed chambers, if you approve, My Queen."

Jezebel dark eyes jumped from him to Imogene. She scowled and tossed her napkin on the table, then clapped her hands roughly. "Of course, Argus, do not let me keep you."

The male servants rushed in and bowed.

"Clean up this mess!" Jezebel said.

The queen rose and Argus pulled out her chair. He took her hand, but she snatched it away and marched to the throne room. Her heels clicked against the marble flooring.

Argus narrowed his eyes at the queen stomping from the room like a defiant child. He grinned at Imogene and gently helped her from the chair. "You must forgive my queen. She is very upset over Conell's escape. Our entire kingdom is in fear of him and the barbarians."

He looped her arm under his and escorted her into a hallway covered in gold mosaics. A cockroach scurried across the clean floor. *What did the Attiyq say?* The words hung before her like scribble on the wall. She laid her head against his arm.

"Are you ill?" he asked.

"I'm tired. I really want to go home."

Portraits of people lined the hallway. He stopped before one picture and pointed to the man. "This was King Efuko, Conell's father."

The King bore a resemblance to Conell. Efuko's strong yet gentle eyes were like Conell's and his long silver hair was tied back in a braid. Where was Conell? Watching clouds? Someone watched clouds. "I don't understand, why would Conell not tell me about the family?"

Argus shrugged and led her down the hallway. "He is a liar. Why should he tell you any truth? Imogene, each day I have seen your pain." He stopped and his dark eyes fastened to her's. "I can give you all that you want—popularity, a family, a home, and acceptance. All you have to do is stay here with me. Conell can only give you burnt rabbit and a life of running from the queen. Is that what you want?"

The angel's face waned and Imogene lowered her head. The room spun.

His arms pulled her to him and he whispered in her hair. "No longer would the cheerleaders call you names or the young Lord Kyle ignore your glances and longings. You would live with me, Imogene, honored and adored by me and others. That is what you want, is it not?"

Yes, she wanted honor, respect, acceptance. But what about Conell and Émer? Frigg and Momma? Her head was spinning.

Argus's dark voice rebounded from a deep tunnel. "Your mother never calls you, never sees you. You mother, your aunt, your uncle. They have all forgotten about you, Imogene. Conell is a liar and will travel onto the sea and across it to escape the queen. He will not come for you. Or my guards will catch him and he will die in prison. Tell me what you want, Imogene." He leaned down and as if to kiss her.

She pulled away before their lips could touch and leaned her forehead on his chest. "I think I need to lie down."

He guided her down the hall. "Of course. You have traveled long, you must be tired."

Her mind was in a fog and it made her feet stumble. His arm slinked tighter around her waist. They strolled down other halls, past closed doors and stain glass windows. The chill lingered. The shadows slithered on the walls and floor.

A large picture of a muscular man sitting on a white horse hung at the end of the hall. A phantom wind blew his short dark-graying hair. *The same man was in the throne room tapestries and on Mount Rushmore, or was it someplace else? Why would a man be on a mountain? Was he a president?* Her voice was weak. "Who is this?" Her memories danced through her mine. Nothing made sense.

"That is King Broden," Argus said flatly.

Like King Efuko, Broden's piercing blue eyes also stared straight ahead.

Argus was her savior, her angel. Nothing else mattered.

He stopped before a closed door and pulled a key from his pocket and unlocked it. The click echoed down the hall. He stepped aside, allowing her in.

The darkness stayed far from this room. Instead, the sunlight burst in through the windows. The small bedroom was a princess room with the large four post bed with a red velvet canopy top. The pink silk bedspread covered the mattress like a pink sea. Large and small fluffy white and yellow pillows were stacked neatly at the headboard. Black leather books sat on a small table positioned perfectly near a cushion chair cuddled in the corner. The roaring fire in the fireplace did little to chase away the chill.

"I pray the quarters are up to your satisfaction, My Lady." He rubbed her shoulders and her neck.

His touch made her heart beat faster. She walked to the window where she could catch her breath. The lush green land of Ezasu stretched out to the horizon. Questions bombarded her mind. *Was this Peoria?*

Imogene pushed aside the linen curtains. "It's beautiful."

"Would you like a bath?" He opened a door and a large wooden tub sat in the center of the bathing room. Steam rose from the water. "Please, My Lady, pamper yourself. I will have a servant tend to you."

He gave her a slight bow, pivoted on his heel, and left the room. After he shut the door she heard a familiar click. *Did he lock the door? Why would he lock the door?* She sat on the bed and rubbed her eyes.

The warmth from the steam drifted into the room. The sweet smell of jasmine filled the air. This was the life. A warm bath, a princess room, a man, or an angel, who adored her, her world was perfect.

She walked into the bathing room and closed the door. She stripped from her old clothes, and slid into the hot water. Her eyes closed. A small tap on the door pulled her from her thoughts.

"Come in," Imogene called.

The same young servant girl from the dining hall entered the small room. She curtsied before Imogene. "The queen said I was to help you."

Imogene smiled.

The servant pulled a pitcher and soap from a shelf and dipped the container into the water. She knelt beside the tub and poured some over Imogene's head. Her small hands scrubbed Imogene's hair with the soap and rinsed it.

Imogene wiped the water from her face. "The queen said that Conell killed a family, is this true?"

The girl plunged the sponge into the water. "If that is what the queen has spoken, then, yes."

"But is it what really happened?"

"If it is her words, then, yes." The girl said nothing more as she cleaned Imogene's body.

A scent of lilac filled the room. Imogene took in a deep breath. The aroma calmed her nerves and she slid into the water. "That soap smells nice. Is it lilacs?"

"Yes," the girl said.

"What's your name?"

The girl paused and furrowed her brow. "I am called, Girl."

"Why do they call you Girl?" Imogene asked.

Girl squeezed water down Imogene's back. "It is the name Lord Argus gave me."

"Okay, well, I'm Imogene. The land here is lovely."

She nodded her head and gave her a weak smile. "So others have told me."

"So you've been told? Haven't you been out? I mean surely the queen treats you well?"

"There is something I need to do." She gathered Imogene's clothes and slammed the bathroom door behind her.

Did she say something to upset Girl? She sighed. What would it feel like to have others respect her? Maybe fear her? To always be called first in the PE games, to have a date at prom. To have a *date*.

She smiled. Her and Argus sharing a pizza at Avanti's or hanging at Northwoods Mall, listening to poetry readings at a nearby bar with the college kids. Cruising in a small red sports car through Bradley Park and meeting the cheerleaders from the high school at Pizza Hut after a football game.

A heat covered her cheeks. Everyone would be jealous of her especially Momma. The Paparazzi would snap *her* pictures instead of Momma's.

Argus also said Momma abandoned her. She frowned as she dribbled water down her knee. Maybe he was right. Three years passed since Momma left for New York and still she refused to let Imogene come and live with in New York, claiming she was "too busy." Momma was always too busy. Even the day she left, she was "too busy."

*Thirteen-year-old Imogene stood on the porch, shivering in the frigid Illinois winter day. Momma skipped down the three chipped cement stairs, her hair pulled back in a tight bun and her tight jeans poured over her long legs. Her black high heels clicked on the stoned walk.*

*Momma stopped in front of the little red sports car she bought with Imogene's college money and waved with a huge smile on her face as if to say, "so long, sucker! I'm off to the Big Apple. Good luck and God bless!"*

*"I need to find myself, darling. I'll come back one day, you'll see," Momma said earlier in the gray morning as she packed her bags. "I see myself as an old withered mother and not as the woman I am supposed to be. And don't worry about the college money. You can get a job and you have your scholarships. You understand, dear."*

*She slipped into the car and raced away. Momma's little red car grew smaller and smaller. Maybe Momma was playing a joke and the little car would turn around and pull up to the curb in front of the house. Momma would sit in the driver's seat and laugh. She'd open the car door and they'd drive to McDonalds for a Big Mac and fries.*

*The little red car steered around the corner and disappeared and she has stayed away for three long years. Gone.*

Tears formed in Imogene's eyes at Momma's parting words. Momma left for good. Imogene was now alone in an unknown world. She must have done something to upset her. Momma saw her as an idiot or a fool and ran off to find a better daughter or even a better life. If only she studied harder. Momma probably thought it was her fault Daddy left. Or was it Èmer who left? Or Cián? Broden?

*Aunt Laurie stood beside her and wrapped an afghan around her shoulders. "Come on, child, come out of the cold. Your Momma's no different than your Aunt Imogene."*

Imogene slammed her fist into the water. It splashed into her face and over the side of the tub. She hated Aunt Imogene Louise Martin. Each family member sang the praises of the great and mighty Aunt Imogene. The eighteen-year-old run-away who ruled the sixties and lived with some weird guy named Charles Manson somewhere in California, but left when he started talking about killing people. She visited a place called Woodstock and smoked pot with a guy named Jimmie Hendrix who played guitar, went to sit-ins, lifted signs as protest against some war in the seventies and died a hero at a college called Kent State while protesting against the same stupid war.

Everyone in the family expected Imogene Katherine Reasley to dance in Imogene Louis Martin footsteps. When Imogene K. became a clumsy nerd, whom the cheerleaders passed over due to her flat chest, hadn't slept with a boy by the time she turned fourteen, would rather attend a library reading than attend an Occupied Wallstreet Meeting, and worse, longed to go to University of Chicago to study medicine, they berated her saying with pitiful voices, "the poor thing." Imie had her aunt's name, but not her aunt's spirit. Momma left because Imogene Katherine was unable to follow in Imogene Louise's path.

Momma saw Imogene K. behaving like her dad, a coward who ran away when the going grew tough. When the bills came in and the money dwindled away and they ate TV dinners while Momma enjoyed *Entertainment Television* and boasted about how one day she'd be on that show. Daddy left when he grew frightened, running for the borders from the queen. She paused. No, Conell ran for the borders, not Daddy.

The warmth from the tub pulled her away from him. *And what about the Attiyq? Did he trick the people?* He probably perpetrated this entire charade and yanked her into this horrid place. She nodded. He brought her here to hurt her. He plopped her in the midst of Conell, a child murderer. He forced Momma to leave years ago on a cold gray day. She shrugged and stretched her arms over her head; Argus would solve her problems. He was a friend, her knight in shining armor. She closed her eyes and smiled. "I could stay here forever," she whispered.

Girl hurried down the hall to Lord Argus's private parlor. She paused and took a deep breath before knocking on the door. Lord Argus's temper raged like rabid wolf when his anger rose. It raged when he was pleased. She knocked again and mumbled a prayer to the Attiyq. She bit her lip and twisted her fingers.

"Enter."

She opened the door, but stood in the doorway. Argus's large frame loomed before the window across the room, making her shrink to the size of a bug he could crush between his fingers.

He studied something out the window. "Did you find my medallion, Girl?"

"My Lord, I have gone through her clothes and the room as you requested. I did not see the medallion."

He slipped his hands behind his back and rocked on his heels. "You went through everything?"

She kept her gaze to the floor. "Yes, My Lord, just as you instructed."

He nodded his head. "Did you steal it?"

"No, My Lord, never."

"Girl, if you lie to me, I will know."

Her breath caught in her throat and pushed out the words. "I am not lying, My Lord."

He paused. Her heart raced. She held her breath and twisted her fingers.

"Conell must have it," he said. "How clever of him."

She let out her held breath and placed her trembling hand on the doorknob. At least she was safe for today.

"You have avoided me, Girl. Do you now despise me? After all I have done for you?"

She bit her lip and focused on the floor. With his mind focused on the prisoners' escape, she prayed he would ignore her scurrying past his door in the evenings. But Lord Argus's eyes saw everything.

"Is the answer you are looking for engraved in the floor? Or have you lost your tongue? If you do not wish for my company, then perhaps you would enjoy the Slave Traders' embrace more than mine." He tapped at the glass window.

"No, My Lord." Her throat tightened and her eyes watered. If only she could rip the skin from her body so his cold cruel hands could no longer squeeze or tear at her flesh. Argus's promises were lies; he never trained her in the art of the handmaiden for the queen. Instead, he shamed her before the elders. The clan would no longer recognize the daughter of Fillian. Their would scowl at her impurity and would shame her.

She would love to see her father one last time to touch his face, hear his old stories over and over. She squeezed back her tears. Lord Argus's fists taught her years ago to weep silently in her quarters.

"Tend to my guest, finish bathing and dressing her and then bring her to my quarters this evening," he said. "Do not be late. I would hate to see what the barbarians would do with such a lovely girl. And who knows, perhaps I do have a wonderful future for you."

"Yes, My Lord." She shivered. He knew and saw everything.

"And Girl? If you try to help her, I will give you to the Slave Runners, understand? They will not be as gentle with you as I have been."

She nodded and quietly shut the door.

Argus waited for the door to close before he released an exasperated sigh. Everyone seemed against him, even his own servant girl, as useless as she was, failed in her quest to find the medallion.

He crossed his arms over his chest and glared into the Attiyq's throne room. The Great and Mighty God mocked Argus's eminence. The Attiyq was nothing more than a proud chicken sitting on her eggs.

Argus's upper lip twitched and yet, here he was the great and mighty Argus, sharing a bed with his puppet and a slave, forced to slither on the ground like a snake. Everything he once owned ripped from him like a parent taking away a child's toy. He clenched his teeth. He wanted his own kingdom as opposed to being the Attiyq's footstool.

He lifted his chin and glowered at the Attiyq. Soon, very soon, all would pay for their insults, including his once "Master." No longer would he be forced to stand behind that insolent woman, Jezebel, bobbing his head like a hypnotized bird. "Yes, Your Majesty. No, Your Majesty, what is your bidding, My Queen." Soon he would be free from his bondage, free to sit on heaven's throne, and Broden's throne on Ezasu. He would be Master.

He nodded. Master would be his new name once he destroyed the Attiyq. The Attiyq's surviving angelic warriors would bow before him and his excellence. Yes, things were coming together now. He lifted his head and marched from the room.

Fear not, said the angel to King Broden. You have favor from the Great One who lives forever.

~ From the *Words of the Attiyq*

## 11

Conell tossed a rope to Émer. "Tie his hands."

"Moji Conell," Ruárc said. "My loyalties are now with you. There is no need to tie me like a prisoner."

Émer yanked Ruárc's arms behind his back and tightened the rope around the guard's wrists. "Be lucky I do not slit your throat, Dancer, and let you join your brother. I am sure he enjoys dancing with his sword."

Ruárc growled. "You will pay for those words, Maúl."

"Remember," Émer whispered in his ear. "That the Maúl rise like ghosts in the fields." He jerked the knot tight, making Ruárc wince.

The castle sat at least two weeks' journey east by foot. The witch's temper would destroy Imogene. Conell let Imogene fall off the cliff and into enemy hands. He cursed.

Frigg helped Ruárc to sit. "Any plans, My Moji?"

"Émer," Conell said, "We need horses. Are there any this north of the hills?"

The priest wiped the blood off the blade and slid it into its sheath. "Do not worry, My Prince, the Attiyq's wings cover the girl."

Conell clenched his fists. *The Attiyq who stood back and allowed a demon to steal away a young, frightened girl. The Attiyq who left his family to die years ago. The Attiyq who laughed while Jezebel betrayed him, tossed him in the queen's rat's nest.* "Do not waste your words on me, priest. If the Attiyq cared for her, He would not have allowed Argus to take her."

"You walk by what you see, not by what you believe." Mumbled words fell from his lips as he sat on a nearby stump.

Conell rolled his eyes. What a crazy old man. "Émer?"

"Nay, My Lord, there are no *qooche* this far north."

"Are there horses in the mountains?"

Émer rubbed his chin. "Perhaps. The Mountain people have them, but most stay hidden. They do not trust us. Besides, we would have to find food to give them. If we cross *Shez Chez*, we might find a few *qooche*. It will take us days. I fear Imie does not have days."

The old man gestured with his hands. "If you will but have faith, the Attiyq will carry you on wings to save the girl."

Conell growled and drew his sword. Émer placed himself between the two men. "Moji, you know I will fall upon my own sword for you, but I will not allow you to harm a Chosen of *Vajie*. Please, My Lord, listen to him."

Conell let out an exasperated sigh and shook his head. The captain fell under the same spell and believed in the one who threw him into prison.

Émer's purple eyes pleaded with him. The young captain would protect the Aho; his Maúl heritage demanded it from him. The deaths of the Maúl lay on Conell and left one small boy behind to carry on their clan. He owed it to Émer to keep his vows as a Voobo-Maúl.

Conell held up one finger. "One chance. He has one chance, then I will leave him here. Understand?"

Émer nodded. "Please, Aho, continue."

"You have no faith in the Attiyq. Yet, you have faith in your sword and in horses."

Still the old man made no sense and demanded more than Conell could ever give in his lifetime. "And?"

"Moji!" Frigg's eyes grew wide.

He spun and drew his sword. Four creatures appearing like horses stood behind them. The blowing of the wind in the trees was the only sound he heard. The creatures materialized like stars emerging on the black canvas.

He blinked. The creatures seemed more like beings from a madman's imagination. A black beast had splashes of white spashes covering his torso. He had the upper body of a black-haired lion. Another had a pure white horse body with a torso of a man. The gray one had gray eagle's chest and head, but horse's body; and the solid black horse's trunk looked like a bull with horns. They had four sets of wings, the feathers the same color as their bodies, which rest at their sides and a set of human arms and hands extending from their horse-chests.

They bore a resemblance to Argus, demons from Jezebel. He could not easily defeat them. Still Conell raised his sword and grounded his feet. If these satanic beings wanted a fight, he would give it to them.

Émer gripped Conell's hand and lowered the Moji's blade. The captain boldly approached the man-beast and bowed. "Forgive me, Áepoo, I thought you were myths."

Áepoo raised his brown bushy eyebrows and stomped his narrow white forelegs. "A myth?"

Áepoo looked like a man jammed into a horse's body. His long brown hair flowed down his neck like a mane, but grew from his head like a human. He raised his clean-shaven chiseled jaw and his black eyes held a sense of authority unlike Argus. Those same eyes held Émer's wide purple gaze. Áepoo crossed his muscular arms over his chest and laid his brown feathered wings against his body.

Conell cautiously approached the beasts. "Émer, what are these things?"

"They are the Great Beasts of the Attiyq. They stand before the Great One day and night giving praise and honor to Him. I thought they were just stories. I never thought…" He paused. "The one with the eagle head is called Asechi, this one with the lion's head is called Etta, the Bull is called Oota."

The creatures bowed their heads. Asechi let out a loud screech and ruffled the feathers on his head. Etta shook his great black mane and roared. Oota snorted, lowered his head and pawed at the ground.

Conell slipped the sword back into its scabbard. "How do you know them?"

"I've read about them years ago when we lived in the castle of your father, but I never thought I would see them."

Cián rose from the rock and made his way to the group of angels. He gave Conell a fatherly grin. A kindness and understanding sat in the old man's smiling eyes. "Do you see now what faith can do?"

"Áepoo, welcome." The old man bowed.

"Great Priest, my eyes are pleased to see you again." Áepoo placed his hand over his chest and lowered his head. "You have summoned us?"

"Yes, my friend," he said. "We need your help. Jezebel has taken a young girl who will die if we do not move quickly. Please, help us to rescue her."

Conell studied the old man, then the creatures. "Cián, how do I know this is not a trick of Jezebel? Argus has wings and flies the same as these beings. I will not take the hand of anyone who will be my enemy."

Áepoo glowered. "You dare to compare us to the insect, Argus?

Why do you insult us?"

"Moji," Émer said. "Please, I studied these creatures; I believe the Attiyq sent them to us. We have no choice, we must get to Imogene. She will not live if we wait." Conell rubbed the bridge of his nose. Of course, Émer spoke true words.

"You remind me of your father, Prince Conell DeCapris," Aepoo said. "And you are as wise as he. He too would question us before taking our hands. But I give you my word; the Attiyq has sent us to help you. We will not betray you, just as we would not betray Him."

Émer grinned at him and motioned to the beasts. "My Lord, please."

*He did not resemble his father or walk in his ways. Father's bloodied body leaned against the stoned corridor, Mother curled in the corner of their quarters, her hand still protecting her unborn child. A weeping boy knelt at his father's side, the blood stains forever etched on the child's hands. Émer stood over him while holding the shocked Frigg in his arms. Conell was the descendent of King Broden and stained as a coward because he ran from the enemy. Broden disowned and would not claim Conell's name.*

The Aho placed his hand on his shoulder. "Moji, trust me."

He brushed off the old man's hand. "If you betray me, I swear, not even the Attiyq will be able to protect you."

Cián smiled and grasped Conell's forearm. "I will take that deal. Now, we must save your young friend."

Ruárc struggled to his feet and his tied hands twisted behind him. "Wait! You cannot leave me here."

"No, we will not." Conell slipped his sword under Ruárc's throat. "You will lead us to this secret passage. If you try to signal the guards, I will cut your throat."

Ruárc's Adam's apple quivered as he swallowed. "Yes, Prince Conell."

Conell snorted. He stooped to the ground and placed a rock before him. Émer and Frigg gathered around him and knelt beside him. Conell motioned to Cián and Áepoo, who stepped into the small group.

Conell pointed to the rock. "This is the castle. If we come in from the south, we can land a mile from the castle, here." He pointed to a spot near the rock. "Then we go on foot." He nodded to Ruárc. "Where is this secret passage you spoke of?"

The soldier waggled his head to the left side of the rock. "Here. It is covered with bushes. It leads to the dungeons."

"More than likely, she will keep Imie in the dungeon," Émer said, "before transferring her to *Ioole Chaj*."

"And if she is not there?" Frigg asked.

"Émer," Conell asked. "Do you still have friends in the castle?"

He messaged his chin. "Perhaps those who kept quiet about us still live. Or we could try to bribe a servant to lead us to Imie."

He nodded and rose. "We will try the dungeons first."

The others stood to their feet.

Émer extracted out a small knife and jammed it into the guard's side. "Remember my Moji's words."

Áepoo pawed the ground. "When do we leave, My Prince?"

"Now," Conell said.

He smiled. "Come, I will carry the son of Broden."

Conell eyed the man/horse but swung up on Áepoo's back. Cián chose the bull, while Émer and Ruárc took the lion and Frigg, the eagle.

"Hang on," Áepoo said.

The four beasts galloped across the field and their four wings expanded. They rose as the wind whipped around them. Conell's eyes grew wide and a smile spread across his face. They climbed higher. He resisted the urge to holler. The bull-horse came along side of them.

Cián grinned at Conell. "Do you still doubt the Attiyq?"

Conell chuckled. "My doubt is slowly dying."

The flying beasts soared over the same mountains they crossed to escape the queen and into the Voobo-Maúl lands. Conell spied Émer discerning the once held Maúl Lands.

Émer pointed to a large three-story wooden building in which the wooden slabs grew white from exposure. "Moji, there it is, the main Maúl Temple! Father took me there when I was only three years old. He became my *Gaevee* and had me sit on a large stool. The elders questioned my faith in that building. It was there that my journey began."

Conell smiled and nodded. He had heard this same story hundreds of times and never grew tired of it.

They passed from Émer's land and into the *Yueg* Territory also called the Northern territory and home of the king's castle. The lush vegetable fields growing corn and wheat raced below them.

The travelers followed the main roads with hauls of corn and wheat to sell to the Southern Lands, but something seemed different.

The people brushed past each other on the roads. Years ago the travelers would stop on the sides of the roads to play instruments, eat, share food, or sell their wares. Gone were the colorful wagons of the Wanderers selling silks of forest green, dark blues, deep purples and reds from the Southern Lands. Everyone anticipated the Wanderers, shifting through their wares with wide eyes. Now, the people simply moved down the roads, ignoring one another.

"Where are the Wanderers?" he called to Cián.

Cián shouted over the wind. "Jezebel chased them from the lands. She said they were bad for the people. Now, everyone fears everyone and refuses to buy from those in the villages."

King Efuko claimed the Wanderers brought everyone together. His dream consisted of one day uniting the South with the North.

The heavy scent of the purple and red flowers of The Field of Blood nestled between Three Son's Lakes drifted up to them. Conell smiled. Finally, he understood the name. The flowers brighten the field, which looked like a sea of blood. He spoke the field's forbidden name: *Voba to Je*. He hoped the wind would slam them into the witch's dead-pale face.

Conell smiled. Mother's favorite place in all Ezasu was this field and she would pack him up with Émer when father needed peace in the castle. Émer and Conell would hide in the flowers playing Barbarian and Maúl; Conell acted the part of the Barbarian each time.

Mother said Efuko asked for her hand in marriage in this field. Conell chuckled. As a child, he had asked his mother why father only wanted her hand. Mother laughed and smothered his face in kisses and called him a wonderful child. How he longed to feel her hands touching his face. Mother insisted Efuko protect and preserve her beloved field. Conell wished she could see it now, she would smile.

Two small mounds covered with red flowers sat in the center of the red mass. Mother and Father. Together forever. His throat tightened.

The field drifted behind him and the great walled city of Jeemie came into view. The large capital of Ezasu always took his breath away. Mother had forbid him and Émer to venture into the city alone and always insisted they take a guard. She claimed it was too dangerous for children to explore alone. Looking at it from a birds-eye-view, Conell understood her fears. The city stretched out for miles on each side. Her ancient walls cocooned her citizens like a large hand protecting a flock of chicks. The small, stone shops and homes of the rich sat nestled inside the large ramparts. Cobbled stoned streets snaked through the town.

Jezebel's large blue banners waved from each tower and smaller ones hung from every store and home. The flags were meant to bring the people together as one being. Individuality, she said, was a sin, but collectiveness was a blessing. The city bustled with men and women, who sold wares and buying items. They rode in large carriagesand wore nice clothing of silk and cotton fabrics. The rich and the poor had become richer.

He itched and wiggled on Aepoo's back. This was not what he expected. Shame covered his heart. A part of him longed to see the city in ruin and the starving people holding hatred for the queen. He saw the opposite. A people dedicated to the new queen. His stomach flipped. Broden's people forgot their king and now lay in the lap of a deceiving witch-monarch.

Cián gave him an understanding nod. "The people believe Jezebel saved them after your father's death. It was her who sent out Argus's men to kill those who slay your family. Now, they follow her completely. She keeps those loyal to her very happy and rich, while destroying those who oppose her."

Conell swallowed the lump in his throat. His people, Broden's people, had forgotten his father and his ancestors. This was no longer his city; he was the alien in Father's kingdom.

He had seen enough. "Áepoo, take us higher," he said. "I do not want Jezebel's eyes to see us." The beasts rose up into the sky until they reached the queen's castle, the House of Broden's light shied away from the white stones as if it feared what dwelled behind the fortress walls and hid its face. The sky-blue spirals once piercing the heavens now seemed ice cold as if the queen's chilled touch had captured them. Hundreds of Jezebel's filthy blue flags hung lifeless from the walls.

The same sinister gloom covered the queen's forest. The plants planted and tended by Mother and Grandmother and her mother down to Broden's wife had withered and died. His mouth dropped open.

This was Mother and her handmaidens' secret garden created only for the Queens of Esazu. Mother had pointed out to him each plant his grandmother and great grandmothers had planted. She always cautioned him about racing down the moss-covered stone stairs that led from the castle to the forest below. Only now that green moss was brown and the stairs were chipped and broken. The small bubbling brook that ran beside the stoned steps and eventually tumbled over a ridge was dried up.

Even Mother's small bridge that crossed the creek was now broken and rested on its side. Conell shook his head. Mother loved that old wooden bridge. Father made it for her on her birthday. She would dangle her feet in the cool water.

The morning mist would cling to the trees and the forest seemed to come alive with visions of fairies and sprites. Mother said the fairies lived in these woods and when the moon stood full, they would dance in the moonlight. A smile lingered on Conell's lips. He and Émer snuck out of the castle one night and sat under the bright moon waiting for the fairies. To this day, both men swear they saw movement amongst the evening trees.

Now, the fairies refused to dance and the mist drifted away. The trees drooped with the weight of evil and all the flower bushes withered. Jezebel added her rotten touch to the king's forest and stole its soul.

But none of this mattered. The House of Broden became the House of Jezebel and she could have it. He came to rescue Imogene, not to examine the condition of his old home.

He signaled to his captain. "We land behind the castle near *Ech to Nio*."

Émer nodded his head. The great beasts followed Áepoo and landed in the forest a mile from Jezebel's castle.

Conell slipped from Áepoo's back. In the past, the witch knew each move Conell and Émer made, yet now she seemed blind to their actions. He mentally questioned Áepoo. The beast could be a traitor waiting to betray them.

Áepoo lowered his head. "I have not betrayed you, Son of Efuko. Nor would I."

Émer and the others dismounted the beasts. Émer held his knife in the guard's side. Ruárc pouted and kicked at the ground, but stayed in his place.

Conell nodded towards the trees. "Émer, scout the area, see what lies before us."

His captain handed Frigg his knife. Ruárc watched the captain slip into the woods and leave. The guard studied Frigg from the corner of his eye. Conell glowered at him; Ruárc looked away.

The blue tipped pinnacles of *Broden Aquga* rose above the treetops. Conell shielded his eyes from the sun's brightness and his gaze followed up the walls to the castle peaks.

Father would stand on the larger squared tower called *Opale* and scout the lands. His presence loomed over Ezasu and the wind blew back his long silver hair. The young Conell would rise on his toes to peer over the tower wall and scan the green, lush lands of *Ezasu*. The men of the family guarded from the top of the world.

"We must guard against the enemy," Father said. "We never know when they will attack."

Frigg pushed Ruárc forward. The young advisor's eyes shone as he gazed at the mammoth structure. "The Tower of the *Opale*. I remember going there once. I was frightened by the height. I thought I would tumble to my death. It is still majestic."

Conell grinned at him. "As was I. I remember getting lost in the castle. I used to stay on the eastern side. I even made a map. It is still as massive as I remembered."

Frigg chuckled. "It has been ages since we walked the great halls of *Broden Aquga*. I can still hear the footsteps of the king down those drafty halls."

Conell stepped away from the massive castle. "But we did not come here to remember; we will never live here again."

Cián strolled up to Conell and pulled him away from the others. "You said you felt something when Argus stood in our camp. What did you feel, son?"

He tugged his arm away and turned to rejoin the others. "I felt...nothing. Let me be."

The old man whirled Conell around. "Now is not the time to allow bitterness to rule your tongue. That young girl is in grave danger. What did you *feel?*"

Conell looked over at Frigg. Ruárc sat on a log, but kept his eyes on the ground. Frigg stood over him. Conell met the old man's angry eyes and let out a great sigh. "I do not know. He held me in a grip, a fear. I felt like I was falling into a pit, suffocating like he would win. When he reached for the girl, I saw a hand—a white claw."

Cián nodded. "He uses your weaknesses against you. You must fight him. The Attiyq fights for me. But you are as one who stands in battle with no armor. All I can do is pray He will protect you.

Remember, Argus lives in your imaginations and thoughts."

Conell gave an impatient sigh. "I do not wish to enter this religious debate with you."

"And I wish I was at home with my family."

"I did not ask you to come here. You chose this."

"I chose because my God asked me to come and I obeyed."

Conell looked away. His eyes flickered back at the insane man. "Then what do you wish me to do?"

"Stay close to me. I am in His hands; His protection surrounds me. Do not look into the demon's eyes and take care of the thoughts entering your mind. He uses weaknesses to snare you."

Conell finally nodded. His eyes drifted to the castle. Mother's screams still echoed from the stoned structure. "I have done things in my past that shame me and the house of Broden. Things Émer and Frigg do not know. I have hidden these things from them. I fear losing them."

He placed his wrinkled hand on Conell's shoulder. "I know, the Attiyq told me something had happened years ago. That shame you carry has now become the demon's key to your heart. If you cling to it, then he will use it to destroy you. Remember, the visions you see are not real."

Émer slipped from the trees. "My Moji, the guards are on the upper walls, and a few surround the castle. We must be careful. Someone saw me, but kept silent. I think it was a woman, she may alert the guards."

Conell gave Cián a strong pleading look.

The old priest grinned. "Your secrets can remain hidden." He nodded a humbled thanks to the old man.

Frigg tugged Ruárc to his feet. Conell pulled out his sword and motioned to Ruárc. "Lead us. And do not think to call the guards, or I will enjoy slitting your throat. Cián, come with us."

He said to Áepoo, "You said you would serve my father, so now I am asking you, will you be here when we come back with the girl?"

He lowered his head. "The Attiyq ordered us to serve you. Aye, we will be here."

Conell nodded. "We will rendezvous here. Be ready to leave. Jezebel will not be pleased, and she will send her demons after us."

Áepoo smiled and rubbed his hands. "I hope she does."

Émer shoved Ruárc. Conell followed. The priest trailed behind him and Frigg took the rear.

The forest grew wild since the witch hauled them off to prison. Thick vines covered the ground and the intertwining tree limbs hid the sun from view. A fog drifted along the floor of the woods and gave off a chill that made them shiver.

The hairs on the back of Conell's neck rose. His skin tingled and he gripped his sword. "Émer! Do you feel it?"

The captain nodded and also drew his blade. "Aye, my Moji. It is black magic, mind your steps."

Something poked at Conell's foot. He shook his leg. The fog slithered on the ground like white worms. His brow furrowed and he took a soft step.

"Émer, what do you hear?" he asked.

He stopped and cocked his head. "Nothing, Moji."

Frigg jumped. "Something touched my leg!"

Conell dragged his foot through the vapor, but nothing moved. "Émer, what moves beneath this fog?"

His captain stepped beside him. "I do not know, Moji."

A trail of white fog glided up a tree trunk. It settled into the branches and coiled like a snake that was ready to strike.

"Moji?" Émer asked.

Conell examined the branches. "Be on your guard."

Ruárc trembled at the mist that gathered around them. "I want to go back." His once proud voice sounded like a whimpering child. "Jezebel is here."

Conell shoved him. "No one goes back without the girl."

The strange fog grew denser. The trees disappeared in the white shroud.

"Stay close," Conell said.

His group pressed their arms against one another and held their swords before them.

"We do not want to get lost in this," Conell said.

The fog wrapped around the group. Conell brushed his hand through it. It dissipated and regrouped as if it played with them.

Frigg grabbed Conell's arm and gasped. Conell whirled. His friend's eyes grew wide. White fingerlike tentacles strangled him. His face faded into a light blue as he clawed at the white fingers gripping his throat. Frigg dropped to his knees. Conell knelt beside him and swatted at the ghostly fingers wrapped around Frigg's neck. His hand slipped through it. The fingers pressed harder. Frigg wheezed. He lowered his head to the ground.

"Cián!" Conell shouted. "What is this?"

The old man placed his hand on Frigg's shoulder. "Release him!" The long fingers drew back and eased onto the ground. Frigg raised his head and gasped for air.

"Aho, send this cursed spell to hell!" Conell rose to his feet and pulled Frigg up. The castle, which once stood before him, now vanished in the fog. A white wall surrounded them like a ghostly sentinel.

Cián grabbed Conell's arm. "Nay, Lad, I cannot! I can defeat one, but not this great mass. Only the Attiyq can destroy such magic. Do not run or you will lose your way in the demon's haze."

A dirty-white hand lowered from the trees above his captain. Its bone-like fingers snaked over the captain.

Conell stepped forward, but a long arm appeared before him and held him back. "Émer, above you!"

The captain raised his eyes. He yelped and jumped aside. The fingers jerked away as he swiped them with his sword. The white phantom grabbed his blade. Émer snarled and yanked his weapon downward, but the fog-hand held tight. The mist glided down the blade to Émer's arm, making him drop his sword. The mist rose and struck, but Émer leaped away. It glided into the branch. Émer kept his gaze on the white snake as he snatched up his weapon. "Moji, there are demons in the fog!" He moved beside Conell. Both men held their swords before them.

"How do we defeat it?" Conell asked Émer.

"I have never fought these demons before. It plays with us as if we were children. Aho, help us," Émer said.

"The book of the Attiyq says…" came the priest's voice from the mist, "do not fear the terror of the darkness, for you lie in the palm of the Great One's hands."

"How does that defeat this demon?" A grip embraced Conell's ankle and wrapped around his leg. He tried to kick it off. Fingers cut into his flesh. A thousand needles raced into his skin. "Cián, get it off me!"

White arms slithered over Ruárc's shoulders and down his chest. The fog-demon yanked him to the ground. The guard screamed. The arms squeezed his ribs. He arched his back. "*Oozeka*, help me!"

Cián raised his head to the sky. "Attiyq! Hear my cry. I do not fear the evil that stalks the night, but trust in Your compassion for us. Help us!"

The fingers fled Ruárc's body and the grip released Conell's leg. The mist parted like an old woman sweeping away dirt. Hands with fingers spread wide appeared suspended on both sides of the small group as if the ghostly palms were trapped behind an invisible barrier. The hands crawled up and down tried to smash the strange barricade. More and more fists crowded against each other, pushing each other aside as they banged on the clear wall.

Émer tried to touch the blockade, but Conell pulled him back. "Let us not linger."

The group jogged to the end of the transparent tunnel and slipped from the forest into the bright sun. The mist evaporated and left behind a dark forest.

Émer placed his hands onto knees and closed his eyes. He raised his face and smiled at Cián. "Thank you, Aho."

Conell ignored a chill sweeping over him and pointed at Ruárc with his sword. "Lead!"

Ruárc nodded to the point. "There is a secret entrance behind the bush."

Conell motioned to Émer. "See if it is true."

The captain slithered on his belly toward the shrubbery. Once there, he pushed it aside and peek in. He waved to the small group. The four men crept to the opening as Émer pulled away the twigs. They slipped into the castle.

"Stay away from the windows," cried the little girl. But the other girls refused to listen and the wolf ate them all.

~ *The Girl who Faced the Wolf* by Merryn, Daughter of Margh, a scribe for King Huw, Thirteenth King of Ezasu in the year 590.

# 12

A small tapping on the bathroom door pulled Imogene from her daydream. She smiled; she hadn't left heaven. "Come in."

Girl slipped into the room. A pale white covered her elfin face and her small hands trembled.

"Are you okay?" Imogene asked.

Girl snatched a towel off a shelf. Her voice was tight. "Lord Argus comes. I must get you dressed."

She held out the white towel and Imogene pried herself from the warmth of the bath. After Girl wrapped the towel around Imogene, she led the way into the bedroom. Girl took a bottle from the dressing table and poured

187

lotion into her palm. "I need to put the lotions on you and help you to dress."

Imogene smiled. "I can manage, thanks… um, Girl. You can't tell me your real name?"

Girl shook her head.

Imogene shrugged, scooped the lotion from the girl's hand and smeared it over her body.

The servant girl opened a large red amour with carved roses on the top and the sides. Floor length medieval style dresses of deep red, blue and black velvet and soft silks hung from the rod.

"These are beautiful!" Imogene fingered a burgundy velvet dress with a burgundy and silver silk center. Small silver swirls were embedded in the silk and beads hung from the end of the long wide sleeves.

Girl thumbed through the dresses. "These belonged to the former queen while she lived. We keep them for special occasions such as now."

Imogene's skin crawled. "Maybe I should wear something else. I mean I don't want to wear the poor woman's dresses now that she's dead."

"It is Lord Argus's orders," she mumbled.

Girl selected a pale blue silk gown layered with light blue silk edged with lace. The back of the dress bunched at the waist. The top had tiny silver and white beads sewn into the soft fabric and flowered lace and beads edged the long wide sleeves hanging down to the waist. She laid the gown on the bed and took out underclothes from a drawer and shoes and stockings from another cabinet.

Imogene winced. These belonged to Conell's mother. It seemed wrong wearing a dead woman's clothes then it hit her. *Special occasion?*

Girl helped Imogene into the underclothes and slid the silk dress over Imogene's head. The tight top clung across her chest and neckline hung low showing a peek of her cleavage, but the middle was fitted at her waist. The long thick sleeves almost covered her fingertips. The silk skirt spilled to the floor.

Imogene admired her reflection in the large standing mirror. She twisted, trying to see her back. "The queen must have been beautiful."

"I do not know. She was dead when mmm…Father brought me here."

Girl's brow furrowed "Your father?" Imogene noticed her sadness.

She kept her eyes on the floor as if struggling for an answer. "Please, I do not wish to speak of it. I need to do your hair."

Imogene pushed up the sleeves past her elbows.

Girl stopped her. "What are you doing? You must not do such things. You are *TTisho* now." She brought down the sleeves and pulled the cuff over Imogene's fingers.

"A *TTisho*? The guys I was with kept saying something about a *TTisho*. What is a *TTisho* anyway?"

The young servant gawked at Imogene as if she had grown three heads and an extra pair of arms. "A woman of the courts. A Lady of Honor."

"So you all got a thing against arms showing?" Imogene tugged at the shoulder of Girl's dress. "You show your arms."

Girl looked away. "I am no longer *TTisho*."

Imogene lifted Girl's chin. "Of course, you are. My friend always says every woman is a princess."

She shook her head. "Women are not princesses in this castle."

"You're still a princess no matter what anyone says," Imogene said.

Girl blushed and gave her a soft smile.

"Well, I just wish I could do my nails. They look awful." Imogene wiggled her fingers.

Girl's confused eyes locked on her.

"So painting nails is out too. But this is okay?" She tapped at her cleavage.

Girl's face flushed. "I know, I am sorry, it is Lord Argus's command. He likes the gowns to be without the *Ajoosho-Acajo*,

189

covering-lace. I know you should be covered, but we must obey."

"So there's supposed to be lace here?" Imogene ran her fingers across her collarbone.

Girl gave Imogene a small smile. "Your nurse never taught you such things? All *TTisho* wear the *Ajoosho-Acajo*. Only women of low statue, *Zuusho* as I, expose themselves."

How could anyone call this girl a slut? "So he wants the *ladies* showing, but not the arms?" Imogene moved her hands up and down over her chest.

Girl covered her lips as a giggle escaped her.

Imogene pointed at her. "You do know how to smile."

She swallowed her chuckles. "I am not allowed to laugh; do not let others hear us."

Girl led Imogene to a large wooden dressing table with a full sized mirror hanging above it. Imogene sat on the cushioned wooded seat. Her reflection in the mirror changed into Aunt Imogene Louise and Momma. She saw a similar thread running through the three Martin-Reazley women. Each of them ran from a life too difficult to live.

Aunt Imogene ran from Grandma who wanted Imogene Louise to attend college. Imogene Louise longed for freedom at a place called Woodstock and died as a protestor at the same college Grandma wanted her to attend as a student.

Momma dreaded the stay-home mom charade, seeing it as a wasted life. Here sat Imogene Katherine Reazley the runaway nerd who refused to stand up to the bullies at school.

All three women fled from themselves. Each of them sought something they thought they wanted and left their loves ones in a pile of tears. Aunt Laurie positioned as the rock of the family would pick up the pieces left behind like a broken mirror reflecting their faces.

*Stay with the prince.*

She closed her eyes as the words dug in her heart and mind. Those were the Attiyq's words, plain as day. And instead, she ran again to something she thought she wanted.

This pretend life of popularity, a lover from a Manga, a servant named Girl who was too frightened to raise her gaze was a sham. She wanted Aunt Laurie, an education, her old life back. She'd even take back the bullies.

The Attiyq and Conell tried to help her and she refused their assistance. She pursed her lips and lifted her chin. When the going gets tough, the tough get going. Maybe the Attiyq wanted her to take the hard road instead of the easy one of luxury, popularity and love. The judge's orders waited for her in the park.

Imogene placed her elbows on the top of the table and rubbed her forehead with the palms of her hands. "Girlfriend, I've made a terrible mistake. I have to go back to Conell and find my way back home. I have to face the judge and finish my probation."

Girl frowned at Imogene in the mirror as she slipped a pearl necklace around Imogene's neck and fastened it.

Imogene's gaze dropped to the items on the table. Necklaces and bracelets made of gold, silver and pearls sat in a small wooden jewelry box embedded with roses and the name Naomh engraved across the front. Bottles of perfume, a hand mirror and a silver brush with strands of black, brown, silver and red hair clinging to it sat beside the box.

Who used this stuff, she wondered. *Did the items belong to Conell's mom? It was wrong to use her stuff without his permission.* She squirmed in her seat.

"What do mean?" Girl asked. "You have made a terrible mistake?"

"I have to go home and face the music, so to speak."

"Music?"

"I have to face my own punishment for breaking the law. I can't run anymore."

Girl pushed a brown wooden bracelet up her arm. She gently combed Imogene's short hair. "Imogene, please do as Lord Argus demands. You are a kind person and it will go better for you if you obey him."

She picked up a flowered barrette and clipped it in Imogene's hair. Her small fingers used a thin stiff brush to apply blush on Imogene's cheeks.

Imogene caught Girl's worried eyes in the mirror. "Girlfriend, why are you so frightened?"

Girl's eyes watered, but she blinked them away. "Please Imogene, you must stop asking so many questions. You endanger both of us."

A small knock thumped on the door. Girl gasped and fumbled with the brush. She scurried to the door and opened it.

Argus's large frame filled the doorway. Girl bowed her head and moved aside allowing him entrance. He eyes roamed over her, making her swallow. He took long strides into the room. The sound of his thundering footsteps echoed off the wooden floor.

Girl gave Imogene one last plea with her watery eyes before exiting the room.

Argus closed the door. His dark gaze roamed over Imogene from her feet up to her face.

Her cheeks burned. The same fog growled at her unyielding mind. The Attiyq wanted her with Conell. The days of running ended at the mirror. A pain tugged at her heart. She would have to say goodbye to the magical castle with a magical man.

He caressed the curve of her face. Her heart beat faster. She ambled to window.

His arms slipped around her waist and he kissed her neck. She closed her eyes and leaned against him. He cocooned her against his strong body. His hands caressed her stomach. She belonged in Argus's arms and she melted against him.

Her gaze rose to the wooden ceiling. No, she belonged home, picking up trash and celebrating her birthday with her aunt and uncle, not lost in this world. She took a deep breath and buried away her feelings.

She pried his arms off her stomach and confronted him. His

dark eyes dug into hers and her knees wobbled. She had been the wallflower left alone in the corner while the popular girls danced with the popular guys. Now, she was the popular girl asked to the dance floor by the handsome hero. She tossed it aside because of a vow she had made to a faceless voice. Foolishness.

"Argus," she said, choosing her words carefully. "I appreciate all you have done for me. You're so wonderful, but I can't stay here with you."

He lifted her chin and raised his eyebrows. "Not stay?" His thumb caressed her cheek. "Where will you go?"

Goosebumps raced across her body. "Home. I have to do my probation. I can't run away anymore." She lowered her head and broke his touch.

"I see." He walked to a side table and poured the red wine into a stemmed crystal glass. "Wine, my dear?"

"No, thanks."

Argus seemed sophisticated, a renaissance man. Kids in high school seemed immature and stupid when compared to this being.

He held the wine glass by its stem and examined the red liquid, then waved the goblet under his nose. "A fine brand, from the Lands of the South, very rare. Are you sure you will not have a glass?"

"I'm too young to drink, but thank you. Please take me to Conell or my home, whichever is closest."

He shrugged. "I will need the medallion to speed you to your home. Do you have it?"

Her fingers traced her throat. "No, I gave it to Conell. He thought I would be safer if he wore it."

He swirled the red liquid in the glass container. "Pity, without the medallion, I can do nothing for you. Conell is a murderer so you must stay here with me. We seem to be in a quandary." He sipped the wine, but kept her in his vision. "You must stay here with me until I can find the medallion." He placed the glass on a side table.

She scratched her head. "Oh, okay, well, now what?"

"I have a gift for you, My Lady." He extracted a purple cloth from his pocket and handed it to her.

A small grin spread across her face. How sweet. "Argus, you don't have to do this."

He placed the small package in her palm. She opened the cloth. A thick wooden bracelet with letterings carved onto the side sat in the silk wrapping.

"Argus," she said. "It's pretty."

"It is my gift to you, Lady Imogene." He took the item from the cloth, opened a small latch on the bangle and slipped it onto her wrist. The clasp clicked shut and echoed around the room.

A voice deep inside her whispered, *"Don't."*

This was Argus, her new boyfriend, whom she would leave behind in a strange world, their lives apart for eternity, she argued. Her memory gift of his love—like in the movies.

She smiled. "Thank you." Her cheeks felt warm again. *Why did she toss him away?*

He kissed her cheek. "Your blush is as soft as the sunrise." She giggled and covered her cheeks with her hands. "Come, lie with me." He took her elbow and led her to the bed.

She pulled her arm from his grasp. This wasn't what she had expected. He moved too fast. They needed to go to dinner first, perhaps a walk in the garden like in the Jane Austin books, not romp with her in bed on their first meeting.

"Argus, I can't do this, I mean, I can't do *this*." She opened her arms and spread her palms wide over the bed. "I'm not ready."

He caressed her jaw line. Tingles spread to her toes.

"You do not wish to be with me?" he whispered in her ear.

His lips were an inch from hers. She closed her eyes. "I do." She lowered her head and broke his spell. "But, not now. You're moving too fast."

He raised her chin. "You speak as if you have a choice, My Lady."

*Imogene, please do as Lord Argus demands.*

Something seemed wrong. Imogene stepped back. "I don't think

I like where this is going. Maybe you should leave, give me time to think. Please."

He picked up the glass and sipped from it, then banged the crystal on the table. "Leave?" The liquid swished over the rim. "I have no intentions of leaving."

His footsteps clicked on the stoned floor and he towered over her. The handsome angelic face darkened and his soft eyes became hooded. His voice was gentle, "When I give you a command, I expect you to obey it."

She took a step back. "Obey? Argus, I don't understand. I mean, I thought—"

"Thought what, My Lady? That I loved you? Cared for you?" He grabbed her arm and held up her wrist. The brown bracelet slipped down her arm. "Do you know what this *pretty bracelet* means?"

She shook her head. Girl wore one on her wrist. *Oh God, what did I do?*

"It means you belong to me." He breathed into her hair. "And when I say sit, I mean, sit." He shoved her onto the dressing room chair and placed his hand on the back of the seat. "My Lady." His voice was a soft whisper and his breath smelled like sour wine. "What did the Attiyq tell you?"

The Attiyq's words slipped from her mind. Argus's eyes grew dark. Piercing. The dream came back to her. Argus dragging her into hell. Flames ripping at her skin. The demon laughing.

"I don't remember," she mumbled.

He slipped his hands behind his back and rocked on his heels. "You do not remember the words of the Great One? A seer who forgets?" He grabbed her wrists and yanked her to her feet. "I suggest, My Lady, you begin to remember."

"Let go of me!" His long fingers dug into her soft flesh. Her fingers tingled and her wrist ached. "I'm going to tell the queen!"

"What did He say!" The harsh words slipped over his sharp lower teeth protruding over his bottom lip. His face grew long and red. His brow, wrinkled.

She gasped and tried to find the words. "Stay with Conell! He said He wanted me to stay with him!"

His eyebrow rose. "Really? And you disobeyed. How will the Attiyq ever forgive you? You are of little use to me now, Seer. But you can serve me in other ways."

He threw her onto the bed and stood over her. She crawled to the other side, but he dragged her back and climbed on top of her. His lips pressed onto her mouth. She clawed his check. He slapped her face. A burning sensation covered her jaw. She clamped her eyes shut. He ripped open her dress. His cold fingers ran over her skin.

"No!" She arched her back and pushed away his hands.

A tap on the door. "My Lord Argus," came a man's voice from the hallway.

Argus lifted his head. "I am busy!" His sharp voice echoed in her ears.

Someone was here. Oh God, please! "Please, help me!"

"My Lord, this is urgent," said the man's muffled voice.

He cursed, but rose, made his way to the door and swung it open. The feathers on his shoulders rose.

*Get up, get up, get up! This is your chance, don't blow it.* She grabbed a statuette from a table and rolled off the bed. Her legs buckled, dropping her to the floor. She grasped the side of the bed and hauled up her shaking body. Words from the man at the door floated across the room. "Conell…Woods" Conell! She hid the statuette behind her back. The other hand held together her ripped dress.

Argus slammed the door shut and pivoted on his heel. His eyebrow lifted. "You disobey the Attiyq and now me?"

"This stops now." Sweat dripped down her arm and onto the statue.

"Really?" He took a step towards her. `

She lifted the figurine and brought it down towards his head.

His arm shot up and blocked her attack. His other hand grabbed her raised wrist and squeezed until a dull pop rippled down her arm. She screamed as a sharp pain shot into her shoulder.

He took the statue and tossed her to the ground. "Would you really destroy an antique statue, Imie? This one is my favorite." He placed it on the dressing table. Shifted the item to the left. Stood back. Admired it.

Imie. He knew her nickname. Only Conell, the guys, Aunt Laurie, and her friends at school knew it. He stole it and allowed it to slip off his nasty tongue.

"How do you know about my nickname?"

He cocked his head and smiled as if he knew a secret.

*Oh God, he's been spying on me this whole time.* That's how he knew. When she bathed, slept, walked, talked. She cradled her broken wrist against her chest as she limped away on her hand and knees. He was crazy. The Attiyq tried to warn her, point out Argus's nastiness. *Stay with the Prince.*

"Oh, God, help me," she whispered.

"You are so foolish to fight me, Imie." He walked beside her crawling form and knelt before her. "Why must you make me hurt you? You are no different from the others who come to me. You too must learn to obey." His cold fingers stroked her hair.

She slapped his hand away. He snarled as he dragged her to her feet and his fist slammed into her face. She weaved against him, and then smashed face first into the flat stones. Lights popped in front of her eyes. A burning sting spread up her jaw.

He cradled her in his arms. "Imie, do you know who stood at my door?"

*Do as he says. Don't fight, not yet.*

"It was my guards. They have killed Conell and the others."

Her eyes closed. He couldn't be dead, not Conell, not Émer. Émer was a Voodo something. He couldn't die.

"My men found them and killed them." He kissed her head and laid his cheek against her hair. "You have no one but me now, Imie. Your mother left you as did your father. Your friends are dead now. No one cares for you as I do."

She crawled out of his arms and looked back at him. "Go to hell!"

He smiled and rose. "I own it, My Lady." His strong fingers grabbed her hair and dragged her to the door. It swung open.

She grabbed the doorframe with her strong arm. He yanked at her wrist clinging to the frame, but she held onto it. He snarled and punched her broken wrist.

A hot red poker raced up her arm. She screamed. He planned to kill her.

He tugged her passed the portrait of King Efuko. The old Monarch's head swiveled as Argus drag her down the hall. *If only you obeyed. Now, you are left in the loving arms of the devil. What a shame. And my poor son tried to help you. So many people are disappointed in you.*

Imogene's eyes locked on the picture and she shook her head. "No, no, no!" Men in paintings are just paintings, not real people. So why was he real? He shouldn't be real. Efuko died years ago. Oh, God why didn't she listen?

"So sad," came a whispered voice down the empty hallway.

"If only she had listened," said a ghostly female. "What a fool."

Laughter rippled down the vacant corridor, making Imogene cringe. Argus's feathers lay down on his shoulders as if stroked by an invisible hand. The demon snuggled his cheek against an unseen palm. He nodded as if hearing a phantom's whispers. Argus was a crazy man residing in a haunted house. She was locked in the castle-madhouse and he would drag her into his hell. If only she could find her way back to that small village.

Imogene dug her heels into the floor and tried to yank free from his grasp. He frowned as if the action insulted his ego and jerked her forward, making her tumble onto the cold tiles. Jolts ran up into her knees the cartilage grinding.

A woman with long greasy black hair knelt beside Imogene. Blood trails marked her once pale face and one eye was missing. The fine lady's once stunning yellow gown was covered with worms that wiggled across her frame. "Where is your Moji, *Tamo Chuoha?*"

Imogene screamed and tried to scurry away. Argus stomped on her back. Her chest and stomach hit the stoned floor. Pain ripped across her back and the stones stole her breath. Argus hauled her to her feet. Her head spun and her feet stumbled. The demon's long nails chewed into her bruised arm.

Her eyes grew wide at the colorful stained-glass windows of the brave Ezasu knights as their beady glass orbs followed them. Shadows waltzed around her and Argus. Darkness caressed Argus's wings and nipped at her heels. It raced ahead of them and pointed at them from the ceiling.

A woman's screams and her panicked cries echoed down the bare hall. "Please do not harm my baby!"

Imogene closed her eyes as the pleas rebounded along the stones, then diminished into the wind howling through the windows. Goosebumps spread across her frame. She kept her head down to avoid seeing the paintings move.

"Please, Argus," Imogene sobbed. "Please, don't. Please, God."

Argus stopped before a flight of stairs looking like a gaping mouth, shrouded in darkness. He shoved her down. She tumbled and landed in a heap at the bottom of the stairwell. A deep moan escaped her and she rolled onto her back. A sharp pain raced into her ribs, making it hard for her to breathe.

Argus's boots pounded on the stoned stairs—Satan's footsteps. He stood over her. Red-demon eyes shined through the darkness.

"Please, Argus, please don't do this," she whispered.

He squatted beside her cowering form. "I demand obedience from my women including you, Seer. If you wish to disobey me, then you pay the price."

Tears slipped down her face. She should have listened. "Argus, please let me go."

He wrapped his fingers in her short hair and wrenched her to her feet. His sharp claws dug into her scalp.

The demon had just begun.

He dragged her into a dimly lit corridor. A stench like rotten meat slammed into her face and made her stomach lurched.

"Argus, please, don't, please."

Rats scurried in the torch light. One stared at them before slipping into a hole in the wall. Argus unlocked one of the closed doors and shoved her into the cell. He slammed the door behind them.

She fell on the floor and landed on her broken wrist. A sharp stabbing pain raced up her arm. Argus's footsteps crunched on the floor behind her. She crawled to the far wall and pressed her back against the cold and wet stones.

Argus knelt and caressed her face, making her flinch.

"Imie." His voice was low and soft. "I want to give you the luxuries of this life, let you live in that nice warm room, but you chose the prison cell instead. And this is where you will stay until you learn to obey me. Then, you will live in such luxury." He smiled sweetly. A deep sigh escaped him as if she was a disobedient child and he brushed away her short bangs. "But for now, you must beg for the Attiyq's forgiveness and hear from Him again. My women bore me after a while and I would hate to toss away such an innocent being." He kissed her temple.

She cringed. *Don't pull away!*

He whispered in her ear. "I must retrieve my medallion from Conell's dead body. You will hear from the Attiyq and together you and I will rule *Ezasu* and beyond these shores. Do not worry, my love. Soon you will see I am right and this is what we must do for the good of everyone." He kissed her lips.

Her fists balled at her side and pressed them into her thighs. If only she could rip out his cold heart. "I hate you. I'll never help you, never. I don't care what you do to me, I won't help."

"Really?" He lifted her chin. "Imie, your mother lives in New

York and your aunt in a place called Illinois, correct?"

She licked her lips and nodded.

"Would you wish for me to slip the brown bracelet on their arms? Please do not force me to do such a thing. I do not enjoy old women."

Momma and Aunt Laurie trapped here? He wouldn't dare. She glared at him through her tears.

His eyes slipped into narrow strips. "Do not tempt me, Seer. I have only to use the medallion, which is now mine, and I will bring your loved ones here. They will be my women until I bore of them, then they will belong to the Slave Runners." He kissed the tip of her nose. "Old women do not fare well with them."

This madman was serious; he would bring Momma and Aunt Laurie here and trap them in this hell. She had to protect them. A tear slipped down her cheek. She closed her eyes and nodded.

His cold fingers wiped away the tear and then moved across her neck and down her body. A wave of nausea swarmed over her stomach.

He rose to his feet. "Good. I hate old women, I prefer the younger ones. I will be back for you, my lovely Seer. Then you can please me as you hear from the old one."

She focused on the dirt on the floor and pulled her knees to her chest.

His boots trampled the rocky floor. The door slammed behind him. A loud click. The squeaking of rats broke the silence.

"Are you there?" asked a whispered voice.

Imogene's eyes slowly took in the empty room. Shivers exploded across her arms. "Who are you?"

The voice giggled. "You should have listened."

More voices joined into the laughter and became louder. She pressed her head to her shoulder, covering her ears. "Go away!"

The laughter stopped as quickly as it started. A deadly hush pressed into her eardrums, making them ring. Her tears started small before rushing down her face. *Was it worth it*, her mind whispered?

*Do you want to sit at the cheerleaders table this much? Is this what you want? A psycho boyfriend who lives in the old Bartonville State Hospital? All this just to date Kyle?* "Please, Attiyq, I'm so sorry, I was so wrong, please help me. God, please help me," she sobbed.

She hobbled to a corner of the room and vomited.

Conell stepped into the tunnel and stared at the dirt ceiling. Jezebel stalked the halls and waited for him. The reek from the prison rose in his nose. The shrieks of dying prisoners and squeaking rats echoed in his ears. This time Conell and his companions would not survive. Broden would frown upon him and Father would turn away. Conell's curse would be to sit in that cell for eternity.

He cut the ropes binding Ruárc and shoved him. "Lead."

Ruárc rubbed his swollen wrists. "I need a light. How can I walk in the dark?"

"He is right," Frigg said. "We do not want to get lost in here."

Émer grabbed a dead torch from the wall, knelt on the ground and rubbed two flint stones together, setting a small fire on the end of the old wooden stub.

The priest picked up a white rock and drew an arrow on the stoned wall pointing to the exit. "And we will need a compass leading us back to the light."

Conell raised his eyebrows. "You *are* resourceful."

The old man grinned. "Yes, I am."

"We need to guard against Argus." Conell paused. The red orbs flashed through his mind. "And the witch. I would not be surprised if they knew we were here."

Émer gave Ruárc the torch and the guard led the way down the darken corridor. The dirt and stoned walls lining the tunnels looked ancient, yet Father never spoke of them nor did he or Émer find them as children.

Conell said to Émer, "Did you know of these tunnels?"

The captain shook his head. "Nay, my Lord. Rumors always claimed that King Broden dug many tunnels around *Ezasu*. But this, I have never seen."

"The old king dug them because of his many enemies," Cián said. "But the later kings boarded them up. Jezebel must have unearthed them."

"Cián, could the barbarians have used them when they attacked the castle?"

Cián shrugged and drew another arrow on the wall. "Perhaps. How do you know of these, Ruárc?"

Ruárc chuckled. "You really think I will expose my secrets?"

Conell poked him in the back with his sword. "I suggest you do."

He arched his spine and winced. "If you insist. My brother and I stayed in these tunnels as children when the weather became too cold for the tower." He whirled. "Remember those days, *Moji?* When *you* and your sweet companions slept in warmth of spacious bedrooms and my brother and I barely survived? You claim to be so righteous, yet you are nothing more than an indulged child. You found favor in Clemwyn's eyes, who ignored my brother and me. We begged him for training, but he always stated he was too busy with you and your pampered pets. But I was the one who rose above the others without the great Clemwyn's training. And it was I who defeated him. Who do you think gave the queen the information that killed him?"

Émer growled and raised his sword to Ruárc's stomach. "You will die for your treason!"

Conell pushed the weapon aside and gave his captain a strong look. "We need him to find the girl. Then your blade can own his heart."

Ruárc laughed. "Treason? No, it was not treason, *Peasant* Émer. The queen gave us favor and took us from the guard tower. *I* am the one who now lives in luxury while you freeze and starve. What a nice turn of events, would you agree, Prince Conell DeCapris?"

Émer's eyes drove through the guard. "I will enjoy tearing your heart from your chest, Traitor."

Again Ruárc chuckled. "That is if you have the training."

Cián stepped between the two men and held them apart. "Enough! We must think of the girl. Ruárc, take us to her."

Ruárc sneered at Émer, and then strutted down the hall. Émer gave his Moji a long, aggravated sigh and followed the conspirator.

"I hope you lead us in the right direction," Conell said. "I would hate to see my captain kill you in your cherished tunnels. After all I did promise him your beating heart."

Ruárc grunted. "Not as much as I would enjoy seeing your blood flow first. You killed my brother."

"He tried to kill me first," Conell said.

He whirled. "You will not leave this castle alive."

Conell slid his blade under Ruárc's throat. "Lead."

He growled, but ambled through the tunnel.

Cián would stop and draw arrows on the walls until they reached a stoned dead-end.

The guard stopped and pressed his fingers against the rocks. "The prisons are just beyond these walls. I cannot remember where the door is, somewhere around here." He pushed on a rock and the rock wall opened. "Ah, here it is."

Conell drew Ruárc back and slipped through the doorway. A dim light glowed in the cold hallway. The soft sound of weeping traveled along the stoned passage. More accusing voices whispered along the darken corridor, but he ignored them. Saving the girl mattered more than the pain and the past.

He ducked back to his companions. "I hear her. Be on the guard. Argus could be anywhere. Émer, stay here and find out what opens the rock door from this side, then join us."

Émer nodded as his companions entered the dungeon passage.

"Frigg," Conell said. "Watch Ruárc."

Conell and Cián slipped down the hall. Memories exploded in

his mind. This was his hiding place when Mother shooed him out of Father's study. The dungeon maze was a place where he fought pretend pirates under the careful eyes of the guards. He counted the torches on the wall and stopped at the forth one. He pressed on a broken brick and it popped open revealing a hidden space. He grabbed the small treasures tucked inside including Mother's locket that Father gave her on their wedding anniversary. He kissed it and placed it around his neck. It was all that was left of Mother.

The memories quickly faded and the prince held out his hand. Both men stopped and listened. The sound of sobbing came from one of the cells. They followed the sound and stood before the door. Conell slipped a knife into the keyhole and twisted the blade until the lock clicked. He pushed open the door.

A small torch on the cell wall cast a dim light into the room. A dark figure sat on the floor against the wall, curled in a ball. He stepped into the cell. "Imogene?"

She whimpered and buried her face in her knees. "Please, go away."

Ruárc stepped behind him and chuckled. "Someone has enjoyed her company."

Conell raised his arm and smashed the back of his fist into Ruárc's face.

The guard collapsed onto the ground. "What did I do?"

Conell knelt before Imogene and stroked her hair.

She flinched and dug her face deeper into her knees. "Please, go away."

What happened to her? "*Tamo Chuoha*," he said.

Imogene screamed. "Leave me alone!" Her small hands thrashed at his face and her nails clawed at his biceps.

He shook her. "Imogene!"

Time stopped for an instant as the girl raised her face. Black and blue bruises covered the once soft cheeks and her bruised upper lip bled. "Oh God, they won't leave me alone!" One arm wrapped around his neck and strangled him while the other arm she kept at her side.

He loosened Imogene's strong grip and rocked her as if a child. "It is all right, *Chuoha*, I am here. We will leave now." Conell swallowed the lump in his throat. Mother's favorite blue dress hung on the girl and the top was ripped open. A shudder ran through his frame. What did the demon do to her?

Cián took off his cape and placed it over her shoulders.

"He kept touching me. I couldn't make him stop." Imogene's body shook with her tears. "Oh, God, Conell! I want to go home! I want my mom!"

If only he had stayed close to her side, none of this would have happened. They would be at the ports now and the girl and Frigg would be on a ship sailing to freedom. Instead, she trembled in his arms.

A woman with greasy black hair and a yellow dress covered in worms leaned over his shoulder. Blood coated her destroyed face and dripped from a hollow where her eye once was. "Really, Prince Conell, I should never have indulged you as much as I did!"

Conell jumped at the sight of Mother's deceased personal maid. The visions poured back into Conell's mind of the woman who was like a second mother. Lady Fath's dead eyes had faced the open door as she lay next to her slain mistress. The woman still clenched a sword in her small hand, yet never had the training. Clemwyn had stated that the young maid was braver than all the Kings of Ezasu and she held her ground against the charging Barbarians.

Conell took a deep breath and pushed aside the beloved Lady Fath's destroyed image. All of the kings before him ruled with valor and honor except the son of Efuko. He made a vow years ago while hiding in the closet that his hands would protect his loved ones and friends from the enemy's sword. That promise crumbled apart like breadcrumbs under the table.

Lady Fath's chuckle echoed through the chamber. *"Vows and promises!* Those things are far from you, Conell DeCapris! Where did I go wrong?"

"Do not fear, *Chuoha*, I am here." Conell lifted Imogene's limp arm. A dark bruise encircled her wrist. "Who did this?"

She buried her face in his chest. "He won't let me go."

"Did Argus do this?"

She nodded.

Émer crouched beside the couple. "Moji, someone approaches. We must leave now. I think it is the witch's demon."

Frigg leaned over them. "He is right. I saw Argus approaching."

"Argus said you all died," she said through her tears. "He said his men killed you."

"He lied, *Chuoha*," Conell said. "Come, we must leave. Émer, did you find the secret to the passage door?"

He nodded.

"I will give you a signal, you be ready to open that door." Conell lifted Imogene in his arms and followed his companions from the cell.

Ruárc scrabbled to his feet, but Émer slammed the door and locked the guard in the prison chamber.

"DeCapris! You would not dare to leave me here!" Ruárc shook the bars in the door's small window. "I swear I will not forget this! I will find you!"

Argus stood at the end of the hall and his eyes narrowed at the sight of Conell's small band. The corridor seemed darker.

Imogene winced and buried her face in Conell's chest. Her arm tightened around his neck.

Conell lowered her to the ground. She wrapped her unhurt arm around his bicep. The demon's black eyes drilled into him. But this time, Conell looked at Argus's forehead and avoided the demon's hellish face. Conell renewed his vow in the presence of King Broden. *I give you my word, My King Broden, on your grave; I will protect these people and will face death before fleeing.*

Imogene trembled and pressed her wet face against his arm. Conell slipped his arm from her grip and draped it around her waist.

"Well, Prince Conell," Argus said, "my guard told me you had arrived. You have two things that belong to me. Give me the girl and the medallion, and I will set you and your men free."

Imogene shook her head and buried her face in his chest. "No, no, please, no, I don't want to go with him."

Conell kept his focus on the demon's forehead. "She does not seem to long for your company."

Argus chuckled. "Her wishes mean nothing to me; she belongs to me under the Slave Laws. She wears the slave bracelet. The queen gave her to me."

Conell sneered. "My father abolished the *Joec* Laws years ago."

"But your father died, remember? And you graciously gave the throne to my queen." A smirk played at the corners of the demon's mouth. "My queen wisely reestablished the Slave Laws." He held out his hand. "Give the girl and the medallion to me, Prince Conell, and I will allow you and your friends to leave."

Imogene's legs buckled, but he shifted his weight and steadied her.

"Why do your eyes turn to the girl and the medallion?" Conell asked. "As a slave, she means nothing to you, so let her go. I will give you the medallion, but the girl stays with me."

Argus laughed and eased his sword from its scabbard. "You are still the same sniffling coward. You disgrace the name of King Broden. Your father's face would turn from you in shame, the coward who hides while others perish. What would your father say of your sins, boy?"

A chill swept over Conell. Émer's eyes were locked on him, waiting for the signal. Argus's taunts drifted past the captain.

Conell licked his lips and swallowed. Argus's words rang true. Cowardness ran through his blood, not Broden's valor. The death of the Maúl, Frigg's family, Mother, Father, his unborn sibling, Lady Fath, even the young maids lay on Conell's shoulders. Death-masked faces glowered at him and pointed bloodied fingers at the small boy cowering in the closet.

*Traitor!!*

*Lady Fath stood next to Argus and her bloody fingers trailed the demon's feathers leaving the white feathers red.* "Yes, My Precious Child, tell us of your treason to my king. I must have done something wrong. I tried, but I failed."

Argus chuckled. Laughter from a thousand phantoms rippled down the corridor and send shivers across Conell. No one seemed to notice or hear Lady Fath's jeers except for him. Insanity covered his mind, that's why no one heard Mother's personal maid.

Émer would discover the truth. Conell would lose the man who stood like his brother. The vow before the king crumbled at his feet. Water travels one way, the elders said. A force dragged Conell's eyes to the monster dark red orbs.

"Steady, Prince Conell," came Cián's soft words. "You are no longer a trembling sinful child, but a strong man."

He peered at Cián who stood strong behind him.

"We hide under the shadow of His wings," Cián whispered.

Argus's eye twitched and he winced. *Lady Fath screamed and raced down to the other end of the corridor.*

As a constrictor releases its prey, the demon's spell uncoiled around him. Conell breathed deeply as the visions faded. He no longer cringed like the boy in the closet. Instead, he rose as a man who made a promise to a king. He steadied his feet and focused on the demon's forehead. "No, the girl stays with me."

"Keep your filthy paws off me!" Imogene said through her tears.

Argus's gaze fell upon her. "What did you say to me?"

While Argus's attention focused on her, Conell nodded to Émer. The captain placed his hand on the rock opening the passage door.

The demon gave the girl a sympathetic frown and spread his palms. "Woman, only I can give you all that you long for. You wish to be happy. You must trust me."

"Do not listen to him, Child," Cián said. "He is a stream flowing with lies. He cannot hurt you."

Argus growled at the old man. "You will not leave here alive, priest."

Conell tightened his grip on her waist and slipped his hand under her elbow. He winked at her. "Sorry, Argus," he said. "Maybe another day. Émer!"

Émer pushed the stone and the rock door swung opened. Conell led Imogene through it.

His captain, Frigg and the priest followed. Émer pushed the stone on the other side and the door closed. He wedged a knife into the cracks of the stone and jammed the secret door. The rock wall muffled Argus's curses.

Cián held Émer's torch before him and followed his arrows that led to freedom. The group hurried along the twisting passages. Argus's shouts echoed down the halls. It would take a while for the demon to open the rock door, but yet he might overtake them at the castle's walls.

At last, the bush came into view. Émer held the others back, while he crept past the bush. He bobbed back in and motioned to the others to follow.

Áepoo's word remained true. He stood amongst his fellow beasts outside the hidden doorway. Imogene screamed at the sight of the beasts and stumbled away from Conell.

He grabbed her arm and led her to his mount. "Do not fear, *Chuoha*, they are friends."

Áepoo eyes narrowed. "The demon did this, did he not?"

Conell lifted her onto the man-horse's back and swung up behind her. "Be careful, Áepoo, she is wounded."

"Not to worry, My Lady," Áepoo said. "You will not feel a thing."

His companions jumped on their horse-beasts. The animals galloped a few paces across the field. Their massive wings spread and they rose into the air.

Imogene clenched her ribs.

Conell placed his hand over hers. "It will be all right, *Chuoha*. You can rest once we are away from Argus." He grasped Áepoo's long mane and peered over his shoulder.

Argus and his winged demons rose into the air.

Despite the great beasts' speed, Jezebel's demons grew closer. Argus laughed and slashed the air with his sword.

"Áepoo!" Conell shouted over the shrieking wind, "They will soon be upon us!"

Aepoo slipped to the front of the small group and the remaining three flying animals created a V-shape formation. The thrashing wind ceased and they soared like hawks against a canvas of blue.

Argus and his winged guards also created the V-shape and drew closer.

Áepoo pressed his torso flat and his four wings propelled them forward. Conell bent over Imogene forcing her down. The others followed their leader's example and the wind shoved them forward.

Argus and his demons struggled to keep pace, but one by one, the queen's winged guards dropped to the ground. Argus could no longer keep up and he hovered in the air. "DeCapris! I swear I will kill you!"


Girl stood at one of the large castle windows and watched Argus pursue the prisoners. She dropped the curtain and leaned her head against the window frame. "Be free, Imogene."

Maybe she should have told the guards about the handsome young man with markings on his face? But, she argued, the Attiyq told her to be silent. Surely, He would protect her. She nodded. But what if He pulled away His hand? Then she would endure for His sake. He had a plan.

Argus knew of her betrayal. It swirled in her blood. Her lord's anger would burn tonight and she would feel his fists. She pressed her forehead into the frame and clung to the curtains, letting her tears fall. "Attiyq, give me strength to endure what lies ahead. And protect my friend, Imogene. And the handsome man." She wiped away her tears and cleaned the room.

The Attiyq's eyes roamed over the countryside, seeking one who trusted Him. He found a young man and the Great One strengthen him. He did great deeds in the name of the Attiyq and the Great One blessed him.

*- The Words of Attiyq*

# 13

Conell called over the screeching wind, "Áepoo, we need to enter into *Opize Ech*. The witch's eyes cannot penetrate the mountains."

He nodded and veered to the left. Imogene dropped her head against Conell's shoulder and moaned.

"It will be all right, *Chuoha*," he said, "We will be in Émer's homeland soon. Then you can rest."

The winged animals climbed higher. The mountain peaks brushed against Áepoo's hoofs. The thin cold air caused Imogene to shiver, making Conell tighten his arms around her.

Once over the peaks, the animals soared lower into the warmer air.

Émer's wide eyes fixed on the green, lush land of *Opize Forest*. The woodlands climbed the sides of the smaller mountains and caves dug deep into the peaks. The green trees covered the land to the crests of *Chioopa Cliffs* and beyond to the Lands of the South.

Ten years had passed since Émer saw his homeland and his family. He smiled at Conell and pointed to his home, *Vozu* Village.

"Áepoo," Conell said. "Veer to the east to the village of *Vozu*. We will rest there."

He nodded and swerved. Soon the thin lines of the chimney smoke drifting upwards from small wooden houses came into view. Áepoo circled the village before heading for a small clearing. His pace slowed and he galloped until his feet touched the ground. He slowed his stride and came to a stop. The others soon joined him. He placed his sweating hands on his knees as he tried to catch his breath.

Conell slid off his back. "Thank you, Áepoo."

He nodded his welcome.

Conell cradled Imogene in his arms. "Émer, we need to get her to your mother."

He nodded and jumped from his beast's back. The priest and Frigg followed and gathered around Conell. Small wooden homes stood in a small clearing. Woods nestled around the small village.

A small group of men emerged from the houses. Women and children peered from the windows and doors.

One slender man with gray speckled hair stepped forward and cocked his head. "Émer?"

Émer laughed. "Uncle!" He ran to the older man, threw his arms around him and lifted him off the ground.

"Émer?" His uncle pulled him away and cradled Émer's face in his hands. "The Attiyq be praised. It is you! I heard tragic news; we thought the queen executed you days ago." His eyes grew wide as he gazed at Áepoo and his companions. "What are these beasts?"

A serious and honored look covered Émer's face. "They are servants of the Attiyq, Uncle. He sent them to help us. Please, they need water and food and a place to rest."

The uncle's mouth dropped open. "Moji Conell?"

Conell smiled and bowed slightly. "My eyes are pleased to see you, Niall. It has been too long."

Niall stunned gaze jumped from his nephew to his prince. "We heard of your deaths..."

"No, we escaped," Conell said. "But the girl needs to see Émer's mother. The demon Argus has injured her."

"Of course," Niall said to the men, "Do not fear. Émer Amgets, my sister's son, has come home."

Some of the men gather around them and shook Émer's hand. Others simply went back to their duties.

"Émer," Niall said. "Take her to your mother. Great Beasts, please allow us the honor of attending to your needs. Please follow us."

Áepoo nodded.

Niall slung his arm over his nephew's shoulder. "We will see you at your mother's house. It is good to have you home again."

"It is good to be home, Uncle." He kissed his uncle's cheek.

Two women burst from the small home and threw themselves into Émer's arms. The older woman pushed back her graying hair and the lines on her faced deepened as she kissed his cheek.

He laughed and kissed them both. "Mother, Aine! I have missed you so much."

"I thought you were dead," Mother said through her tears.

Conell grinned. Aine, Émer's younger sister, no longer wore her black hair in tails, now it flowed down her back like the night sky. The young girl whom he teased had blossomed into a lovely woman.

"Last time I saw you," Conell said, "you wore your hair in tails and I enjoyed pulling them."

Aine separated from her brother's embrace. A large, toothy smile covered her thin face and her purple eyes shined. "Moji Conell and Frigg! It is good to see you alive." Her smiled disappeared when her gaze fell on Imogene. "What happened?"

Émer guided his mother to Conell. "Mother, Imie needs your

help. The demon, Argus, hurt her."

"He did more than hurt her," Conell said, shifting her weight. "The coward beat her as if she were a man. Laoise, she needs your help."

Laoise nodded. "Quickly, get her into the house. Aine, get me my herbs. Émer, get me fresh water."

Conell followed Laoise into her modest home. They passed into a small room with a table, five chairs, a chopping block, a spinning wheel and stool, and a small hearth. A tiny room opened from the main living area containing a single bed and a small chair.

Laoise pulled back the multi-colored quilt and Conell placed Imogene on the fresh sheets. She took off Imogene's shoes and covered the injured girl with the blanket. Aine slipped past the men and handed her mother a basket filled the fresh smelling herbs. Émer followed with a bucket of water.

Imogene moaned and opened her eyes. "Conell?"

"I am here." He stroked her hand. "I think her wrist and ribs are broken."

Laoise felt her forehead. "She has no fever. I will need you to leave while Aine and I tend to her. This is no place for you."

"No." Imogene grabbed his arm. "Don't go, please don't leave me."

He swallowed the lump in his throat. "I will be in the other room, *Chuoha*. I will not leave you."

Laoise gently pried Imogene's grip off his arm and escorted him and Émer from the room. Conell faced the door as Laoise shut it.

Argus knelt before his queen in the eerily quiet throne room. Word spread throughout the castle regarding the prisoners' escape.

Once again, the servants hid from their mistress' wrath. Jezebel sat on the king's throne and drummed her long fingernails on the chair's golden arm. Her black eyes burned with anger. Argus stiffened a chuckle. He enjoyed seeing her simmer.

Her dark eyes drilled through him. "How could you have let them escape?" Argus hid his grin behind his frown. Her jealousy burned like fire. "It seems he had help from Ruárc." His calm demeanor seemed to fuel her wrath. "The coward showed them one of the secret passages. But it was *you* who let them go."

He shrugged. "Perhaps, but I have sent the Slave Runners after my girl. Once they find her, they will find the medallion. It is only a matter of time, My Queen."

She clicked her tongue. "The more they chase freedom, the closer they come to solving the medallion's mysteries. Conell would have great power at his fingertips and you and I will be no more. Is that what you *want*, Argus? Or is it something or someone else that you seek?"

He smiled sweetly. "You are all I want, My Lady. But I cannot allow my slave to escape, nor would I ever disobey your commands."

Her eyes narrowed. "I wonder?"

He chuckled and lifted his gaze. "You know my loyalty is to you, My Lady, ever since I found you years ago. Very soon, you will have the true Throne of *Ezasu* and the mysteries of the medallion, and I will have my girl."

She narrowed her black eyes and cocked her head. "Let me ask you, Argus. Did you enjoy your new whore? Does she satisfy you more than I? What about the amulet and the powers it holds? Does that mean nothing to you?"

He laughed. "It sounds as if you are jealous, My Queen. And yes, I do care for the girl. She is…"

"Young? Pretty?"

He grinned. "You are jealous. Nay, My Lady, she is an Oracle of the Attiyq and is needed to read the medallion's mysteries. But you, My Queen, are my heart's beat and my love. You always have been.

217

She is my toy, but you hold my heart."

He rose and caressed her cheek. She lifted her dark eyes to him. He weaved his spell over her and she drooped in his hands. He placed his lips against her hair and his words were soft like a summer breeze. "It is you who makes my heart beat faster and blood boil in my veins. Let the Slave Runners find my girl and they will find your medallion. Then we both can have her, but for different reasons." He smiled. "Let me do this. The girl is just my toy, but you…"

He kissed her. Her eyes fluttered open and she gave him a soft smile. He touched her cheek. She was as soft mud. "Of course, Argus. Forgive me for doubting you," she whispered.

He dropped his arms to his sides. "My Lady, there is still the problem with Ruárc. He led the prince here. I fear he may have compromising loyalties."

Her eyebrows rose. "Do you truly think he is working with DeCapris?"

He lifted a shoulder. "Could be. Shall I bring him in?"

She nodded. "Yes, let us hear what he has to say."

Argus snapped his fingers. A guard opened the outer doors and waved to someone in the hall. The sentries dragged Ruárc into the room and tossed him before the queen. The guard landed with a plop on the stoned floor. He sat on his haunches and bowed. Argus stepped beside his lady and his large body engulfed the smaller, fat man. "Do you know why you are here?"

Ruárc trembled as he slowly sat upright, but kept his head bowed. "Forgive me, My Queen! I had no choice; I had to lead them here. They would have killed me!"

Argus chuckled. The queen rose from her throne and dragged a long fingernail over Ruárc's cheek. "You had no choice? How sad. But now what? Because of your fear, the medallion and the girl are gone. This is the second time you have let them escape."

Ruárc swallowed and shivered. "But, My Queen, that first time, Toál and I did not guard them. We were only patrolling the grounds. Why blame me for others' mistakes?"

She released a loud "humph" as she made her way to Argus. Her long nails stroked the feathers of his great white wings. "Argus, what happened to the guards who let the prince and his friends escape?"

"My winged men? I ate them." The demon licked his lips. "I enjoy my meat fresh."

"That is right; you and your winged army desire human flesh."

Ruárc bowed before the queen. "My Lady, please, I beg for your mercy. It was I who brought you the girl in the first place. If it were not for me, you would never have known about the medallion."

"True," she said, "but it was you who brought them here and it was you whom Argus found in the prison."

"I can help you!" Ruárc said. "I have friends amongst the *Upe-* I mean, Barbarians, who know the land and its people. DeCapris killed my brother and he cannot find peace until I revenge him. Please, My Lady, give me one more chance, I beg of you."

She gave a quick nod to Argus, who pointed to Ruárc and motioned to the door. The guards dragged him from the room.

"My Lady, please!" A sentry shut the door behind him.

"What do you think?" She eased onto the throne and flipped her black hair from her face.

He folded his hands. "You could use the barbarians' help. The Attiyq's beasts flew south, to the land of *Opize*. You cannot see beyond the mountains. Once you or my soldiers enter the area, DeCapris and his men, along with my girl and your medallion, will cross the Eastern Borders. You need spies, My Lady, to search for them and bring them home."

Her long fingers rubbed her forehead. "Where in the world did those beasts come from? Who summoned them?"

"I think the priest may have summoned them. But do not despair, My Lady. Once I hunt them down, the priest will be the first to taste my blade." His jaw tightened. *Cián will pay for his actions. Harming a handsome demon such as himself.*

She collapsed against the back of the chair. "It seems a powerful magic is at work. First, the medallion chooses the girl who appears out of nowhere, then a powerful priest of the Attiyq resurfaces from seclusion and summons the mythical creatures. Perhaps, we have lost this time."

He narrowed his eyes; the puppet was slipping. He blinked and forced a smile on his face. "Is that what you think, My Lady?" He caressed her cheek. "Power flows through you, My Lady, and yet you wish to give up so easily."

She kissed his iced palm. "It seemed so easy years ago. I killed the king and queen and then took over the kingdom. Everything belonged to me. No one stood in my way." A smile spread across her pale face. "I remember the first time I found you. You were so strong and brave. You chased all my pain away. You gave me this life. Do you remember?"

Argus grinned and stroked her face. "Yes, I remember."

"You destroyed those who would destroy me. You showed me truth about my family and gave me a second chance at life." She lowered her head and broke his soft touch. "And now it's like a snowball, rolling down a hill and it gets bigger and bigger until it smothers us all. I don't want to lose all of this. I could never do this without you, Argus. I don't want to lose you."

His fingers lifted her drooping head and he kissed her. "Do not give up, My Queen. Take Ruárc's sword. And remember, you will never lose me."

She nodded and cupped his face. Argus motioned to the guard. The queen's sentinel opened the door and the two sentries hauled Ruárc into the room.

Ruárc dropped to his knees and bowed his head. "My Queen!"

"I have decided to take your offer," she said, "Get the Barbarians to help you. But if you make one more mistake, I will kill you myself. And you will report to Argus all your finds."

Ruárc closed his eyes and breathed a sigh of relief. "I give you my word, My Queen; I will not let you down."

Conell turned away from the closed door. How did things turn so wrong? He took a seat at the wooden table across from Cián. The old man stuffed tobacco into a pipe.

Émer leaned back in the chair beside him and grinned. "It is forbidden to smoke the *ine*."

The priest took a piece of timber for the fire and lit the tobacco in the pipe's bowl. "Well, then it is good the witch is not here." He sank against the chair's back and sucked on the pipe's mouthpiece.

Conell placed his elbows on the table and rubbed his eyes. "I should never have left her side."

Cián pulled the pipe from his mouth. "And I should have taken care also. All of us should have seen it coming, but our eyes were blinded."

Conell narrowed his eyes and cocked his head. "I thought you held the Attiyq's ear and yet the demon captured her. You claim the Great One cares for us, yet see what the demon has done to her."

He pulled the pipe from his mouth and pointed it at Conell. "But it could have been worse. You could have died and the medallion in the hands of the queen. Then the girl would belong to Argus. Would that be better?"

He rubbed his forehead. "No, but if He truly cared for her, then this would not have happened to her. What if the demon did join his body with hers? What if she truly does belong to him in body, not just as a possession?"

Laoise cracked open the door. "Émer, there is water in the kettle on the fire. Pour some of it into another bucket of cold water so it will not be too hot and give it to me. And hand me the soap and towel next to the stove. She needs to bathe."

"Bathe?" Conell asked.

She shut the door.

"Why would she need to bathe?" he asked as Émer rose and poured the water into a bucket.

Émer knocked on the door and handed her the wooden pail, soap and towel. She shut the door behind her.

"Who knows, My Moji? Mother probably needs to give her an herbal bath?"

Cián crossed his arms over his chest. "And where will you go, Moji?" The smoke from the pipe curled around his head.

"We are close to the border now," Conell said. "We will pass into the Lands of the East and follow to the edge of the world. She cannot follow us forever."

"Possibly." Cián clenched the pipe with his teeth. White smoke escaped through a crack in his lips. "And if the demon did join his body with hers? If she is no longer pure, then what?"

Conell watched a small green lizard scurry across the cross beams on the ceiling. "Then I will take her for my bride." He met the old man's gaze. "No man will accept her if she joined with another who is not her husband. She will not survive on her own."

A smile crept upon the old man's face. "You never answered Argus's question. Why do you care so much for her?"

He shrugged. "I do not understand my own actions, but I feel that I must do this. The choice is not mine. It is…a duty."

His smile broadened. "It is because the blood of King Broden flows through your veins. Your father would do the same, as would his father and his father to the great king himself. You would rather face the disgrace of marrying a blemished maiden than to throw her unprotected into the streets."

Laoise stepped from the room and placed her hand on Conell's shoulder. "The demon did not join his body to hers. But he planned on doing it without her permission. She has a broken rib and I think her wrist is also broken. Beyond that, I think she is unhurt, thank the Attiyq. She is asking for you, Moji."

Conell ran his hand through his hair. How could he face her after what he caused? If only he stayed by her side, if only...

*Lady Fath sat across from him and noisily stirred the tea in a cup. "Yes, you should have stayed with the girl just as you should have stayed with us."*

"Moji?" Laoise asked. "Did you hear me?"

He startled and nodded his head. "Yes."

*Lady Fath sang a song she had sung to Conell as a child to help him to sleep. Only the words now were changed and told of a traitor.*

Conell avoided the maid's mocking face as he opened the bedroom door, stepped inside and shut the door behind him. Lady Fath's cruel laughter slipped through the wood.

Imogene wore a large woman's nightgown which hung on her thin frame. The quilt covered her legs and her dull eyes started at the wall beside the bed. A bandage wrapped around two sticks supported her broken wrist. The bruise on her face grew darker, purple and black. She looked like a broken bird.

He cleared his throat and she turned to him. Tears danced on the edge of her eyes.

"I'm so sorry," she whispered.

"No, *Chuoha*, no, it is I who must apologize." He sat on the edge of her bed and gently took her hand in his. "It is I who allowed you to fall into a pit."

Imogene's bottom lip trembled and a tear inched its way down her black-and-blue check. "You said he was bad, but I kept hoping..." Her voice cracked. Conell slipped his arm around her, and she nestled her head on his shoulder.

Conell rested his head on hers. "I too was secretly hoping that he was honorable and trustworthy."

Tears rolled down her cheeks. "He kept touching me. He said the bracelet meant I belonged to him, and I can't get if off." She tugged at the bracelet and scraped the skin on the sides of her hand. Conell pulled her hand away.

"He said once he had the medallion, he'd make me do what he wanted. Oh, God, Conell, he kept touching me. I can't get rid of his smell. I feel so dirty." Her tears raced down his shirt and her body heaved in his arms. "He stole my name; it's mine and he stole it."

A hot anger raced through his veins. It traveled across his mind and through his heart. His fingers longed to feel the hard steel of his blade slicing through the demon's flesh. The spell from Argus's dark eyes would not save him. "I swear to the Attiyq, I will not allow him to harm you again."

She pulled away. "Jezebel said you killed a family."

He sighed. "No, I did not raise my hand to anyone. She killed the family, then blamed Émer and myself for the crime. That is why she threw us into the prison. The only way she could take my father's throne was to eliminate me. But she could not raise her hand to me unless there was a reason; it did not take her long to find that reason."

She nodded and leaned her head back on his shoulder. "I wish I never found that stupid medallion. I saw something in the castle hallway. It, it was a picture of your dad."

Conell nodded and grinned. "Mother insisted that Father have that painting done when I was very young."

"I think he's mad at me."

Chills spread down his arms. "What do you mean?"

"When Argus was taking me to the dungeon, your dad yelled at me in the painting and said I was a disappointment to others and that I should have listened to the Attiyq."

Conell's mouth dropped open. "Imogene, my father is dead."

"Yeah, I know. But he seemed so mad. And I heard a woman begging for her baby's life. Other paintings of knights seem really angry too. They kept saying this was my fault."

He swallowed and suppressed a tremble. "More of the demon's tricks; that is all. My father would not be mad, nor would his warriors. Go to sleep. Do not think of this again."

He held her until her breathing became slower and her chest slowly rose and fell. How could the girl have seen Father speaking from a painting or even know Mother's dying words? None of his father's warriors would scoff at a child's pleas for help, especially Clemwyn, who taught him and Émer the honor of protecting the weak and ill. The old guard would be the first to rescue a young maiden. Conell gently laid her on the bed and covered her with the blanket, then crept from the room and quietly closed the door.

Aine cut vegetables on a board and Laoise used a large wooden spoon to stir soup in the black kettle over the fire. The smell of cooked meat and baked bread waffled in the air. The men sat at the table and pulled pieces from the loaf. They stopped eating when he entered the room.

Émer stuff his mother's bread into his mouth. "How is she?"

"She blames herself for what happened." Conell collapsed into a nearby chair and rubbed his eyes with the palm of his hands. "All she could say is he kept touching her."

Aine dumped the vegetables into her mother's pot. "But you stopped him, Moji. There is not a man in the village who would have done what you did. You saved her honor and her life and that is what matters."

The priest nodded. "I agree. But Argus said the witch brought back the slave laws, which means she also brought back the Slave Runners."

*Lady Fath giggled. "I am so grateful I died so I would be free of them. Of course, your little princess is a different matter."*

Cián followed Conell's broken stare to what he saw as an empty chair. The old man's gaze came back to the prince. "It is good though that the Great One is more powerful in me, than the one who rules this world."

*Lady Fath groaned, rose from the table and slipped into the floorboards.*

The priest said, "I do not have to tell you what they will do to the girl. They will join their bodies with her. When they send her in chains to Argus and she is blemished, they will blame it on you or others. They do not respect the land's borders and will hunt her down. Will you be able to fight so many?"

Conell looked away. Cián's words ran with truth. The Slave Runners would have no mercy on her. "What do you suggest?"

As expected, there was no good answer.

A man who believes he cannot win, cannot win.

~ As overheard by a guard from King Kane,
fourth King of Ezasu to his son in the year 343.

# 14

Ruárc knelt before his campfire and threw another log into the blaze. The twig burst into flames as the red and orange fire consumed it. Crickets chirped in the darkened woods around him and the night birds' caw echoed across the valley. The stars lay out above him as *Ookéza* slept for the evening.

Argus's face rose before him. He snarled. The twisted angel believed he rose above others. The demon was nothing but a child's toy for the queen. The way she gawked at Argus made his stomach churn. Obviously, the two joined in the flesh. Now the creature pursued *his* girl. He should have asked for her the first day he saw her. *Ookéza* would give him strength. Toál's

227

presence wrapped his life force around him and protected his older brother in life and now in death.

A twig snapped from the woods behind him. His gaze followed the sound and his hand grabbed his sword. A man stood in the light of the fire.

Ruárc rose and motioned to the camp. "Nute, my friend, please come join me in the comfort of my fire. I have been expecting you."

Nute held back his brothers who gathered around him. Moonlight reflected off the *Upeshis'* bald heads and small white horns. Red and black tattoos of swirling circles, jagged lines and strange symbols covered their massive bare chests, arms and legs. Father once told him and Toál these marking represented the souls of animals and past loved ones who guarded them. Thus, they had no use for armor. They preferred the modesty of a loin cloth made from either human or animal skin to cover their waists. Toál once said, "An enemy who does not wear armor is insane and unpredictable and not afraid to die."

Ruárc swallowed hard and prayed for his god's protection. They carried their weapons, long curved swords pounded from hard metal stolen from the Southern Lands. No knives, axes or arrows.

Ruárc handed him cooked deer meat. "I have food for you and your brothers, please share my feast."

A young boy, appearing no more than twelve and with no tattoos on his body, took the cooked meat in his dirty hands and gave it to Nute. The leader raised the meat over his head and cried out gratitude to the beast who gave its life to feed them. Ruárc bowed his head in reverence. Once the prayer had ended, the boy cut off a portion for Nute and gave the rest to the warriors. Following their tradition, the boy would not partake in the meal until his elders had eaten.

Nute sat cross-legged on the ground across from Ruárc and devoured his portion. Ruárc forced a smile; barbarians tore at the meat and chewed with their mouths open. If not for the treaty Ruárc's father made with them many years ago, Ruárc would have nothing to do with them.

Nute wiped his mouth with the back of his hand and pulled a leather water container from his side. He plucked a cap from the top and downed the liquid. Red fluid flowed from his mouth and onto his naked chest. He passed the jug to Ruárc.

Nute would be insulted if Ruárc refused. And if he insulted Nute, the barbarians would use his skin to clothe their children. He prayed to *Ookéza* that the flask was made of animal skin and real wine filled the flask. He swigged down a gulp. The liquid stung in his throat, but he forced it down.

The warriors laughed and gathered around the campfire. Ruárc retold the tale of their brothers dying in the recent battle with the estranged prince. Some pursed their lips, while others nodded and mumbled chanting prayers.

"But it was I, my brothers, who led the prince and his cowards into a trap set by our queen. I told them I would lead them into the castle where they could kill her majesty. But just as I was about to slaughter them all and take the young girl for myself, the fool Argus blundered and the cowards escaped. So the queen has asked for your help, Great Nute. The prince stole a piece of jewelry from the queen and she must have it back. The girl belongs to me; she is my slave and must be brought back to me." He prayed to *Ookéza* to cover his lie.

Nute rubbed his chin. "Our slain brothers will one day visit us as the birds in the air. We rejoice in seeing them. As for your request, give us something in exchange. The girl could bring us money as a slave. Yes, I want the girl; I could sell her in the Eastern Territories. The *Joec* Laws have made us very rich."

Ruárc nibbled on his lower lip. There was nothing left to trade. Except…"What if I gave you two strong men as slaves? They travel with the prince. One is a young advisor, only fifteen years, the other is DeCapris' Captain of the Guard. He is older, around twenty—the last of the Voobo-Maúl warriors. Both are strong with the sword. Of course, you will have to break their spirits, but you have done this before. And the captain has a sister and a mother who would make acceptable slaves. The girl is very young, around eighteen I believe, and very lovely from what I have heard, and the mother is a healer. Will you agree?"

The Barbarian raised his eyebrows and nodded. His fellow brothers also gave their approvals. "Two women, a boy and a Voobo-Maúl? The Maúl have always been an enemy to my people ever since the days of Anu. Many *Upeshi*s have died by their hands. We would enjoy sprinkling his blood over our brothers' graves."

The warriors huddled around Nute as he explained Ruárc's offer. The group nodded and laughed. One pointed at Ruárc and grinned. "Why would one so fat want a small girl? He cannot walk, how will he break her?"

Nute laughed. "Lessrama needs someone to cook his food and clean his house."

Ruárc took in a deep breath and pushed the anger aside at the obvious insult. No matter what he and Toál did, Nute always saw them as small ones in the land of giants and claimed the brothers were tiny bugs trying to destroy the giant bird.

"Do you accept?" Ruárc asked.

Nute raised his chin and nodded. "Tell the queen we want all in the *Opize* territory, or we will not help her."

"It may be difficult to capture all of them. Even the queen cannot see beyond the mountains surrounding the lands. It is said that the Great Attiyq rules over the area and His Hands cover the land like a mother's blanket."

Nute laughed. "You think that I fear the Attiyq? He is nothing to us. We are the *Upeshi*. Tell her we want the people of *Opize*, or we will not help her."

Ruárc bowed his head. "It is as you have asked. I am sure she will agree. But remember, the girl is mine. The prince and the jewel belong to the queen."

Ruárc grasped Nute's hand and shook it. "It is done."

Argus knelt on branch above Ruárc's campsite. The wind nudged the words of the *Upeshi* to him as a mother corralling her children. He grinned. So the coward blames him for the escape of his girl. Such was the heart of one who sniffs the ground as a dog. Let the *Choo* place the blame on him. It made no difference. What mattered were Imogene and the medallion. Let the fools run ahead of him and track the land. Once the dead lay on the ground, he would step in as the true king of *Ezasu* and take back what once belonged to him.

His queen summoned him. He spread his great wings and lifted into the air.

Cián stirred his tea with his spoon, then shook away the droplets and laid the utensil on the table. "You do not wish to hear the answer, so why should I spread it before you?"

Conell shoved his seat back, stormed from the house and slammed the door behind him. The chilled night air made him shiver and the sound of the animals chirped in the blackness. He gazed up into the dark sky. The same stars he saw for years blanketed the heavens. One fell leaving a silver streak behind it. What did Imogene say? *Wish upon a star.*

He breathed in the cold air. At least here, the queen could not pursue them and he gave thanks for the strange magic surrounding this land. He sat on a log and rubbed the back of his neck. Of course, his ears rejected the answer. Lead the people. But how? His ancestors chanted from the grave: coward.

The door to the house opened and the leaves crunched underfoot. The smell of tobacco lingered in the air. Cián eased onto the log and studied the starry sky.

He puffed on his pipe. "You know, some say others live on the stars and the stars themselves are actually like this land."

"Maybe we could go there?"

He chuckled. "It would be a long walk."

"So you think I should lead the people into battle?"

"It makes no difference what I think. What do you think?" The barrel of the pipe glowed red as Cián inhaled the smoke.

"I cannot lead. I am a coward and I have made a painful mistake."

The old man grunted. "The Children of Broden are not cowards."

Conell's gaze lowered to the ground. "When I was seven years old, I heard two guards speaking of an attack on the castle. I had harsh words earlier with my father and my anger burned. I decided to keep the secret to myself. That night the *Upeshi*s attacked the castle. My mother," he paused. "They killed everyone, including Frigg's family, the Maúl warriors, and Émer's father."

Cián nodded. "I seem to remember a celebration that evening to honor the Maúl."

"Yes, all of the great warriors assembled there. When the *choo* attacked, Father and Émer's father put Émer and myself into the closet, telling Émer to guard me. I hid while my family and friends died."

"So you believe that the actions of a child equate a coward as an adult?"

"Yes. I never told Émer. I fear losing him. What if he discovers my secret?"

"The captain is a strong man. He will endure and understand you were just a child. He will not leave you."

"I think Argus knows, but I have never told anyone."

Cían shrugged. "Do not worry about that demon. He cannot

hurt you." He crossed his arms and stretched his legs. "If all the men of this land fled at the first sign of battle, then all of us would be labeled as a coward. But you have led Émer and Frigg and protected a young girl from a demon. That does not equate a coward. You are stronger than you believe and Broden speaks from the grave. Will you not heed his words? And what of the mark of Broden upon your arm, will you also ignore that?"

Conell rubbed the bandage covering Broden's sign. The tattoo father placed upon his arm. The old man refused to give up his fight. He gestured with his hands. "But you still do not hear my words. Jezebel was my guardian after my parents' death. She gave me all that I asked for, sweets, meats, toys, animals; it was a child's dream. But she withheld the use of the sword; that is where the guard Clemwyn stepped in. He taught us what he could before she killed him."

Conell gestured. "If only I could see father's battle scrolls and books, then maybe I could learn battle scenarios and I could lead an army. But Jezebel destroyed them saying I did not need them. But even if I did possess them, I cannot push away this guilt of my past sins, what I did to Father and Mother. And to my friends. How can I lead when I know I destroyed their lives? Aho, I believe I have slipped into insanity. I…see things, people who died in the castle: Lady Fath, a young maiden named Afanen and my cousin Peta. They all accuse me of killing them. When we were in the prison, I heard mother's screams day and night. Now, the insanity has slipped to Imogene. She claimed my father's painting spoke to her and that she too saw the dead speak in the castle. How can I help her when I too am slipping away?"

"What do these people say to you when you see them?"

Conell shrugged. "Mostly that I am to blame for their deaths. Lady Fath sat across from me at the table, but disappeared when you said the Attiyq was great within you. What power is that?"

Cián grinned. "I suspected as much. Argus has wanted to destroy us all and has started on the Child of Broden. He wants the last of the king's heir destroyed, so his queen can take over the throne. The

Attiyq's power is greater than Argus and that frightens the demon and his children. You did not see the fair Lady Fath this evening, but Argus's child. Let me know if you see them again. The demon uses his forces against you and now he has used them on the seer. Argus took yours and her pain and cast spells against it, making you and her see things that are not there."

Conell nodded. "So these visions are not real? How do I stop them?"

"You must realize you are not to blame for their deaths. A child is not responsible. And how do you know that the result would have been different if you had told your father?"

Conell opened his mouth, and then closed it. That never occurred to him. "But I cannot lead."

The priest took in a deep breath and let it out slowly. "I understand your problem, son, but it will not hold back the witch. You must release these useless thoughts and lead. Books and journals do not make a strong warrior." Cián removed the pipe from his mouth and pointed it to the bandage on Conell's arm. "Do you remember on your fifth birth-celebration when your father carved the sign of Broden on your arm?"

Conell nodded. "Yes, it was a great day, a large celebration with magic men and animals from the south. Father brought in merchants and foods."

"Yes, it was. I was there. You stood on the balcony overlooking the courtyard while all of *Ezasu* watched below. Your mother stood beside you and your father carved the markings into your arm. You stood so strong, never once weeping, although I have heard, it is quite painful. You endured because you are of Broden. So now will you ignore the markings because you do not have journals to read?"

Conell moaned. The old man made sense, but still the murmurings of his heart told him another tale. "But what if I cannot lead an army into battle?"

The old man grunted. "Do you remember your father?"

"I remember a lot about him. He was strong, almost

overpowering, but gentle to mother and myself. What I remember the most are he and his advisors pouring over war strategies and maps. He hardly left that room. I snuck in one day and rummaged through those maps. I could see his fingerprints inked in the scrolls. The scrolls themselves smelled of dust." He chuckled. "I pretended I was Broden. I must have fallen asleep, for I awoke in my own bed. I wonder if I dreamt it."

"An interesting dream," the priest said, chuckling. "Perhaps you are right, perhaps you will never be that warrior. But what of Imogene? As you said, the Slave Runners will cross the borders to find her. She will not escape them."

Conell shrugged his shoulders and shook his head. "I do not have that answer. I know I must protect her, Émer and Frigg. Now I must also look after Aine and her mother. There are so many now."

The priest nodded. A small animal chattered in the trees, then scurried off in the woods. "It seems even now those loyal to you are growing. Will you turn your back on them?"

"No, I cannot. Broden's spirit pushes me forward." He placed his elbows on his knees and rubbed his hands together. "Imogene said something in the room. She said Argus told her once he possessed the medallion, he would rule. Do you think the demon wants the medallion for himself?"

"Who knows? There is more to that demon then his outer clothing. I fear that if he does get the medallion, he may do worse than the witch."

"What do you know of this medallion?"

He sucked on his pipe and blew the smoke from a crack in his lips. "Not much. Many legends surround it. Some priests say the Attiyq created it before He created this world. Some say it contains the power of the Ancient One, others claim it will give the wearer great strength, enough to rule all the territories. But some, including myself, say it will lead the bearer to a weapon of great power, something of the Attiyq. This weapon can defeat even the queen and her great powers. No man or being can stand before it."

"Is that what the Attiyq wishes to show Imogene, where this great weapon is hidden?"

His dark outline shrugged. "Who knows?"

"What do you know of Argus?" Conell asked.

Cián sat back and crossed his arms over his chest. "I met him only once, after your father died. He stood next to Jezebel on her coronation. I, along with other priests, did not agree with her crowning and protested the ceremony. He took us into another room in order to discuss the problem, but instead betrayed us. He killed the other priests, but I managed to escape. I have discovered he hates the Attiyq and His word binds him like rope and blinds him like acid." He took another puff from the pipe and exhaled the smoke from the corner of his mouth. "There is something evil about that creature. The Attiyq has kept the demon's true nature hidden from me. I only know horror follows that demonic being."

The light from the neighboring houses twinkled in the darkness. The scents of cooked meats and breads made his stomach rumble, reminding him that he forgot to eat dinner. "It would be foolish to give the witch the medallion if it meant the girl's life against a piece of old jewelry, perhaps it is an option?"

"Would Argus give up his slave so quickly?"

"No." Conell rubbed his chin. "My options are dwindling."

The old man laughed. "Now you sound like your father."

"How did you know him?"

"Have you not yet solved this riddle? Your father worshiped the Attiyq as did his army, staff, and family. He and his army would scour the countryside, seeking the enemy and often they would stop at the temples to worship the Attiyq. Many times, he came to my village and my people planned a great celebration. It was an honor to have your father sit under my teachings. Many knew of your father and his great deeds. They depended on him for protection and support. He was a great man and he loved his people."

"If they loved him so much, why did they turn their faces from us? The witch threw us into prison, and while all of them remained silent."

"I see." Cián nodded. "So you are reluctant to help them because they did not help you."

"You do not understand. I saw the witch change the laws set down by my father. Émer and I would travel throughout the land, despite her protests. I saw their sufferings and gave her my words, but she pushed me aside, saying Father had indulged the people and they would not submit in the years to come."

"And you believe her?"

"I questioned her answer, but kept my peace." He kicked a small rock. "She was my guardian and my father's priestess.'

"Is that what she said? That she was your father's priestess?"

"Yes."

Cián sighed. "Then perhaps you are not like your father after all."

Conell scratched at stubble on his face. "What do you mean she was not my father's priestess?"

"Do you remember her in the castle when your father ruled?"

He shook his head. "No, but she said she practiced away from the castle."

"She was a priestess, but not your father's. He never trusted her. She came to us as a thirteen-year-old girl and a priest took her under his wing and raised her in the ancient's temple. She grew strong in the teachings, and rose to high priestess. Then your father and mother died and she stepped in as Regent Queen." The old man grunted and his teeth clattered on the wooden pipe stalk. "It is strange, the Attiyq's power did not settle on her, as if she did not know Him and He did not know her."

"Then how did she come to guard over me?"

He pulled the pipe from his teeth. "I am not sure. After the royal family died, she stepped in and claimed to be the king's priestess. Since all of the castle staff, guards and family were dead, no one could dispute it. Because she was a high priestess of the Great Temple, she claimed she must become your guardian. Some of us priests questioned her decision, but she used her influence to quiet us. Now, I wish I had been stronger." He shrugged. "I was young and naive."

"She did raise me, but to be weak and a coward."

"Who can bear that burden?" He paused and sucked on the pipe. "It is strange. She rose so quickly to the office of high priestess as if she wove a spell over all involved. It is not simple to become High Priestess. A priest takes a child no older than three years of age much the same as the Maúl. The child lives in the temple and a priest becomes the child's mentor, teaching him or her the Attiyq's ways. Then when he is older, at least in his twenties and has never known a woman, then he becomes a priest. But this was," he paused again, "strange. Jezebel was much older, at least twelve when the priest took her in. Much too old for an apprentice. And she uses blue for her banner color, while Broden and all the kings after him used yellow."

Conell raised his eyebrows. "If I remember correctly, yellow represents the Attiyq's power given to the king, while blue is another's power given to the king. Perhaps something did happen."

"Who knows except the Attiyq?"

He chuckled. "Again you claim the Attiyq is all knowing. And again, we come to the same path. If the Attiyq cared so much for us and was all knowing, then why allow Jezebel to rise to power? Why kill my family, the Maúl and allow the people to turn towards Jezebel? Imogene now weeps from the pain caused by the demon. No, the Attiyq cares only for Himself. His ears are closed to our cries." He placed his elbows on his knees and rubbed his temples. "I have done all I could for Him, I worshiped Him, even after Father died. Here I sit, my throne gone, the girl hurt, I have nothing and I race to the safety of the borders. I do not understand this."

"And as I said before, he did not join with her. You are safe as is the last of the Maúl warriors and the girl. You must help her hear from the Attiyq. If you speak such ill words to her, then she will surely crumble and the demon will truly own her."

Conell dangled his hands between his legs. "What do you wish for me to do?"

"That you help Imogene hear from Him and find the weapon. Use it to defeat the witch and take back your throne." The priest chuckled. "I warned you."

"Yes, you did. But again, how can I lead an army when I have no knowledge of war?"

"I never said lead an army, I said use the weapon to defeat the witch. As you said before, leaving really is not an option."

"Perhaps."

He emptied his pipe bowl on the ground and rose. "It is late and I am an old man who has had a long day. All the rest of the world sleeps and I think I will join them. Think about what I have said. You do have your father's heart and Broden's as well. Their courage resides within you. Use it." Then he shuffled into the house.

Conell sucked on his lower lip. *It would be difficult searching for this strange weapon. What if this great weapon did not exist? And if it did exist, how would he use it? Where did it hide? Ezasu covered much land. And what of the girl, Émer and Frigg? Maybe he was sane after all, but how would he fight off Argus's mind traps?*

A deep growl rose from his throat. He would give his life for them before allowing Argus to touch them. The borders called out to him. Their strong arms would hide them from Jezebel. If they must, Frigg and the girl would take a ship to foreign land while he and his captain tried to survive in the Southern Lands. Jezebel could have this land, Broden's castle, even the Maúl temple. He rose and made his way back into the house.

A small fire burned in the fireplace, giving the place a soft glow. Émer and Frigg slept on mats on the floor. Conell quietly closed the door. Émer's eyes flicked open and he sat up. "Moji? Is everything all right?"

"Yes, Émer, go back to sleep. Where are the girls and the Aho?" Conell asked as he poured stew into a bowl and grabbed a hunk of bread.

He pointed to a closed door. "My mother and sister sleep in my mother's room. The Aho is in my sister's bedroom."

He nodded and entered into Imogene's room. The moonlight spilled onto her prone form hidden under the covers. He made his way to the window and tried to see past the dark trees. Aimlessly, he ate the stew and bread, not tasting Aine's rich broth. The only sounds were Imogene's soft snoring and the wind rustling the branches outside. Argus and his witch waited for them on the other side of the mountains.

Conell dropped off the bowl in the living area, picked up his sword and slipped back into Imogene's room. He sat on a wooden chair under the window as the girl slept.

The priest's words echoed in his mind. *Use the Attiyq's weapon.* The Attiyq kept His hands far from him, He would not extend them now. He abandoned Conell like an orphan in the storm. The Great God was the coward of *Ezasu.* Conell alone would lead his small group as soon as soon as the girl could walk. They would run on the edges of the earth if they must.

A yawn slipped from his mouth and his eyes grew heavy. His head nodded and dropped to his chest. He took a deep breath and opened his eyes wide, but sleep, a gentle mistress, wooed him to her bosom and wrapped her calming arms about him. His chin fell to his chest and he drifted to sleep.

*"Moji Conell," said a female voice.*

*It pierced his dreams. His mind dismissed it.*

*"Moji Conell."*

*He snorted and forced his heavy eyelids to open. "What is it, Imogene?"*

*A woman with long blond hair sweeping over her shoulders stood before him. Her long white cloak pooled onto the floor. Great wings spread open from her small back and a light from a million suns filled the room. Conell gasped and reached for his sword. But his arm remained frozen at his side.*

*She smiled at him as if she were Connell's trusted friend. "Hello, Conell."*

*"Demon, how did you get in here?" He tried to wiggle his fingers, but the thing bewitched him. "I swear I will cut you in half if you hurt any of them."*

*The woman clicked her tongue. "I am not a demon nor will I hurt your friends. The Great Attiyq sent me to give His message." The angel exhaled a dragging breath as if dealing with a disobedient child. "He understands your anger and pain, but now you must leave the past where it belongs. He forgives you as does your father, and so should you. The lives of all who live in this land depend upon you and your great courage. Trust in the Old One's strong arms and allow Him to show the girl what she must do to destroy the enemy. For the Attiyq Himself will go before you and will fight for His people. But if you run to the borders, all of you will surely die."*

*"What of Argus? He has a spell on me. I cannot fight him. I see the dead and hear their voices."*

*The angel frowned at him like an adult scolding a toddler. "Argus is nothing, a child who plays with wooden toys. Do you truly think he is stronger than me or the Attiyq? Why do you fear one so small?"*

*"If you are an angel, then tell me yourself what I must do. Stop toying with me as if I were a child."*

*The angel tilted her pretty head and winked. "But would you listen if I told you?"*

Conell's eyes flew open. The room was once again dark. Imogene's soft breathing broke the deep silence. He tried to move, but could not as if a stoned blanket lay over him. The heaviness penetrated in the room and pressed him in his chair.

It seemed like hours as he sat in the darkness. The being's words wiggled in his mind like trickling water. They oozed past the rage and throbbing pain from his broken heart and calmed him like Mother's soft voice. The presence lifted and he jogged from the room.

He woke Emer and both searched for the intruder. But they found no one.

# Do not ask me to turn back, for I will not listen.

~ Words of King Broden, first King of Ezasu in the year of 265 before the war against the Southern Lands. *It is said that the enemy's army ranged to ten thousand, yet the Great King's army consisted of 300 archers, 2000 spearmen, 1000 swordsmen, 2000 calvary, and 1500 sling shot warriors, giving the king 5000 men. He defeated the great army through the strength of the Attiyq, leaving the King of the South in ruins.*

# 15

Conell's eyes fluttered open in the morning sun and he stretched his stiff arms. He groaned and cracked his neck as he rose from the chair. Sleeping in a hard chair jolted his back more than sleeping on the ground. The strange visitation seemed so real. The heavy presence had lifted, but a soft lilac scent filled the room.

Imogene still lay curled under the covers. He placed his hand on her forehead and exhaled as he felt her cool skin. Her bruised face swelled over the night.

He left her room and entered the small sitting area. Émer sat at the table and sipped from a cup. The priest and Frigg sat across from them. They stopped

243

chatting when he entered. Aine watched him take a seat, then placed the blankets into a cupboard.

"Morning," Conell mumbled.

Aine smiled. "I heard something happened last night."

Émer shook his head and mouthed "no."

Conell rubbed his eyes and sat in chair at the table. Aine poured him a hot cup of tea. He smiled his thanks. "I do not know what happened last night. I believe it was a dream. I question my own mind."

The old priest sipped from his cup. The steam drifted up from the hot liquid. "This is twice the Attiyq has moved on your behalf. What did the angel say to you?"

Conell massaged his forehead. "She said I am to allow an unknown God to speak to Imogene and if we try to escape to the borders, then His hand will slay us all. He will spill our blood if we do not obey Him."

Émer scrunched his face. "Moji, surely you do not believe your own words."

"What did the angel say exactly?" the priest asked.

Aine studied him as she flipped the meat frying in a skillet over the fire, but said nothing.

Conell swirled the dark liquid in the cup. "I do not remember. You are the one who hears from Him, you repeat His words."

The priest grinned his toothless smile. "As I said before, sometimes He makes me ask. What did she say exactly?"

Conell sighed and wrapped his hands around the mug. "He will fight against the witch and I am to help Imogene find the weapon." He took a sip of hot tea. "All I wish is to run for the borders."

Émer nodded. "I know, Moji, but if the Attiyq told you to do this, then maybe you should."

He frowned. "And if it was just a dream? Then what?"

"And what if it is not?" Cián asked.

Conell gritted his teeth. "You ask me to trust a girl who has a sick mind? Have you not heard her words? She speaks of phones and a place called New York. A beast with a nose the size of a small tree?"

"And how do you know this New York and a beast with a long nose are not true?" Cián asked. "How do you know that she was not brought here from a far-off land?"

"By a magic medallion?"

"Is it so impossible?" asked the Aho. "And do you think the Slave Runners will simply allow you to cross the seas? Do you not think they will search the coasts to find her and you? Cut her hair, change her clothes, it will make no difference. They will come for her."

He gripped the sides of the warm cup. The old man's words rang true. The Runners would find them. But to trust the words of a sick girl, to find a weapon that may not exist spoke against his very soul. Would Broden take such a horrible risk? Would his father? "But what if you are wrong?"

"And what if I am right?"

Aine placed the meat and eggs on the table. "Moji Conell, forgive me for speaking, I know it's not my place, but I need to say this. Imogene spoke of a girl last night as I tended to her wounds. She said the girl wore a bracelet like the one she now has. Her father brought her to the castle when she was very young, but after your mother's death. Imogene said the demon calls her Girl and forbids her to use her real name. The child feared Argus terribly. Imogene is convinced the demon hurts her, forces her to…She feels horrible that she left Girl behind." She paused and wiped her hands on her apron. "Anyway, Girl said Argus brought other women, visitors I think she called them. Argus orders the women to dress in your mother's clothes, and then he would…join with them and enslave them, just as he tried to do with her."

Conell's body became numb. "The demon joined other innocent maidens without their consent?"

Aine picked up her brother's empty cup and handed it to her mother. She refilled it and placed it before Émer. "No one has stopped Lord Argus because no one can. He is allowed to do as he pleases. Young poor women go into the castle with promises to become handmaidens and store owners, but their families never see the women again. No one will stop him because the women come from poor families. No one cares for the poor anymore. The merchants have said that the *Upeshi* take these young women into slavery. Many young women have simply disappeared. If their fathers seek their daughters, then the demon lies about them or worse, kills the family left behind." She knelt beside him. "Please, My Moji, do not leave us. I do not wish to disappear."

"That poor child left behind." Laoise shook her head. "May the Attiyq have mercy on her."

He swallowed and his gaze slid to Cián, Frigg and Émer. How did this terror begin? He placed his elbows on the table and dug his palms in his forehead. How could he now turn from lost maidens? How could he as Aine said, simply let them disappear? Argus could move upon the wind.

"Moji." Émer wrapped his hands around the cup. "You cannot allow the demon to dishonor these women. I will not leave my sister and mother behind." He reached below his chair and picked up a weapon the size of a large hammer with a jagged head on one side and a long hooked point on the other. A pointed spear three inches long extended from the top. "It seems my uncle stole father's *atabo* from Jezebel and kept it hidden all these years. I wish to use it against the enemy."

Conell gave him a grin.

Cián's old eyes twinkled. "You have three men who are willing to fight by your side, Moji. And the girl will lead you. What is your decision?"

Aine rose to her feet. "If you do not help us, then we all will die."

Cián leaned forward. "You do not need to lead an army, only help the girl read the medallion."

"Who is insane? Find the weapon and defeat a demon. You sound like a child." Conell rose and exited the house.

The sweet scent of summer flowers drifted across the forest, mixed with damp dirt and moss. Sun beams stretched through the trees limbs and raced to the ground. He smiled and vowed to enjoy each morning until he rested with his fathers. He sat on the wooden bench outside the house and listened to the birds chirping in the trees.

Cián spoke true words; the Runners would come for her and him. Imogene would not survive the Slave Runners or Argus. Use an ill woman to find His weapon and defeat the demon. But if the Attiyq did not exist, or if He refused to help them and him and her would perish. How could Conell fight against Argus's visions of the dead?

The Angel's words echoed in his heart: *Trust in the Old One's strong arms and allow Him to show the girl what is needed to destroy the enemy. For the Attiyq Himself will go before you and will fight for His people. But if you run to the borders, you all will surely die.*

He tried to fight Argus on his own and instead the demon tricked him and stole away Imogene. He beat her and tried to rape her. Conell failed as he failed in the past.

He rubbed his fingernails against his chin. Argus asked for Imogene and the medallion. It made no sense. He understood Argus wanting Imogene for his slave, but the medallion meant nothing to the demon.

The door to the house closed and the sound of shoes crunching the grass approached him. With a deep sigh, Cián lowered himself on the small bench. "It is a hard decision."

Conell smiled. "It is one that speaks of insanity. Still, a question nips at my mind. Why would Argus and Jezebel want her and the medallion?"

The old man waved away a fly. "Maybe they know something you do not see?"

"You mean they believe she can read the medallion?"

"They obviously do not believe she is insane. Have you seen her shoes? What if she is from another world?"

Conell furrowed his brow. "She is not insane? Then that would mean..." His eyes grew wide and he jumped from the bench. "Then that is why they long for her and the medallion. They believe this weapon exists." He eyes captured Cián. "Do you truly believe this thing exists? Truly?"

Cián nodded. "Yes, Son, I do with all my heart."

What if this thing did exist? What if the Attiyq brought Conell here? Broden's face appeared in his mind's eye. The old man smiled at him. *Father and Mother joined him, grinned and nodded. Mother held a cooing baby in her arms and she blew Conell a kiss. Peta giggled and slipped her hand into Afanen's and the two children skipped away.*

*Lady Fath, dressed in her lovely yellow gown, her black hair piled high on her head and her smooth cheeks glowing, smacked at his head. "Stop being such an idiot! I died so you could live. I expect you to move on. Do not disappoint me, Moji Conell."*

He winced as he always did when she scolded him. "Yes, Lady Fath."

The picture changed to a small boy no taller than the waist of his father, hiding in a closet. The child's anger burned towards his father, but still thought the great man would win the battle. Efuko was the king and the king always wins every battle. An adult does not bare the mistakes of the child.

The shame and anger peeled away. Father, Mother, Peta, and all the others did not blame him. He closed his eyes and took in a deep breath of the wood's scent. Broden would follow the Attiyq' words as would his father. He nodded. "Yes, Aho, I believe they exist also."

He marched into the house and flung open the door. Laoise dropped her large wooden spoon into a pot of boiling water and Émer spilled his tea on the table.

"Laoise," Conell said. "How long before Imogene can travel? We need to find those weapons."

Émer smiled as he wiped the tea from his shirt. "We will not leave your side, Moji."

Conell crossed his arms over his chest. "I would not have it any other way, My Captain."

Conell slipped into the bedroom where Imogene lay sleeping. Light pierced the windowpane making her hair glow with each touch of sun light. He watched her breathe wondering what was coming over him.

He knelt beside her and removed Mother's locket from around his neck. "Attiyq, I have never followed You and have tossed You from my life. I do not care for my life, but I care deeply for this one. Please do not let Argus take her. I have lost so much. Please, do not take this one from me." He dangled the locket over her palm as she slept, but paused. "When you are ready, I will be here." He tucked the necklace into his pocket as he gently kissed the back of her hand.

Brón's tears dropped to the floor as her trembling form knelt before her father, Argus. "Please, Father, forgive me. I did all I could, but the cursed Attiyq…"

Argus kicked her across the room, slamming her into the stoned wall of his fortress. "I do not accept excuses, cursed daughter. You will have to work hard to gain back my favor. You may have lost my only chance of regaining what was stolen from me."

Handsome Amhras wrapped his arms around his father's waist and gave Brón a sneer. "Allow me, Father, to fix my sister's mistakes."

Argus snuggled against his son. "Yes, My Son, fix your sister's mistakes."

End of the first passage of

## The Chronicles of the King

Volume 13 in the year 1033 as told by King Bran fifteenth king of Ezasu to his scribe.

NOW ON SALE ~ Book Two, The Last Maúl

# Author's Notes

I started Hidden Secrets as a novel for teens who longed for something adventurous and fun and the novel became Hidden Secrets. At first it was to be about Imogene, but soon I discovered it was about Conell and conquering his demons. The book became a living being and sprouted wings. This is my first novel and it was such an amazing adventure. I'm looking forward to the next ones.

There are so many I need to thank for this novel. So many folks who have come and gone in my life who have some part in this book. Tiffany, Tanya, Wandalea, Alisha and the elephants (haha), Amanda, Danielle, Deb, Michelle who is funny comedian, just to name a few who have moved on to bigger and better things but will live on in this novel. They listened to my concepts, gave me ideas, Tiffany edited the book for me (and she did a great job).

Most of all I thank my God, Jesus Christ who gave me inspiration and wisdom in writing the novel. Next is my amazing church family and Pastor John King at Riverside Community Church who inspired me, kept me accountable, and always ask, how is the novel going? Thanks, gang!! You all rock!!

To my friend Kim and her husband Darren who taught me fencing and always had a yearly amazing Sword Seminar for my writers. My very good friend Donna who said, Kim, when are you going to do all the things you said you were going to do? Thanks, Donna for all your encouragement!! You rock!! Suzanne who edited the novel and taught me how to write. Thank you!! And thanks to my writing buddies on facebook: Rita, Andy, Nike, Teresa, Nichole, Jenn, Megan, Kyle, and to my new group of writers, AFCW group in Peoria and to Jackie who owns the Her Majesty's Tea Room at Fairchild's where we meet (And yes, I am advertising her place. Look her up on Facebook and then go check out her place. You won't be able to leave.) To my friend Laurie, who keeps wanting to me to read my book at her library and yes, Laurie and her husband are based on the Aunt Laurie and Uncle Tim in this novel. To my Friend Angie and her boys, who keep me going, thanks, gang!! To Kristian Lamb who taught me how to market using social media. To Kip Edwards, who draws great maps and cover pages. Thanks for making the art work and the maps!! To my three friends named Vicki two whom I miss a lot.

In 2009, I attended classes at Karitos in Chicago, Illinois, a Christian Arts Festival where they have different classes about art, writing, drama, etc. There I met Patty Hickman who had two days of writing classes in which I learned the fine art of writing. So I thank the organizers of Karitos who put the festival together. I don't think I'd be here if I didn't attend Karitos. Ruth Ann from Karitos is also someone I need to thank, as she keeps inspiring me to keep going.

Then there's my amazing writer's group, The King's Pen. I started it around 2009 as a small church group for writers and we became a family. They listened to me, prayed with me, supported me and stuck with me. I am forever grateful which is why I dedicated the novel to them. (Let's just say, they put up with a lot of stuff. Not to mention, they brought the snacks.)

I can't forget my family, my mom who always keeps me accountable to writing and is my biggest fan, my wonderful Aunt Polly who encouraged me to keep going, my Uncle Joe and Aunt Judy who always ask about the novel, my cousins and their families who also ask about the book and want to support me, my dad and stepmom who encourage me. Thanks to all of you.

I also want to thank the folks who have come and gone on Absolutewrite.com. I learned a lot about writing from those folks. Thanks, gang. From Dancre.

# About the Author

Illinois native Kim Kouski has been writing since she was a teen, and as an adult, ventured into the YA speculative Christian Fantasy realm. Her desire is that every writer finds his or her way to publication, and fulfills all that God has for them.

If you enjoyed this book please post a review for it on Amazon.com. This helps the author tremendously! Thank you, The Publishers

# Also from Little Roni Publishers
## *Award-Wining Christian Fantasy Fiction*

Check out our *Christian YA Historical (American Civil War) Fiction!*

*Kim Kouski*

Send correspondence to:
Little Roni Publishers
submissionsLRP@gmail.com
www.LittleRoniPublishers.com

www.ingramcontent.com/pod-product-compliance
Lightning Source LLC
Chambersburg PA
CBHW022033240626
47154CB00007B/2393